PRAISE FOR M. L. BUCHMAN

Tom Clancy fans open to a strong female lead will clamor for more.

— *DRONE,* PUBLISHERS WEEKLY

Superb! Miranda is utterly compelling!

— *BOOKLIST,* STARRED REVIEW

Escape Rating: A. Five Stars! OMG just start with *Drone* and be prepared for a fantastic binge-read!

— READING REALITY, MIRANDA CHASE
SERIES

The best military thriller I've read in a very long time. Love the female characters.

— *DRONE,* SHELDON MCARTHUR, FOUNDER
OF THE MYSTERY BOOKSTORE, LA

Meticulously researched, hard-hitting, and suspenseful.

— *PURE HEAT,* PUBLISHERS WEEKLY,
STARRED REVIEW

A fabulous soaring thriller.

— TAKE OVER AT MIDNIGHT, MIDWEST BOOK
REVIEW

Buchman has catapulted his way to the top tier of my favorite authors.

— FRESH FICTION

Nonstop action that will keep readers on the edge of their seats.

— TAKE OVER AT MIDNIGHT, LIBRARY
JOURNAL

M L. Buchman's ability to keep the reader right in the middle of the action is amazing.

— LONG AND SHORT REVIEWS

The only thing you'll ask yourself is, "When does the next one come out?"

— WAIT UNTIL MIDNIGHT, RT REVIEWS, 4
STARS

I knew the books would be good, but I didn't realize how good.

— NIGHT STALKERS SERIES, KIRKUS
REVIEWS

FINAL TASTE

A KATE STARK THRILLER

M. L. BUCHMAN

Previously published 2014 as Dead Chef #1, One Chef!

SIGN UP FOR M. L. BUCHMAN'S NEWSLETTER TODAY

and receive:
Release News
Free Short Stories
a Free Book

Get your free book today. Do it now.
free-book.mlbuchman.com

Other works by M. L. Buchman: *(* - also in audio)*

Action-Adventure Thrillers

Kate Stark
Final Taste
Ice Burn
Knife's Edge

Miranda Chase
*Drone**
*Thunderbolt**
*Condor**
*Ghostrider**
*Raider**
*Chinook**
*Havoc**
*White Top**
*Start the Chase**
*Lightning**
*Skibird**
*Nightwatch**
*Osprey**
*Gryphon**
*Wedgetail**

Science Fiction / Fantasy

Deities Anonymous
Cookbook from Hell: Reheated
Saviors 101

Contemporary Romance

Eagle Cove
Return to Eagle Cove
Recipe for Eagle Cove
Longing for Eagle Cove
Keepsake for Eagle Cove

Love Abroad
Heart of the Cotswolds: England
Path of Love: Cinque Terre, Italy

Where Dreams
Where Dreams are Born
Where Dreams Reside
*Where Dreams Are of Christmas**
Where Dreams Unfold
Where Dreams Are Written
Where Dreams Continue

Non-Fiction

Strategies for Success
Managing Your Inner Artist/Writer
*Estate Planning for Authors**
Character Voice
*Narrate and Record Your Own Audiobook**
Beyond Prince Charming: One Guy's Guide to Writing Men in Romance

Short Story Series by M. L. Buchman:

Action-Adventure Thrillers

Kate Stark
Miranda Chase Stories

Romantic Suspense

Antarctic Ice Fliers

US Coast Guard

Contemporary Romance

Eagle Cove

Other

Deities Anonymous (fantasy)

Single Titles

The Emily Beale Universe
(military romantic suspense)

The Night Stalkers
MAIN FLIGHT
The Night Is Mine
I Own the Dawn
Wait Until Dark
Take Over at Midnight
Light Up the Night
Bring On the Dusk
By Break of Day
Target of the Heart
Target Lock on Love
Target of Mine
Target of One's Own
NIGHT STALKERS HOLIDAYS
*Daniel's Christmas**
*Frank's Independence Day**
*Peter's Christmas**
Christmas at Steel Beach
*Zachary's Christmas**
*Roy's Independence Day**
*Damien's Christmas**
Christmas at Peleliu Cove

Henderson's Ranch
*Nathan's Big Sky**
*Big Sky, Loyal Heart**
*Big Sky Dog Whisperer**
*Tales of Henderson's Ranch**

Shadow Force: Psi
*At the Slightest Sound**
*At the Quietest Word**
*At the Merest Glance**
*At the Clearest Sensation**

White House Protection Force
*Off the Leash**
*On Your Mark**
*In the Weeds**

Firehawks
Pure Heat
Full Blaze
*Hot Point**
*Flash of Fire**
Wild Fire
SMOKEJUMPERS
*Wildfire at Dawn**
*Wildfire at Larch Creek**
*Wildfire on the Skagit**

Delta Force
*Target Engaged**
*Heart Strike**
*Wild Justice**
*Midnight Trust**

Night Stalkers Reload
*Guard the East Flank**

Emily Beale Universe Short Story Series

The Night Stalkers
The Night Stalkers Stories
The Night Stalkers CSAR
The Night Stalkers Wedding Stories
The Future Night Stalkers

Delta Force
Th Delta Force Shooters
The Delta Force Warriors

Firehawks
The Firehawks Lookouts
The Firehawks Hotshots
The Firebirds

White House Protection Force
Stories

Future Night Stalkers
Stories (Science Fiction)

ABOUT THIS BOOK

Ex-Secret Service agent Kate Stark owns the #1 cooking network on television. When a chef and a guest judge are poisoned on her show, all fingers point to Kate.

Except she's nowhere to be found.

Drugged, kidnapped, and loaded into a shipping container, Kate's next port of call? North Korea.

From New York TV studios and her Chrysler Building penthouse suite to the Panama Canal and a DPRK smuggling ship, Kate desperately recruits her team as she races to stay alive: a geek, a Marine, her con-man twin brother, and a very handsome chef.

It will take all their skills to survive.

Previously published as Dead Chef #1, One Chef!

———

A list of characters and locations may be found at:

M. L. BUCHMAN

https://mlbuchman.com/people-places-planes#KS
And return afterward for a free bonus story
and a recipe from the book.

*To my favorite chef to cook beside,
the lady I share joy with in the kitchen
and in my life.*

Note
*The Cloud Club, Office 39, the bulk carrier ship Chong Chon Gang,
the counterfeiting, and the fate of Choi Eun-hee are real.
The rest? Well, this is a work of fiction.*

PROLOGUE
13 HOURS AGO

MARIANNE RIMALDI SCOOPED A SCANT TEASPOON OF THE GRAND
Marnier chocolate ganache and drizzled it atop the single bite
of chocolate truffle cheesecake. The perfect final bite for the
meal she was creating.

A glance at the competition clock.

Two minutes.

She plated three more desserts for the judges. The
television cameras filming *Kate's Kitchen from Hell* hovered close
by—two on her, two on her competitor as the final seconds
ticked away. One glass-eyed lens had an angle that showed her
the cameraman wasn't focused only on the food.

Precisely according to plan.

Marianne needed victory on America's most popular
cooking show, which meant winning over at least two judges.
More than that, she lusted after *Kate's Kitchen* "Blazing Knife"
stamp of approval on her career, which required all three
judges' nod of approval on all three courses.

She'd made it through the five runoff contest episodes, one
by the skin of her teeth. But now in the final? Winning was *not*
enough. She lusted after that three-vote knife and the prestige

that it came sheathed in. For a shot at that, she applied other...ingredients.

The heat of the competition kitchen—the flaring burners and blinding stage lights—simply *forced* her to pull at the cross-shoulder buttons of her confining chef's jacket, which now hung half open. She wore a loose-necked satin blouse beneath, no bra. She'd chosen an emerald green to contrast with the fire-red of the winner's jacket that she intended to be hers at the end of the show. It also stood out well against her unadorned ash-black jacket of a contestant, but she wanted the red.

However, mere party tricks wouldn't work on the show's main judge.

Marianne had to capture Kate Stark's approval. With her, nothing counted except the food itself.

Kate Stark, the blue-eyed, black-haired goddess of television food on the nation's most popular cooking network. She'd founded the show and served as its perennial judge. Always front and center on the panel. That she also owned the entire network only added to her aura of ultimate power.

Deep inside Marianne didn't want to merely win Stark's vote, she wanted to impress the hell out of her. She'd sell her soul to the Devil if needs be; this was *Kate's Kitchen from Hell* after all.

Don't think! Focus on the food...but don't forget the theater.

Marianne's slight build made the least view down her blouse a revealing one. Bent over her dessert plates, the satin draped away from her body allowing a deliciously cool ripple of fresh air to course along her front. Her build might be far less substantial than the one that had made Mom such a success on the *wrong* side of Hollywood, but she'd certainly watched her mom and learned what sold. It had been an educational upbringing, if not a typical one.

Three judges.

Two of them were easy.

Zania, the guest taster, sat in the role of the *every-person's* palate so necessary for engaging an audience. She gave the viewers someone to identify with, among the professional chefs. Of course, her palate was the only thing on Zania *not* extraordinary.

She was the hottest new Hollywood starlet—who Marianne suspected to be a closet butch. It wasn't too dangerous a bet because Zania's mother worked the same side of Hollywood as Marianne's and word got around about what truly happened after the bedding was rumpled in erotic film.

During her intro, Tinsel Town's hot new box-office draw had announced she was centerfolding for *Playboy* next month in the same sultry breath as promoting her new tight-leather, sci-fi thriller movie. Marianne knew that anyone who pegged Zania as an airhead had a nasty surprise coming; she absolutely knew how to market herself. In every way.

However, hints to the actress of possible woman-on-woman bonding that would allow Zania to prove exactly who was the *ultimate female among women* offered definite possibilities for leveraging the star's vote. It looked as if she'd bought into Marianne's careful seasoning of her performance with hints and suggestions.

Marianne's own tastes, however, were for the second guest judge; the professional chef.

Harold Merritt, with his Michelin-starred *Chicago's Merritt* restaurant, was both distinctly handsome and notoriously single. Win or lose, she'd make a point of chatting him up after the show. That broad chest and short dark crewcut gave him a deliciously tough look; she could find many uses for him outside the kitchen, or in it—two bodies, a touch of olive oil, or maybe chocolate sauce...

A careful peek from behind the screen of the jet-black dyed bangs of her blonde hair revealed both Zania and Harold's attention remained fixated on the monitors of the show's live feed rather than gazing benignly over the competition kitchen floor. Their attention remained precisely where Marianne wanted it. On her.

Kate Stark posed a different problem.

The Number One slotted television chef on any network, not merely the one she owned—also watched the monitor, but with a slightly amused smile that Marianne would pay good money to understand. Kate's startling blue eyes, aquiline nose, and straight black hair brushing her shoulders and framing those well-defined cheekbones, also made her one of the most attractive faces on television, cooking or not.

She was a notoriously deadpan judge, at least on this show, so that wry smile must mean something.

For good or ill, Marianne would not find the answer on this side of the judge's table.

The camera judiciously, or injudiciously, spying down her jacket, pulled back, ready to seek another shot. To maximize her own airtime over the competition, Marianne *accidentally* dribbled a large dollop of the orange-chocolate ganache onto the back of her hand. She licked it clean as if too hurried to wipe it away, making sure the camera could see the pleasure on her face at the success of her own work. The guy behind the lens stayed focused on her.

Damn! She'd nailed the ganache. Marianne would win on taste alone. But she'd have to play the meal presentation carefully, spiking the odds even further in her favor with both of the two guest judges.

The competition buzzer sounded as she shaved the last of the zest of a blood orange using a nutmeg rasp. Even as Marianne held up her hands to show she was done, the camera focused in on the cloud of orange dust, sprinkling through the air like snowflakes.

Her shiny dark green satin blouse made a perfect backdrop, which had *somehow* slipped out of another button. Somehow...

because she'd enlarged the buttonhole last night to ensure that it popped free when she raised her arms.

Nailed it.

She had to close her eyes for a moment to steady herself.

Light-headed.

She needed to eat.

Her normal technique of shrugging it off didn't work. Even lowering her arms and subtly bracing herself against the table didn't help clear her head.

Her hands were shaking.

Her hands never shook.

———

Franco Lamar cursed.

The damned bitch wasn't supposed to taste her own food, at least not that big teasing lick off the back of her hand. A small taste and she'd have been fine. For a while. Long enough.

From where he stood, he could see Marianne Rimaldi wavering. He and his men lurked in the shadows of the television studio, far behind the judges' table and well clear of any camera's eye.

Bitch pissed him off.

He held his breath, keeping his men in place. He had a Plan B, but he hated when that happened. Especially because he didn't have a Plan C.

Rimaldi made it through the male competitor's meal service by clutching the edge of her worktable, rousing herself to high-five her sous chef, but not much else.

The studio emptied. Last shoot of the day. Competitor headed for the bathroom after the judges finished critiquing his lame ass. Already a given he'd be going down after that review—not a flicker of emotion from the head judge.

The main kitchen staff and cameramen drifted out precisely as Franco hoped.

Now the room held three judges, two cameramen, one floor director, and dumb bitch Rimaldi.

When she served, the ohs and ahs and cheerful commentary among the sappy judges bolstered her reserves.

Franco could feel his fingers digging into his opposite arms where they were crossed. He always hated this part the most.

In Marine Force Recon, they'd parachute behind enemy lines, observe, assess, and report. They could be weeks on the ground playing cat-and-mouse games with enemy security and military forces. That was fine. Even lying low between Command's final *Go!* and the actual zero-hour start of the operation never bothered him. Find a willing local female, or an unwilling one, and lay her low until it came time for the shit to hit the fan.

The gap between the actual start of an operation and the launch of his own role in it? He utterly despised that mandated inaction.

Full lock-and-load, then sit on his ass? It had sucked in Recon. It sucked now.

Rimaldi wavered again...but kept going. Tough broad. Her body was shutting down on her and she'd have no idea why. Her brain was going, which meant she'd be past caring.

C'mon bitch. Hold it together long enough to deliver the dessert clean.

She nearly dumped the final plates to the studio's cement floor, earning gasps of surprise from the judges and cameramen that they'd have to edit out.

But she recovered and made it to the table.

Franco held his breath as she stumbled through her presentation. The drug was allowing so little oxygen to her brain that he couldn't believe she remained upright.

Delivered.

Now the tasting.

C'mon, judges.

The movie star wench did even better than he could have hoped.

She ate the poisoned dessert in two neat bites. Then the stupid whore picked up her plate to lick up the puddled chocolate sauce with a long, sensuous move that sent a shiver up his balls.

Licking that plate clean, in addition to the dessert itself? No longer a knockout drug—now a major overdose.

She didn't even wobble. Instead, she collapsed forward, face onto the plate.

Shit!

The actress hit the table so hard that one of her awesomely impressive breasts—only marginally contained in her sheer top —popped free.

Franco looked at the other two judges as the studio exploded in panic.

Kate Stark's hand rested on the male judge's arm to keep him from eating.

The two primary targets both sat there—undrugged.

Rimaldi's body finally figured out that it was already dead, and the chef collapsed to the floor.

That put paid on the two secondary targets: Rimaldi and Zania were past recovery.

Stark and the guy sat there unmoving.

Franco nodded to Jason.

Jason Mann pulled out a dart gun and shot them both in the back of the neck.

They each flinched in turn, then slumped in their seats.

Franco signaled his men to move in. When the studio lights blacked out, the four of them pulled down the night-vision goggles perched on their foreheads. The studio was now visible in a hundred shadings of green.

They pulled the darts out of Kate Stark and Harold Merritt and dragged them back.

Jason stopped to grope Zania's errant breast. He looked ready to do more until Franco hissed at him to get moving.

Their timing must be perfect for this to work, or Plan B would be a worse bust than Plan A.

Down the elevator that their inside man had locked in place for them.

Along the basement corridor.

The moment the hired truck backed against the loading dock; Vince used bolt cutters to cut off the diplomatic-pouch door seal on the empty shipping container. Manuel held the door open as they dropped the two bodies on the mattress inside and Jason injected them with the antidote.

Doors closed, a new seal slapped on—identical to even the registration number—crimped into place, and Nicky shooed the truck driver on his way in under fifteen seconds.

They dumped their gear into a couple of lawyer's briefcases, and each took a different route to the parking garage.

The container and its cargo were on their way.

They were done and damn well paid.

———

FBI AGENT MARCUS REYNOLDS AND HIS PARTNER LEONA Edwards were walking along the 50th Street side of Rockefeller Center in midtown Manhattan when a semi-truck burst out of the loading dock and missed flattening them by mere inches.

"Shit!" New York was like that. Let your attention drift sideways for a moment and you're done.

He automatically noted that it was from Express Truck of the Five Boroughs and had a twenty-foot burnt-orange shipping container on its bed. The driver waved them around, his bumper protruding half across the sidewalk, then he roared away, not quite taking Marcus' shoe heels with him.

Marcus' inattention had stemmed from the same cause as always over the last six weeks: Leona. That's how long she'd been his partner, and he couldn't stop looking at her instead of trucks that were trying to kill him.

Leona Edwards' lustrous skin was the color that only emphasized his pale-guy whiteness and would have sent his white-trash parents stumbling for their shotguns. The way she filled out a white shirt and black suit coat was enough to kill a man; definitely custom-tailored—had to be on her frame. No problem hiding a sidearm in a shoulder holster; she had plenty else filling out the jacket for even her Glock 17 semi-auto service issue to be a distraction.

She caught him looking and quirked one of her eyebrows up; damn woman thought she was Spock. He'd been caught staring so many times that now it was no more than a part of their routine. She had too damn much worth staring at—and knew it.

Leona pulled him out of the way of a midnight blue BMW 760Li sedan with dark-tinted glass that shot out of the parking garage and across the sidewalk without touching its brakes.

Twice in half a block. He needed to get his head back in the game.

"What is this *hacker signature* crap again?" Leona knew computers far better than he did. Which didn't bother him any, as long as he kept outshooting her on the range. She came close but hadn't beat him yet.

"Every top-level computer hacker has a style, a unique way of doing things, as unique as a bomber does for wiring a timer. It's their fingerprint or signature."

Damn but he could listen to her rich, low voice all day. No wedding ring, no jewelry of any kind, which didn't signify squat on a field agent. Six weeks together and he didn't know if she was married or had a boyfriend. Or preferred men or women.

He held a door for her, then they headed across the busy lobby of Rockefeller Center to the bank of elevators.

"So, someone with this hacker signature broke into our FBI databases and no one could stop them?" Cyber warfare creeped him out. He didn't like things that made him afraid of his own smartphone.

"They didn't merely break in; they strolled in with such a sophisticated set of tools that the guys in DC still aren't sure how they were hit or what was taken."

"Then how—"

"We've been trying to tag Rafe for the last six months, right?"

The fact that the two of them had been working the case from opposite ends was what finally brought them together. That and timing.

Marcus and Leona somehow lucked into their own elevator and started the climb up the 30 Rock building. He thought of things that two people could do in an elevator if they were willing. Then he thought about the cameras that were probably watching them and stayed focused on the conversation.

"Sure. But I don't understand why we're here when we should be closing in on this creep. Damn, we were so close. Then he guns down poor Jake and vanishes." Jake's death was the reason Leona needed a new partner. His own partner retiring had left him partnerless at the same time. Marcus would have to remember to thank him for that next time they got together over a beer.

"Because—" she stared unblinking at the floor numbers. Tough to the bone. "—that hacker with their *unique* signature, not Rafe's, strolled into our system. Not a random part of it, they walked straight into DITU."

"Shit! I thought that thing was bolted down hard. I

remember a lecture on it." The Data Intercept Technology Unit had to be the scariest damn thing he'd ever heard of. E-mails, phone calls, Internet browsing history, fully compiled and cross-indexed covering pretty much everyone in the country, or anyone whose signals crossed American borders. Or who even thought about logging on. Or using their phone. For anything.

"Said hacker," Leona continued, "apparently read every e-mail and grabbed every phone call we had scooped up on Rafe and a number of others. It's a signature they haven't seen in five years."

"So, we're going to see Kate Stark, the owner of Cooks Network because…" it was finally making sense.

"Kate Stark," Leona straightened her jacket as the elevator slowed, "was a Secret Service agent at the time, in the counterfeiting division. She's credited with taking down this same hacker who popped up inside our network, but there's no record of the hacker's ID—before or after the supposed event."

"WITSEC?"

Leona nodded. "The Witness Security Program shows that she entered protection five years ago. And then she evaporated. US Marshalls lost track of her."

"Until she decided on a bit of recidivism and popped up in DITU. Got it." The elevator slowed as they approached their floor.

The doors slid open on the main floor of Cooks Network to shouts.

A lot of them.

They weren't shouts of surprise.

They were blind panic.

———

Captain Rang Jin-ho stood on the bridge of the North Korean ship *Chong Chon Gang* and shifted his weight to keep it off his artificial leg; it itched horribly. The problem was that it itched in a place that was now made of steel.

But he wasn't going to go below and rest it. They had permission to be in port for three hours and he'd never looked out on American soil before, not once in his twenty years at sea.

I wish you were here to see it with me, Su-jin. His wife would have enjoyed the moment. But, for fear of defection, not even the most trusted servants of Office 39 were allowed to leave North Korea together with their family. One or the other always remained behind.

He'd taken command of the hundred-and-fifty meter ship a decade ago. Perhaps he'd done it a tad brutally, but it had succeeded with no one the wiser, which was what counted. He and the *Chong Chon Gang* had been Office 39's number one cargo and smuggling vessel ever since.

But they were known—no one could hide the purpose of such a large ship forever. So why did the Americans agree to let the premier vessel of the Democratic People's Republic of Korea's most secret and powerful government agency arrive in the Red Hook terminal in the Port of New York and New Jersey?

Were Westerners truly so soft-hearted that they'd allow a known spy vessel into their harbor under the pretense of being a UN food aid delivery?

Perhaps.

Rang would not be so foolish. No CIA ship would ever be allowed into Wonsan harbor.

He had been granted three hours to take aboard and stow one hundred shipping containers. The big cranes were making quick work of the task. But only ninety-one of the containers were in the stack they were loading.

It had been two hours. He had less than an hour left before the hovering Coast Guard cutters would escort him once more to sea, when he spotted the delivery trucks crossing the yard.

Nine trucks bearing nine containers.

No Customs inspections on those.

They were under the seal of the People's Republic of China diplomatic pouch. Each door lock seal was checked as the trucks arrived, but nothing more.

He knew the contents of five of the containers, all forbidden goods specifically against the UN sanctions: two containers of RPGs and other ground-fire weapons, two containing the various parts from which a Bell Cobra attack helicopter might be assembled, and a Tesla roadster to assuage the Supreme Leader Kim Jong-un.

As long as the vicious bastard had his occasional new toys, he left Office 39 alone. And if he didn't, he'd find out exactly who truly ran the Democratic People's Republic of Korea as his father Kim Jong-il had before him.

In his first two years of power, Kim Jong-un had executed the four men his father had appointed to train him. Next, every general in the military who had been one of his father's cronies was removed—very permanently. After that, he had his own uncle, the man's family, actually *most* of his own relatives machine-gunned down. Or fed alive to starved dogs. The reports varied. Over a hundred of North Korea's preeminent citizens removed during a that initial purge.

Never in the mad rampage had the Supreme Leader touched a single family member of Office 39, which proved he was not stupid, merely vicious.

Rang kept an eye on the *loading mix-up* that caused one of the containers to be rejected by his First Officer only after it was lowered deep into the cargo hold.

P'yo kept it smooth.

The moment the container hit the stack, he had the lifting tackle switched to a different container. One which bore the same identifying numbers and seal that they'd brought from North Korea.

Rang watched from his eagle's eye perch on the command bridge.

None of the inspectors of security people hovering about his ship noted the exchange.

A quarter of a billion dollars in supernotes—counterfeit US hundred-dollar bills—would be returned via the PRC's diplomatic pouch to the embassy and be spread out through the gangs of the Chinese Ghee Mun Tong. A simple payment method for the contents of the nine containers.

Office 39's supernotes were the best on the planet and they distributed billions of dollars per year. Yet one more way that the Office kept the DPRK's economy afloat. They could pass the supreme test—the American gambling casinos' machines accepted them every time.

Rang watched the replacement container as it was reloaded onto the truck, which then departed through the gate.

He eased his leg again.

The last four containers' contents were unknown to him. They were labeled for the Council of Five, the leaders of Office 39. A Council on which he intended to sit one day.

His wife Su-jin had instructed him at length on how to spot opportunity when it came.

These four unknown containers? he asked his wife's image in his mind.

Wait and see, Rang. We remain always patient.

Those last containers gave him an ache in his missing knee that he didn't like one tiny bit.

What could possibly be inside them? Opportunity or death notice?

1

NOW

KATE STARK WOKE SLOWLY WITH NO MEMORY OF GOING TO SLEEP.

And absolutely no memory of taking a man with her.

But the body she lay half across was male. A broad, powerful chest. Truly male.

His heartbeat was loud in her ear despite the shirt.

Shirt?

What was the point of dragging a man into her bed if she didn't remember it *and* they didn't get naked?

She tried opening her eyes. No difference. Not one bit. Either she was blind or in the pitch dark. To avoid panic, she chose one item from Column B, thank you very much.

Kate pushed herself away, using the sleeping man for leverage. He grunted softly.

She was dressed too. A hand to her chest—show clothes. She rubbed her fingers over her left breast—the outline of a logo embroidered into her master chef's jacket.

The show!

Kate's Kitchen from Hell.

She'd been judging a show. The final one of a two-week filming stint. First two weeks of June. Three shows a day. A whole season plus Thanksgiving, Christmas, and Kate's birthday specials in the can. The final judging. Two competing chefs. Maxwell and...

The man beside her snorted, not so softly, then shifted and continued his slumber.

And now...? What was she doing?

Her brain was moving through molasses.

Ignoring the head spin that came with it, she sat up on a mattress. A decidedly thin one. Not hers.

They had judged Maxwell first. He was an excellent chef, and his meal had been splendid. His final dessert of mango sorbet served on a strawberry-wine reduction with a flake of a fresh-made chocolate mint sprinkled with sea salt made a delectable denouement to the meal. Splendid...but not innovative. Not exciting.

She remembered that clearly enough and rubbed the back of her neck to try to shake loose more. She hissed against the pain. A mosquito bite-sized lump on the back of her neck and a bruised area the size of her palm.

Kate tried...but couldn't connect it to anything.

Guest judge Harold Merritt with his patrician features, short dark hair, and serious work-out chest—clearly taken in by the progression of flavors, totally missing its lack of original thinking.

To Kate, Maxwell's meal had been most exceptional in not being exceptional.

Zania's palate had been wholly outstripped. She'd declared it "wicked tasty" then realigned her sheerly clad and impressively generous profile to the best advantage for the nearest camera.

Off the edge of the thin mattress, a platform extended. Kate tapped a short-trimmed fingernail—a metal platform. Reaching out into the smothering darkness a foot or so—more metal. Not smooth like a knife's blade or a stainless-steel counter, instead rough and covered with a patina of rust corrosion. And the stench of...fish. Yet not television-show fresh fish. When she rested her palm against the floor, she could feel a deep vibration rumbling through the steel. Diesel engines, big ones, running at cruise—not flat out but not idling. But no bumps of a roadway either. Her inner ear reported a rocking motion.

She eased the collar of her show jacket. The air was tepid—thick and difficult to draw into her lungs—and...tepid was all her sluggish mind could unearth for an adjective. Like tea water with no remaining warmth to comfort or coolness to soothe.

The man beside her grunted and thrashed about a moment before settling. His noises echoed strangely. She snapped her fingers, though it took a couple of tries to make it a clear, sharp sound; her nerves were functioning no better than her thinking. Once achieved, the snap made a bright sound, as if—

She didn't want to jump to conclusions. But neither did she like the one she'd landed on.

Then a second chef had served... Marianne Rimaldi! That was who! Harold and Zania had come to life. Somehow Marianne was managing to work both sides of the aisle with her flair for showmanship.

She definitely played well on camera; a skill Kate always looked for while wearing her network-owner hat.

Marianne's food was also fascinating. Her first dish was exquisite, though her second rated as a partial miss—the chocolate Halibut Mole. *She'd either needed a stronger fish like a swordfish to mitigate the contrast of the protein and the sauce or a sharper* mole *for the contrast to be a statement of flavor—but the first and third dishes were so exceptional and the* mole *itself so rich that Kate, in her judge's hat, decided the contestants were neck and neck on flavor and elegance going into the dessert course. Without question, Rimaldi ruled the innovation category.*

Kate rubbed at her sore neck, unclear what had happened. But the other memories were coming back. Perhaps this one would too. It was hard to be patient while breathing tepid, fish-flavored air in total darkness.

If Marianne nailed the dessert, Kate would invite her onto Two Chefs Chat. *It was a new show she was developing to help chefs take that next step to stardom—a one-on-one master class of two chefs learning from each other, filmed for the public.*

Rising to her feet, Kate wobbled on the unstable mattress and braced one foot lightly on the sleeping man's chest. She also discovered a headache that cried in alarm.

She ignored it.

Cries. There'd been cries of surprise. Each sharply halted on a gasp. Marianne Rimaldi stumbling and nearly dumping her dessert service onto the studio floor as she'd climbed the steps to the judge's stage.

At five-foot-ten, Kate's upward reach was seven-nine. Mattress thickness was negligible. By pushing onto her tiptoes, she discovered exactly what she didn't want to know. At seven-foot-ten above the steel floor was a corrugated metal roof.

Screams.

On the verge of toeing her uninvited companion awake—because Kate always remembered when she invited someone into her bed—she became aware of a new sound.

They hadn't been screams of surprise. They'd been screams of...

2

———

A CLANK, A THUMP, AND LIGHT POURED INTO THE DARKNESS LEVEL with Kate's knees; proof that, thankfully, she wasn't blind. A one-foot square inspection port opened in a sidewall of their shipping container prison, for Kate had no doubt that's what this was.

The flash of light confirmed her suspicions.

They were the sole occupants inside an eight-by-eight-by-twenty-foot cargo shipping container. The rumble through the steel-plate floor probably belonged to a ship's engines. That meant they were at sea, confirmed by the slow rocking motion.

She watched mesmerized as a couple of water bottles and what appeared to be a bag lunch were dropped through the opening.

"Hunh? Hey? What's going—" Harold Merritt. As she'd have guessed if she'd been ready to think about it. Her guest judge belonged to the nice chest she'd been unconscious on.

In half a second, he was going to spook their unidentified provider. There wasn't time to shush him. Therefore, as he sat up, she spear-handed him in the sternum. He collapsed back onto the mattress with a pained but relatively quiet whoosh.

She'd spotted something.

Two things: one past, one present.

Her brain had processed them both, even if she hadn't caught up with either yet. Kate held herself frozen for a long instant.

Then the memory fought its way through her miasma.

There wasn't merely a threat now or in the past, there was immediate danger.

Mortal danger.

Marianne Rimaldi managed to get the desserts distributed, but her hands were shaking.

She was blinking hard.

Kate felt a sharp knot in the pit of her stomach. Marianne's sudden change of mannerism was ringing a bell somewhere.

Not as a cook.

But from Kate's life before that.

Marianne rallied to distribute the plates, but there was no finesse, no flirting that her earlier manners had promised—not with Harold, not with the bombshell Zania. Her explanation of the dish rambled so badly that Kate tactfully cut her off.

The connections finally surfaced.

Training videos from the five years Kate had been a Secret Service field agent.

Videos of poisonings!

The hand that had delivered the food and water reached into the cargo container.

It was far steadier than Marianne's had been.

He was reaching for the other something that Kate's brain had cataloged, even if her conscious mind had not.

A covered bucket stood close by the opening. Their toilet.

As the arm stretched through the small opening to check the bucket, Kate dove, grabbed his wrist—no question of gender by the thickness of the fingers—and bent his elbow backwards against the edge of the opening.

She had managed to stop Harold before he bit into the tiny dessert.

Turning to warn Zania, but far too slowly, as if she was moving in a dream.

The world slowed to an impossible crawl.

Twice in her life, Kate's perceptions had slowed. Neither time had it saved her life, instead it had cost others theirs.

The first time? During the assassination of the newly elected Vice President.

Kate had been close enough to feel the heat of the gunfire and the stinging impact and hot burn of his spraying blood.

She'd taken tackled the shooter hard enough to break four of the woman's ribs and both arms—a mistress with a grudge at not being Mrs. Vice President. Being a familiar fixture had let her slide past the first several layers of security; Kate was supposed to have been the final guarantee.

She'd quit the Service the day the investigations were done. Even though they'd exonerated her, she hadn't forgiven herself.

The second slowdown had been watching the unfolding disaster in her television studio.

Zania made a show of popping Marianne's dessert into her mouth before Kate could warn her. The actress gave the dessert one clean bite with those perfect white teeth, then swallowed the whole thing. She licked her bright lips with an impossibly long tongue, promising immense delights to whoever could conquer her. Clearly, she was "ramping up" to re-engage Marianne's wandering attention.

The bombshell picked up her plate, licked it once where Marianne had pooled the ganache, then set the plate back on the table—and folded forward to plant her face at its center. She hit the edge of the table hard enough for one of her breasts to break free of her filmy blouse, adding disgrace to...death.

Kate didn't need to reach for Zania's pulse to know she no longer had one.

Hollywood was going to need a new super-hot starlet.

It had been too little and too late then...

But not now!

She torqued harder on the jailor's elbow, could feel it would only take the least bit of pressure for it to give and break backwards.

Well and truly trapped, his scream now echoed the others in the studio.

Kate turned back to Marianne.

The chef settled hard to sit cross-legged on the studio floor, tipped to the side, and hit the concrete like a sack of flour. Her eyes popping open to remain fixed and dilated.

Dead. Murdered.

The chocolate ganache.

Kate's last thought then had been that death by chocolate was no kinder than death any other way.

Her first thought now was how pissed she'd be if she'd died over a bite of chocolate cheesecake in the studio. Almost as pissed as she was at being made prisoner in a damned cargo container going God alone knew where.

She eased off the pressure on their jailor's elbow, then yanked inward on his arm hard enough for him to slam his head on the outside of the container. That changed his cries to whimpers.

3

Paul Stark couldn't watch the *Evening News with Vanessa* one moment longer. He leapt out of his Follot armchair to pace the living room of the apartment atop the Chrysler Building that he shared with his sister.

He'd tried killing the television's audio and filling the cavernous silence with Bach.

And then The Boss.

Neither helped.

He turned the news anchor back on.

From behind her small desk, she radiated that perfect mixture of holier-than-thou and barely contained sex.

"Police are looking for heiress and network executive Kate Stark, twin sister of international jetsetter Paul Stark."

"Did you enjoy saying that, Vanessa?" he talked back to the screen. "You sure looked like you did." But all Vanessa's delivery was verbal. Lead anchor or not, she'd been boring as hell in bed.

"The brother and sister are co-owners of the highly successful Cooks Network television station, as well as several others. They currently reside in what is considered the ultimate bachelor pad in downtown Manhattan—"

"Blah, blah, blah, Vanessa. You're just bent out of shape because you didn't get to stay here more than the two nights." She was also clingy as hell and continued to call him multiple times a week though they were months done.

The police had been seriously bent out of shape this afternoon when they'd found Paul home instead of Kate. The FBI who'd followed close behind had been far more serious and far more thorough. Worst of all, the seriously hot woman definitely hadn't taken his word on anything no matter how charming he was being.

That's when he'd turned on the news and started to worry in earnest.

He paced away from the TV.

The curved arc of narrow triangular windows that were the Art Déco signature of the uppermost stories of the Chrysler Building sent the midday sun marching across the polished heart-of-pine flooring in hard-edged slashes. The fitted circular cross-sections of pine tree flooring offered him their rings of history to pace on. He occasionally used them as an excuse for a wandering mind whenever Kate caught him not listening to her. *Contemplating the ages, Kate.*

Bored out of his skull at another harangue and daydreaming about women would be a more accurate assessment, but you couldn't say shit like that to Kate without her tossing it right back full force like a curve ball in a game of fast pitch.

The flooring didn't distract him this time any more than it usually did. He considered going downstairs, but they didn't use the sixty-sixth floor much except for entertaining; he'd fixed it up when they'd bought the place, but it was mostly a party space for other tenants of the building. The five thousand of sixty-seven they'd left open except for a couple of home offices. It served as their living room, dining room, and kitchen. The three thousand square feet of the sixty-eighth were his and Kate's personal apartments.

The Old-World elegance of the former Cloud Club couldn't eradicate either the news of Kate's disappearance or Vanessa's *Look-at-me, I'm-so-damned-cute* voice.

Paul crossed to one of those triangular windows and looked out over Manhattan. But he didn't see one of the most spectacular views in the city.

Instead, he saw the city that was hunting his little sister for the murders in her studio. He could get away with calling her that, since she wasn't here. After all, Kate was thirteen minutes younger and two inches shorter than his six feet.

If she were here, she could pound the snot out of him, so he typically exercised discretion in her presence—at least when they had guests.

"Master Chef Kate Stark and Harold Merritt, a guest judge in *Kate's Kitchen from Hell* studio..." Vanessa restarted the story again behind him as if doing a breaking exclusive of the next World War.

Must be a slow news day for Kate to be stuck as the lead story. And once more, the typically crappy photos—heavily Photoshopped to make them look even more like criminals—were plastered across the screen. Kate had never looked that rough even after the time Paul led her on a curative all-night bender through Manhattan's seediest dives the night she'd quit the Secret Service.

"...are being sought by authorities in the double murder of another chef," who apparently wasn't popular enough to deserve a name, "and the hot Hollywood rising-star Zania."

"Not rising anymore, Vanessa, unless she's planning on rising from the dead." Paul half-waited for his sister's scathing comeback that usually made the tagline on his jokes. Perhaps: *And it's not Hollywood that is* hot, *you airhead.*

But Kate's response never came. Nor the follow-up comment about him stooping low enough to bed such a pea brain.

The film of the victims' last moments had predictably been posted anonymously to YouTube and gone instantly viral. The film was chaotic: deaths, Zania's clothing failure revealing a truly impressive errant breast (shown with the smallest possible blackout square over the nipple), power failure in the studio, then lights back on. Somewhere in those few seconds of darkness, the two surviving judges had scampered, though Zania's breast had remained.

Then they plastered the screen with a shot of the hurriedly edited cover of the next *Playboy* featuring Zania; the publisher had added a black wreath and *In Memoriam* to the cover. With Zania's assets and the free advertising being broadcast, this was going to be a record issue.

Paul did take a moment to appreciate the scantily clad woman in the magazine's cover image splashed across the screen. Her cover-shot halter top required significantly less leather than it took to make the halter for the horse she rode in on. The woman certainly did know how to sell it.

But was she that hot in real life? Unlike Vanessa. Rather, had she *been* that hot in real life?

He'd ask Kate, but...

Damn it! When she hadn't come back to their apartment last night, he'd assumed that she'd shacked up with a cute guy. She did that on rare occasion, well, close to never. And she'd always let him know before. Disappearing for days at a time was more his style than hers.

But now, a morning of silence—and then this.

"What did you get into this time, Katydid?" She hated that nickname, but she hated it less than her middle name, so she let him get away with it. Even with that caveat, he made sure never to use it when she had a chef's knife in her hand. While she might have been dangerous as a Secret Service agent, she was lethal as a chef.

Okay, bad analogy considering the current news for Starlet Zania and the former chef competitor Miss Nameless. They'd flashed her picture once—blonde with black bangs, slim, and a knowing smile that Paul rather liked—making her much cuter than the overstated Zania. But she didn't have the fame to claim any more screen time than that.

Still there was no answer from Kate.

Unable to stop himself, he glanced over at her bent-wood IKEA chair. The woman had no sense of history. If they were going to lease the top three floors of the Chrysler Building— truly the ultimate bachelor-twins' pad—why had the woman bought herself a Swedish box-store chair that she'd had to put together herself? With disposable tools, no less.

"Well, guess I'm going to have to track you down to find the answer to that question, too." He'd better find her before the police did, who were gearing up to create a world of hurt for Katydid.

That meant finding Erika Albert.

Crap!

4

"WHAT'S GOING ON? WHAT ARE YOU DOING?" THE DIM OUTLINE of Harold Merritt came up to Kate as she held their jailor's arm hard against the edge of the inspection port.

A Shakespeare line about a poor player strutting the stage came to mind, but she was too drugged to place it. They must have been drugged for her not to be able to place the speech...*Hamlet? Lear?* She was reasonably sure it wasn't *Julius Caesar.*

Harold was bending over to look out the open inspection door, mostly filled with the whimpering man's arm.

Kate spotted the appearance of a gun barrel, protruding several inches through the inspection port into the shipping container.

Macbeth! The next line of the speech, *then is heard no more,* slammed into her consciousness.

She kicked Harold in the gut none too gently to knock him clear as the gun fired. Mere inches kept his curiosity from killing the cat.

The muzzle flash and the cannon-roar inside the dim metal

container was such a brutal shock to the senses that she barely kept her grip.

Wild shot.

Next one wouldn't be.

The idiot outside was screaming because of the powder burns all up the arm she had pinned.

Thankfully, he'd been dumb enough to reach the weapon through the opening. Despite being momentarily blinded by the muzzle flash, she estimated that the kick of the shot would slam the gun up against the top of the opening. Kate grabbed for the barrel, snagged it by chance on her first try, and wrested it free.

Harold was cowering face-down on the mattress, covering his ears and cursing. She didn't have that luxury. Keeping the pressure on the man's arm, she reversed the gun and stuck it in the man's face.

She knew the revolver by feel, even though her vision was slow to re-adapt from the bright muzzle flash in the container's dim interior. A long-barrel Smith & Wesson 29, Dirty Harry's .44 Magnum. What was it with small men and big guns? At least the VP's mistress had understood the proper use of power with a neatly concealable 9 mm Colt Defender.

"First, empty your pockets through the door," she ordered the man. She didn't wait for him to complain or refuse. Torquing his arm like the handle on a meat grinder, he frantically complied in place of risking the dislocation of his elbow.

He whimpered. There might be others nearby enough to hear, but that couldn't be helped at the moment. At least most of the report of the gunshot had been confined inside the container, as testified by the ringing in her ears.

With the barrel boring into his ear, he dumped dribs and drabs of pocket detritus through the opening. His hisses of pain said she'd hurt his other hand when she'd taken the gun. But under the threat of imminent death, he stayed on task.

A pen knife, a flashlight, his wallet, a walkie talkie, and, *ka-ching,* a cell phone.

"Now, open the door."

"I can no reach," his accent was thick, marginally understandable. One of the Asian languages; she hadn't seen more of him than his arm and his gun. The Asian languages were never her specialty.

"Who else knows?"

"Cook. I pay him extra to food. Him think for stowaway girlfriend."

"If I let you go, can you open the door?"

"Maybe. Maybe. Yes."

She shoved the barrel harder against his ear. "Open it."

5

———————

"You open the door now!" Kate spoke harshly and drilled the barrel of the massive revolver into their jailor's ear. She knelt in front of the cargo container's inspection hatch.

He nodded fiercely, at least she assumed that's what caused the gun to move up and down. Most of the small opening was taken by his arm and shoulder which was making communication difficult on top of his marginal English. She considered telling him to bathe more often as well...but kept her thoughts regarding his stale reek to herself even though it was overpowering the lingering cordite.

She released him slowly, pulling the gun back into the container so that only the tip of the barrel protruded. Shifting both hands to the weapon, she'd make sure he ate a bullet if he tried to tear it from her grasp.

The man could be in no doubt that his life depended upon his obeying.

As their jailor moved away, she ducked low to look out the inspection hatch, cautiously in case he was planning to land a punch and recover his weapon through the small opening.

She faced another stack of containers five feet away, enough

35

space to open the container doors in an emergency, but no more. The light, now that her eyes had adapted, vaguely revealed the steel canyon. They were deep in the container stack.

Apparently, bravery was nowhere in the jailor's job description. He actually moved to comply with her order under the threat of the massive weapon. He didn't even think to slam the inspection hatch closed, not that she would have let him.

Stevedore thinking.

No Special Ops-trained soldier would have missed such an opportunity.

She heard the metallic clank of one of the handle's safeties. Standard Conex shipping containers had two doors on one end, like window shutters. Each door stood four feet wide, eight tall, and was stout enough to survive the impact of shifting internal cargo in rough seas. On the outside of each door were two locking bars that pinned the door in place. Their handles had to be freed from a small keeper latch, then swung outward. Two releases, two raised and turned handles, and the left door would be open. That's all she needed.

Altering her position to keep both the gun and her gaze on the man, he seemed to be reaching for the door handles. It was awkward to follow him as the small inspection door was low enough that it meant she was lying on what she assumed was the bag lunch and had to knock the piss pot out of the way with her head. Thankfully, it was still dry and empty.

The jailor's problem was that it took two hands to unlatch a door and even that was awkward when the container wasn't resting on the ground in front of you. A quick peek out the tiny hatch revealed they were well up in the cliff of stacked containers and he would need one of his hands to hold on.

After an inordinate amount of thumping through the steel door, no doubt exacerbated by his scraped up and burned arm on one side and wrenched fingers on the other—neither of which Kate had not the least sympathy for—he managed to release one of the handles.

But the handle had also been his support and now it swung free. With a brief cry, he lost his grip and fell. Korean from the brief glimpse she had of his terrified features. His head banged hard against one of the containers on the opposite side of the narrow steel canyon.

After that, he fell silently.

6

"Hey, Rikka."

"Go to Hell, Paul!"

Erika *Rikka* Albert hung up the phone wishing it was one of those old-style things she could slam back into the cradle. She'd have to write an app that did that—crashing-down-into-the-cradle sound then disconnect.

For Paul? She'd make it ear-splittingly loud.

Add cathedral bells, crashing semis, and howitzer fire. With a subliminal layer of the T. Rex roar from *Jurassic Park* to make it extra freaking scary, too.

She returned to the order she'd been preparing in her catering production kitchen. There were fifty more pieces of baby abalone sashimi and a hundred of tuna belly to cut. A twenty quick rolls of her spiced salmon and avocado sushi and she'd be done—the avocados so perfectly ripe that she could smell the dusky warmth even though they were still in their nubbled dark-green skin.

Paul Stark's call had cost her a precious thirty seconds: five for shock—it had been two goddamn years since his last call, which wasn't anywhere near long enough. Five more seconds to tell him where he could go, and twenty more resisting the urge to heave a perfectly good phone into the trash because it now was infested with Paul-cooties.

She rammed the phone into the back pocket of her jeans. Could feel its outline there. But putting it in the front pocket of her apron would be even worse.

It rang again, vibrated her butt as harshly as a slap.

She whirled as Paul cracked open the door to her kitchen. Like Lara Croft in the movie *Tomb Raiders,* she heaved three-hundred millimeters of *yanagi* sashimi blade into the door frame to leave it quivering inches from his nose.

Ignoring the blade, he opened the door the rest of the way as he arched a knowing eyebrow at her. A slow smile quirked those strong lips. His sun-tipped blond hair as light as his sister's was dark. He was at least as handsome as his sister Kate was striking. Where her features were precise and elegant, his were an enchanting cross of rugged yet refined.

Rikka stalked over and jerked the blade out of the wood, returned to the chopping block and calmly began to re-hone the edge. Dulling seven hundred dollars' worth of knife over Paul Stark would be a total waste of good steel.

She turned her back on him and, cursed herself for being a total lame-oid. She shouldn't have aimed at the door jamb. What had it ever done to her? She should have stuck him in the center of the forehead with that throw like Lara Croft would have. She'd try to remember that, in case this exact situation ever came up again.

"Already told you where to go."

Rikka could hear him step into the kitchen behind her. He'd learned stealth from his sister, but she heard him nonetheless. The door settled closed with a light snick as he leaned against it.

She tried to cut the *toro* and totally hacked the slice. She had to reshave the slab of tuna belly to make a clean line, a loss of two pieces. At forty-five dollars a pound wholesale, that was an expensive mistake. Raising the knife once more, she paused. No question, this cut would be wrong as well if she attempted it.

Taking a deep breath, she planted both fists, one clenched around the knife, against the heavy cherrywood chopping block specially lowered for her five-foot-zero height.

"What?!" She didn't turn to face him.

"You're looking great, Rikka. You always were hot in a petite Japanese and whatever way, but now you've definitely got something more going on. Smokin'. And I like your hair long on your back like that, the pixie cut never suited you. Brings out the green in your eyes. What are you working on?"

"A five-thousand-dollar order and you're screwing up my timing." She turned with the intention of scaring him off. Maybe she'd throw in a side plate of free Paul Stark sashimi with this order; it wasn't as if it would be *human* meat.

It wouldn't be right though; Matsuko was a good customer whenever he was in town and Paul was a toxic substance. Besides, she liked Matsuko, who also threw a hell of a party. She'd been hoping to find someone there to drag off into her lair for a few days' rough and tumble.

But Paul wasn't back by the door. He stood a half-step behind her, and she had to look way up to see those blue eyes. It was the only feature the twins shared. Paul was blond and blue, Kate black and blue. Both had that mystical Irish eye coloring.

He leaned in, not quite impaling himself on her still-raised and nearly forgotten blade. He inhaled deeply then sighed.

"You always did smell wonderful. Like cinnamon and sea salt on a fine sailing day."

She remembered Paul's scent plenty well, exactly as it had been the last time they'd been this close two years before. Man. That was it. Not leather or wood. Not rock or earth. He was that most refined essence of pure male. She was either going to have to kill him or kill herself. Otherwise, she'd be wrapped around him in seconds and that would be bad. She'd resisted then and she'd resist now, but this particular dry spell had dragged on far too long if she was even thinking such thoughts.

"I, uh," he winced, "I have a problem."

"What's that?" It would help if he didn't look as good as he smelled...

"I appear to have lost my sister."

7

———————

Between a second and a half and two seconds later Kate heard a distant thud of their jailor's body hitting the deck below. His fall had been, she juggled the math in her head, around fifteen meters. They were in the fifth or sixth tier of containers in the stack.

"What happened?" Harold was wheezing from the knife hand to his sternum and the kick to his gut.

Kate ignored him and poked her head out the tiny opening. Fresh air without the least bit like Manhattan mixed in. No, it smelled of the open ocean.

They were fifth container in the stack, three from the top.

No movement in the shadows far below, most likely dead, and not too likely that anyone would come looking for him here. At least not soon, so she had a few minutes to think —hopefully.

The idiot had climbed up five containers high without a harness or safety rope. On top of that, he was in on the kidnap plot, so he'd gotten what he'd deserved.

Twisting her head to look to either side of the steel canyon, she saw blue and blue. Ocean blue. No sign of land.

If they'd been even one layer lower in the stack of containers, they'd be inside the hull of the cargo ship and she wouldn't even see that much.

The sunset to the right gave her the direction of west which told her they were steaming south, for all the good that bit of information did her. Unless their container was facing the rear of the vessel, in which case they were going north. In other words, no clue.

One last thing to check.

Exactly as she'd feared.

The handle closest to the inspection port dangled free. The farther one, the one out of reach no matter how creative or inventive she might be, the one that bore a heavy official seal she'd need tools to cut, remained firmly latched.

8

RIKKA HAD MADE PAUL SIT IN THE CORNER.

"I'm not twelve."

She ignored his protest. Instead pointing with the tip of her blade, turning into that frozen statue thing she did so well, until he complied.

So, he'd found a barstool—carved from a single block of ebony by the look of it—and moved it into the farthest corner of the kitchen without quite giving himself a hernia.

He sat down to wait.

Paul had always been able to find her when he needed to or, he admitted with chagrin, when the whim had struck him. This time he'd cracked the GPS application on her phone. She'd had it off, of course, but he had a buddy at the NSA who'd used what he called *The Find* that worked even when the phone itself was turned off. He'd reached into the system and read off Rikka's location.

The results had led him to the top floor of a warehouse in a bad section of the Bronx, not that he'd ever been to a good section, but Mott Haven was freaky bad. The neighborhood looked burned out, run down, and run over. And that was before he'd probed into the projects built by the New York City Housing Authority.

This rank warehouse won the Worst-of-it-all competition. The only reason he'd been able to traverse it without being mugged was because Rikka must have scared off any indigent desperate enough to squat near her hidden production kitchen.

Which was impressive, because Paul had trouble imagining her scaring off a fly. It's not like you could be a true badass when you were a mere slip of a seriously cute thing.

He also knew from experience that, after his intrusion here, Rikka would never use this space again. An odd habit he'd never found the roots of.

From the outside, her kitchen looked like a hexagonal concrete box in the corner of the abandoned warehouse. The only revelation from the exterior was the ornately etched glass front door.

Inside, the kitchen was perfect. A masterpiece of burnished wood and stainless steel, the air swam with the hints of fine cooking and fresh herbs that could only be achieved through months or years of top-quality meals being prepared in the space. She'd created a six-sided wonder of a high-end kitchen.

Yet within a day, perhaps less, it would cease to exist as if it had never been. Concrete, steel, broken windows, and the musty smell of old cobwebs would be all that remained.

Rikka lived in a shadowed, elusive underworld and could never be found in the same place twice.

That's why he'd waited to call until he'd wended his way through her multitude of security alarms—she had impressive ones—and stood close outside her door.

Given warning, she'd evaporate.

Maybe she had a *Star Trek* transporter beam worked out. With Rikka, not much would surprise him.

It was a pity, though. She had a nice setup here. Pristine stainless-steel counters with massive refrigerator units below.

There were no upper cupboards, instead the rosewood walls were covered with pen-and-ink drawings. A print of the Hokusai wave hung beside a Kudo Shunman butterfly, then a Hiroshiga landscape hung beside...and so it continued around the room. Each piece of art tastefully separated from the next by hand-painted rice-paper scrolls each bearing a single Basho haiku in Kyujitai kanji; the same lettering the poet might have used four centuries ago. He'd wager that she'd done the last herself; they were meticulous, as was everything she did. And these looked far too fragile to survive any attempt to move them.

Her art was from the Edo Period, nothing more recent than two centuries. It was the last reign of the great artisans, before they'd been subsumed by the Meiji Restoration. As if she didn't wish to live in the present.

Despite the room and the mystery, Rikka herself looked as neat and modern as her kitchen appliances. Five-foot-nothing of slender Japanese-Eurasian in form-clinging black with equally dark hair to the middle of her back trapped in a bright pink scrunchie decorated with tiny images of *The Powerpuff Girls* kicking the shit out of cartoon villains.

Her narrow and elegant face that might be mistaken for a child's if not for the penetrating darkness of the greenest eyes he'd ever encountered.

The woman herself was a mystery. No past that his NSA buddy could target even with a data collection finder tool, and Katydid had slammed the door on his most circumspect inquiries. Normally that was the kind of thing that he found easy to discover, but not with Rikka. Her non-past but one part of the intriguing package. Which made him wonder why he'd never pursued her—other than the threat of imminent death and dismemberment.

To distract himself, he read her Basho selections, they were from among the less common of the seventeenth-century poet's vast art, but he particularly liked the one about the crane's thighs splashing in cool lake water. It made him think of—

"I can hear you thinking," she snapped at him.

Before he could open his mouth to protest, she cut him off.

"Don't you dare speak!"

He closed his mouth and watched her flashing knife race through the fish. Each slice neat, controlled, perfect.

He waited until she finished her order.

She slid a stack of trays into a dumbwaiter that he hadn't noticed. It whisked the load noiselessly out of sight to a delivery person with a refrigerator truck, hopefully a heavily armed one in this neighborhood. The knife was scrubbed, stoned, honed, oiled, and slid into the sheath at her waist with a sharp snick. Everything about Rikka was so neat, so planned, so controlled. The sheathed knife was then pulled from her waistband and tucked into its proper slot in the hand-tooled leather knife case he'd bought for her ages ago.

He started to smile at the memory.

"Don't!" Rikka didn't look up.

It was hard to wipe a smile from his memory that hadn't had a chance to reach his lips, but he tried.

When the kitchen was clean to the point of being beyond Zen, she again planted her fists on the chopping block, looked up at him, and opened her mouth.

That's when his phone rang.

9

———

"Sɪs! Dᴀᴍɴ, ɢɪʀʟ!" Pᴀᴜʟ's ᴠᴏɪᴄᴇ ꜰʀᴏᴍ ᴛʜᴇ ᴘʜᴏɴᴇ ᴇᴄʜᴏᴇᴅ ɪɴ the silence within the long, mostly empty shipping container.

Kate held the dead man's cheap flip-phone outside the inspection hatch to get a signal, set to speaker so that she could hear it inside.

"I was getting worried about you. The cops have APBs out on you and a guy who is way better looking than your usual fare. So where are you?"

Kate did her best not to look at Harold. He was grinning at her and he was...Dammit! What was a red-blooded girl supposed to do with Harold-bloody-Merritt crouched beside her after sleeping on him for who knew how many hours? It didn't help that his face was crowded inches from hers so that he too could hear the phone outside the tiny inspection port.

She considered hitting him again, but decided she needed to focus on her tenuous connection to the distant shore.

"I was hoping you could tell me where I am."

"Sis, how am I supposed to—"

"You need to go find Erika Albert. She can—"

48

There was a loud rattle, accented by a hard grunt from Paul, as someone grappled for the phone.

Kate didn't need—

"Kate. Hold tight. I'm tracing you."

Kate knew the voice.

"Rikka!" Finally something was going right with her day.

Her brother was capricious, mercurial, and whimsical. Rikka was a stable rock and had the skills Kate needed.

She couldn't believe Paul had gone to Rikka. He must have been worried out of his mind to have taken such a risk. Or was he dumb enough to be unaware that his life hung by only the tiniest thread in Erika Albert's presence?

She'd bet on the latter. No matter how easily he could charm most of them, Paul could be a thickhead when it came to women.

There was a loud slap, like a hand on a wall in lieu of a fist to Paul's chin that he fully deserved, and then she heard the sharp rattle of a computer keyboard.

Somewhere in the background Paul let out a soft, "Holy shit!"

Kate had only entered Rikka's inner sanctum a few times. The woman could work miracles from a laptop. But what she could do with her full setup must give the NSA heebie-jeebies in the night.

In under thirty seconds, the quality of the sound on Kate's cell phone improved markedly which was a good thing, because it was pretty marginal there at the beginning. She had no idea how far offshore she was.

"I've got you by satellite, because your land-based cell tower is way out of range. Pure luck you managed a connection on it."

"But this isn't a satellite phone."

"There's an NRO satellite above you that has a cell phone repeater. Don't ask; you don't want to know why. But it won't be near you for long."

Great. The only people even more paranoid about security than the NSA was the National Reconnaissance Office. How had Rikka managed to walk through that firewall?

Now wasn't the best time to ask.

10

———

THE FIRST TIME KATE HAD MET RIKKA WAS WHILE BUSTING HER for money-laundering. She'd been using the name Shirō Usagi at the time and working as a nasty Chinese street gang's hidden data geek.

I am Neo, before he takes the pill.

When Kate had asked what in the world she was talking about, Rikka had refused to say anything else until Kate had brought a DVD player and a copy of *The Matrix* to Rikka's holding cell and they'd watched it together.

The cloistered computer genius. She understood that now.

As Shirō Usagi, Rikka—even though she was theoretically mostly Japanese—worked with the New York and Boston Chinese Tong gangs that had exploded into power shortly before the UK gave Hong Kong back to China in '97. All that money exiting China had to find new ground, fertile capitalist ground, and the two largest East Coast Chinatowns had been part of that map.

The North Koreans, not being fools, had ridden in shortly afterward and leveraged the Tongs to help them recover from their dual political and environmental disasters of the 1990s.

The 2002 outreach programs implemented by the DPRK had hooked the Tongs on drug running and the easy money of Office 39 counterfeiting.

When Rikka grew bored with them, she'd hacked her way into an acceptance at MIT (to replace going to the trouble of applying), given herself sole possession of a double *Two Room* on the top floor of Random Hall (because she liked the bay window), and a full scholarship (though she could sweep money out of a bank without them ever knowing any time she was in the mood).

That's where Kate had found her, attending any classes that amused her and doing side jobs for the Tongs. If a computer could crawl, Rikka could make it do the tango while whistling the national anthem of Uruguay.

Like most agents, Kate's first Secret Service job had been in the counterfeiting division. She'd led the bust against a DPRK-inspired, Tong-implemented counterfeiting and money laundering routine. That had led her to Rikka.

Kate had turned her State's evidence then dumped her into the Witness Protection Program when they were done.

After the pissed-off remnants of the Tong—those few that were left when the Secret Service and the Koreans were done with shredding them from both ends—made it through the first layers of Suzi Suzuki's Chicago-based identity, Kate and Rikka had cycled her through again.

This time they'd made sure that not even Rikka's US Marshall's case worker could find her in New York. Their association continued through her second reincarnation, as Erika Albert turned herself into a premier sushi and sashimi *itamae*, not a title lightly granted to American-born chefs, but one Rikka had earned.

That same bust had launched Kate on an ill-fated promotion to the Secret Service's Protection Detail that had ultimately cost the Vice President his life.

Seven years on and Kate still felt gutted by that. Just because she couldn't stand the man, didn't mean he should have died on her watch. She'd been the only woman who agreed to work on his protection detail.

A walking slime mold with wandering hands—hands he learned fast to keep off Agent Kate Stark if she wished them to remain unbroken.

Kate had felt bad for the jerk's former mistress even as Kate tackled her. She performed a justice for womankind. Too bad she'd had to murder a vice-head of state to do so.

Vice being the Veep's guiding principle made it justified in Kate's book. The courts hadn't seen it that way.

11
____

"Got you tracked," Rikka finally returned to the phone.

"Still here," Kate responded but could tell that the signal was fading already.

"You're offshore. International waters. Passing ninety-two-point-seven-two kilometers due east of the Cape Hatteras lighthouse. Since they moved the lighthouse four-hundred-and-sixty meters inland in 1999, that puts you into international waters by—"

"Rikka!" Kate shouted at the phone through the tiny hatch that was becoming decidedly claustrophobic with Harold leaning close enough to…well, close enough for it to be weird that they were dressed.

"Sorry. No need to get so fired up about it. You're aboard…" more computer keys in the background. Then a long pause.

"Would you like us to come get you?"

"Please."

"Okay, it means I'll have to get Sam."

Kate kept her curses under her breath. "Why…do you…need…" She couldn't even get the name out. She could picture the fury suffusing his fair skin to a dark red every time their paths crossed. Sam Fierro was like the modern version of The Duke with a blond crew cut, and only Kate, of all people on the planet, could make him lose his John Wayne-unflappability. How many times had she tried to fix—

"Because, Kate, according to the Marine Traffic site, you're aboard the *Chong Chon Gang.* Which, if you're too disconnected to know, is a big-ass cargo carrier registered to North Korea's Office 39 with your next port of call listed as Pyongyang. So, unless you want to get cozy with the Supreme Leader, we need Sam. We're on our way."

Rikka was already gone, so Kate closed the phone.

She knew exactly what this ship and Office 39 were and could think of only one reason she was aboard. If they'd found her, it was a wonder that she wasn't already dead.

Rikka had better hurry.

12

"WHAT'S OFFICE 39?" HAROLD GAVE KATE ENOUGH ROOM TO GET back inside but stayed well within her normal personal space. Who was the last man she'd let inside her personal space? Long enough ago that she didn't remember easily, a sad statement in itself.

"You've heard of the CIA's Special Activities Division?" She double-checked the phone's battery. Near dead. She shut it off to save power. No way for Rikka to call her inside a steel shipping container.

"Uh, that would be no."

"The SAD does the things that your average American government isn't allowed to do, not even with Special Operations Forces. Office 39 is North Korea's version of that, crossed with Mafia-style tactics. They counterfeit a billion or so dollars a year in undetectable US hundreds. Though when it comes to smuggling, they usually confine themselves to military hardware or drugs. The military gear they take home; the drugs earn them another couple billion."

"Not humans?"

"First time for everything," her straight line made his laugh roll about the container.

Unlike Paul's laugh, that typically made her wish to pound her brother into a pulp or tear the last ten pages out of every volume of his full set of signed Clive Cussler first editions, Harold's laugh was friendly and welcoming.

"Aren't we the lucky ones," he leaned back against the inside of the container door so that they rested shoulder-to-shoulder.

Kate was not amused by the situation in the slightest.

"So, how did we end up here? It doesn't look the least bit like your studio." She appreciated his efforts to keep it light. She didn't need the distraction of a freaked civilian.

"Does your neck hurt?"

"No," but then he raised a hand and checked. "Ow! Yipes! It does."

Had a grown man said, *Yipes?* She was glad of the darkness hiding her smile.

"Do you remember getting shot?"

"Not really... Shot?"

She did, now that the adrenalin had finished clearing the drugs from her system. A sharp pinprick from behind. But a needle wouldn't have created the surrounding bruise. So, a fired dart.

"Marianne and Zania were poisoned. You and I were knocked out by drugged darts and dumped in here."

"They were...what?" Harold's surprise had him shifting aside, finally edging him out of her immediate personal space. She resisted the temptation to move with him. He *was* attractive. She didn't recall sleeping on his chest, but she'd wager that if she did, she'd have enjoyed it. He had a lovely one.

But the dim light of sunset trickling in through the small hatch, revealed the blood draining from his face. "If they're... Then why aren't we..."

"Dead? Good question," one she'd very much like to have answered herself. "I need your belt, Harold."

"You trying to get me undressed, Kate?" He appeared to be recovering...or taking mental refuge from the concept of death. Most people hadn't seen death happen, not violent death. When they did, they were either shocked past functioning, or it turned into merely another *movie scene* in their head—never ever attached to the actual demise of real people. Harold was following the reaction patterns for the *denial* scenario. The problem was, that psychological pattern also often led to highly unpredictable responses when he finally accepted the truth.

As to undressing Harold, the thought had definitely crossed her mind more than once or twice already, but the way he'd phrased it was more turnoff than foreplay.

"Do lines like that work on women?"

Harold was quiet while he pulled off the belt and handed it to her. "Most women. Yeah, they actually do."

"Hello. Not most women."

"I seem to have noticed that about you, Stark," he rubbed at his sternum where she'd had to hit him to keep him out of her way, twice. "It looks good on you by the way."

"Your belt?" He'd folded it in half and laid it across the flat of her palm.

"No, you goofball, you being *not most women*. Looks damn good on you."

Kate concentrated on the problem at hand to give her a moment to consider. Her competence scared off far more men than it attracted. And the ones it drew in were usually the love-to-conquer-a-challenge types. She took those on rare occasion, they could be fun for a short run. Few made it into the category of genuinely interesting.

A category Harold Merritt may have now joined.

13

KATE STUCK HER HEAD OUTSIDE THE PORTAL AND INSPECTED THE problem carefully. Pulling her head back in, she put a loop in the belt. It was the tail end of a deeply ruddy sunset, almost full dark now. The jailor's body lay completely lost in the shadows below. But since she could either see or do—insufficient room to do both at once out the inspection hatch—it didn't matter.

More by luck than skill she managed to snag the handle on the cargo container's door that the stevedore-jailor had died to open. She hauled it back into place, finally managing to reseat it on the latch. With a quick shake, she freed the belt and returned it to Harold.

"Did you lock us back in?"

Kate nodded, "Halfway. Even with your belt, I had no way to unlock the second handle; there's a heavy wire seal on it. So, I relocked the first one. If this crew finds their dead crewmate, I don't want them zeroing in on our container. Now they'll think he was looking for something to steal somewhere in this stack and fell."

She inspected the Korean's rough-leather wallet, nothing of

interest. He must have held back the stash of cash that he'd been paid and was using to bribe the cook. Cheapskate.

Then she found ten US hundred-dollar bills tucked away behind a small flap in the wallet. She flicked on the flashlight to inspect them. The batteries were already fading—couldn't the man even maintain his flashlight?

The bills looked and felt good.

They crumpled properly.

Had the right sound when rubbed together.

They had to be fakes, good ones, but fakes. Real ones would be worth a fortune to a North Korean. Six months salary in ten thin bills.

What was a North Korean stevedore desperately in need of a shower doing with a thousand US hidden in his wallet? Rikka had said this was a ship belonging to Office 39—the world's most accurate and largest scale counterfeiter of American money.

Even back in her heyday as a Secret Service Special Agent they'd known about Office 39. The problem was that the group was so elusive it might as well be myth rather than an ugly reality. The Secret Service almost had them in 2007, but the Bush administration stopped the investigation and even rolled back what had been already achieved because Kim Jong-il threatened to withdraw from arms talks that never went anywhere anyway.

North Korean supernotes weren't merely good, they were notorious. Those Ben Franklins would pass most any test, physical or chemical, and even then you had to know what to look for. If she'd doubted that she and Harold were in trouble before, this removed even a shadow of it.

They were in deep shit.

Kate stuffed the bills in her pocket, hung the wallet across the lower edge of the inspection port, then reached out to ease the small door closed. It didn't latch because of the thin leather, but it did block the bits of light from the ship.

"Do you have to do that?" Harold didn't sound happy over the loss of even such a small amount of connection to the outdoors.

She turned off the flashlight to save the dying battery, figuring that gave her answer well enough.

He didn't protest, but he did curse. Nice to know he had a few good invectives in him so that he wasn't *such* a straight man.

Kate looked to the far end of the container at the tiny spot of blood-red sunset, though it shed no light. The .44 Magnum round had punched a neat hole through the steel. The container now reeked of old fish, cordite, and overripe stevedore. She too wished to keep their tiny supply of fresh air available, but didn't dare.

Harold, finally accepting her answer, handed her one of the water bottles and after a bit of floundering around in the dark, half of the flattened bag lunch.

"Eat the food now," she informed him as she bit into the beef and kimchi on a hard roll, not bad. A good job on the pickling, authentically spicy hot. They had a good cook on board. An extremely good one; there were interesting umami notes that developed the more she ate. The problem was that the heat made her want to chug her water. That wasn't a good idea.

"Do your best to conserve as much water as you can," she told Harold. "We seem to have cut off our line of resupply."

"And after we're done eating?" Rather than arguing, his voice had gone soft and offered a world of promise.

Kate was glad of the dark or he'd be able to see her face. She knew exactly what she wanted to be doing once they were done eating.

14

SAM FIERRO KNEW THEY WERE WAITING FOR HIM. NOT BECAUSE they'd triggered any of his security alarms, but because Devlin hadn't. Sam could set his clock by the alcoholic's ten p.m. perambulation through the Brooklyn alleyway. The past ate away at Devlin's brain every night at this time, and he'd go walking it off with the precision of a nighttime security patrol.

One person wouldn't be enough to make Devlin miss his route to the back door of Sam's charcuterie. He was Marine Force Recon as Sam was—no such thing as an ex-Marine—and could have easily avoided Sam's alarms, but he tripped them on purpose so Sam would know he was coming.

All except one, that no one would be able to see, but he only set that one when he wasn't in the chilled back kitchen of his shop.

Devlin had a weak spot for Sam's strong coffee and his butcher-shop-heaped salami sandwiches. They rarely spoke, there wasn't a need. They both understood. No amount of words or time were going to change the past.

Two strangers showing up would stop Devlin though—shift him over to his deeply trained hide-and-observe mode.

However, two people together definitely would set off Sam's perimeter alarms unless...

He slammed his cleaver into the carcass of aged beef he was halfway through butchering; two pigs hung next in line.

Sam didn't bother picking up the fourteen-inch chef's blade that he used for the finer work. He didn't need to reach for the PB, a silenced Markov pistol that he always kept close to hand. *That* he'd taken off a KGB man who'd been reluctant to let it go. He left the Steyr AUG assault rifle mounted beneath his chopping block that he'd taken from an equally reluctant Mossad agent who'd gone dirty.

With his boot, Sam nudged his *go* bag where it lay beneath the counter. It didn't budge, heavy with demolition gear and his M40A5 sniper rifle case, but he didn't reach for it.

Instead, he opened the back door that he never bothered to lock—his reputation on the streets of Brooklyn kept it plenty secure, and turned back to his butchering table. No point looking out the window into the alley's darkness. While he was waiting, he sorted, wrapped, and labeled the parts of the cow he had finished so that his cousin Nadya would know what to do with them when she opened the shop in the morning.

Paul Stark stepped in. Then made a loud rubbing of his hands at encountering the chilled air of Sam's butchery. The second person's step wasn't light due to stealth; Erika Albert simply didn't weigh enough to tread heavily.

He waited a heartbeat. No Kate. He knew he wouldn't hear her. But he'd feel her, a presence like no other. Except he didn't. If Paul and Erika were together and hadn't already killed each other without Kate standing between them, it meant that Kate was in trouble.

Damn her to Hell.

Sam turned to face them and crossed his bare arms over his apron; his tattoos exposed for all to see. Special Operations Forces guys might hide who they were, Marines owned up to it from the get-go. One arm had the unofficial Marine Force Recon logo, a winged skull wearing a SCUBA breather, over crossed boat paddles. The other arm simply said: *Celer, Silens, Mortalis* in large, ornate Marines-blue lettering—Swift, Silent, Deadly.

"You have access to a chopper, buddy?" Paul looked ready to glad-hand him on the shoulder, but apparently decided at the last second that he didn't want to pull back a bleeding stump.

He had access. And he didn't point out that choppers were motorcycles. Marines rode in helos.

"We're going to need that helicopter," Erika knew the difference, of course. She crossed her arms to stay warm despite wearing a black turtleneck on a warm summer's evening. "Loaded for bear."

Not surprising with Kate involved.

What was she up to this time?

15

IT WAS PAST MIDNIGHT AND WHAT KATE WAS DOING ON THE mattress inside the cargo container was stomach crunches.

Then she heard the change.

The steady background rumble that was the sound of the ship's engines hadn't varied in hours. Now it took on a heavier beat through the steel of their container.

She'd risked cracking open the small inspection hatch so that they didn't suffocate, but the air was as warm and dreary outside the container as inside.

Something had changed, and she had her suspicions as to why.

She nudged Harold awake, "Here we go, put your shirt back on."

They had tried...but not gotten far; they both still wore their pants. What had started out so pleasantly as a natural segue after their meal had been interrupted one too many times— neither of them had been able to hold their focus.

First, the ship's crew had discovered the jailor's body. A ruckus ensued, stopping their first efforts around the time they became interesting. That confusion took an hour and a great deal of yelling to quiet down.

After they thought the ship had settled—and she and Harold had returned to the task at hand, so to speak—someone began crawling over the container stacks on an inspection. Or was someone looking for whatever prize their crewmate had been seeking before his fatal fall.

Whichever, he didn't discover the unlatched inspection port.

That was too bad, Kate had stood poised to take advantage for a long thirty minutes in case their snoop decided to check the unlatched portal and flip it open to see what might be inside. She didn't swing it wide as an enticement in case it was an official inspection and there was a sniper waiting below.

By the time the solo climber finished, the waiting had grown into a tangible presence inside the container. While Harold had displayed a strong willingness to try a third time, Kate felt less than inclined.

He did have good, strong, chef's hands. But when they brushed along her waist, she wondered about the amount of time needed for her brother and Rikka to locate Sam, scare up a helo, and come chasing down to Cape Hatteras.

As he fondled her in places she definitely liked being fondled, she started thinking about Office 39 and North Korea and what on the planet they could have to do with her cooking show. It must have to do with Cooks Network and not her past. Or why else would Harold be here?

Also, if it had been about her past, she'd already be dead.

When he gave up and flopped back on the mattress, clothed from the waist down, she'd rested her cheek on his chest until his breathing slowed and he slept. She enjoyed the brief respite from her chaotic worries.

Then she'd sat up in the darkness and started in on what

those six years of training in the Secret Service had been meant for, thinking.

For all of that effort, she felt none the wiser by the time she ran out of new things to think. There was no possible reason for the Democratic People's Republic of Korea to kill two American television chefs and kidnap two more. It simply didn't add up.

And if they had identified her as the person who had ruined so much of their Boston money laundering network, it made no sense that it had taken them four years to find her.

Unable to make sense of anything, and not daring to sleep in case she missed her own rescue, she did the only thing she could think of—exercise. For the time being, she only had the one set of clothes, so she'd left her jacket, blouse, and bra off in order to not sweat them up.

But with the heavy thud of the approaching helicopter, she dressed hurriedly.

With the barrel of the big Smith & Wesson 29, Kate nudged the inspection hatch open.

16

"GUESS WHAT WENT MISSING," LEONA EDWARDS STOOD IN FRONT of Marcus Reynolds' desk. Her jacket was draped over her desk chair in their cramped office. Her shoulder holster was pulling her white dress shirt tight in all the right places.

The blood from his brain is what had gone missing. He forced his gaze up to her dark eyes.

"Rafe went missing last week," he replied. "Kate Stark and Harold Merritt yesterday. Next thing to go will be our evidence on this screwed-up case. Then our jobs, and we can finally rest in peace in the back alley of forgotten FBI agents."

"Nice try," Leona dropped a single-sheet printout on his desk.

It was past midnight. They should have knocked off hours ago, but when a national celebrity disappeared in the middle of a double homicide, especially one with links to the Secret Service and a high-profile drug case in which an agent had been gunned down, upstairs wanted it solved and solved fast. Any questions regarding the hacker were tabled for now.

He struggled upright so that he could glare at the print.

"It's a flight plan."

"You always were a bright boy, Marcus."

"Screw you, Edwards." Wrong damn thing to say. He surely didn't want that image in his head. Focus on the damn paper. "For a Gulfstream G280 passenger jet."

"Owned by?"

The names stood out like a neon sign once he spotted them, "Kate and Paul Stark."

"Traveling from Teterboro Airport over in Jersey to..."

Damn. When she was teasing him, there was a surprising—and enticing—lightness to her tone.

"Having fun, Edwards?"

"Yeah, mon," she put on that fake Louisiana accent that always sounded so sexy no matter how bad it was. "Me love proving that de woman agent she be smarter than de man agent."

Marcus finally spotted it.

"...to—" reading it twice didn't help. "I don't even know how to pronounce that."

17

———

Kate saw no searchlight.

Couldn't detect anything dangerous through the narrow crack around the shipping container's inspection hatch, so she nudged it wider.

No one shot her and the new sound grew louder. Both points encouraging.

She risked a peek.

A CH-53E Super Stallion helicopter painted Marine Corps gray roared by low overhead. It was the largest helicopter in the entire US military. As Sam Fierro had proved many times, he never did things by halves.

She pulled her head in as Harold came up beside her. "Here," she slapped the dead man's flashlight into his hand, "point that straight up and wave it around. Don't drop it."

"Say please."

"Please or I'll hit you again, extra hard this time." She tried to make it sound funny and mostly succeeded.

"Close enough," then he kissed her.

As she let herself become lost for a moment, she decided that she'd definitely succeeded. Kate had learned that Harold

Merritt's kisses were something a woman did *not* hurry away from. She let herself linger for several long, splendid seconds before breaking it off.

He turned on the light, reached his hand out through the opening leaving as much of the opening clear as he could, and began waving it around.

She powered up the cell phone. When stuck out the opening, it showed no bars.

She tried dialing Paul's cell phone.

Nothing.

The walkie talkie she'd taken off the Korean looked like a bad copy of a cheap radio that she'd found in a box of her dad's childhood toys. She dialed in channel nine, the old Citizen's Band emergency channel and tried it. At least she guessed that's what it was, the dial was labeled with Korean characters, not numbers.

A moment later she heard a voice blasting from above; it echoed and rang along the steel canyon and was incomprehensible. It was a loudspeaker on the helicopter, and it might have said, *Use the phone.*

She tried the phone again with no luck. No bars. Twice the helicopter zipped by, then it came to hover directly over their personal, private canyon of container steel. The downdraft almost ripped the phone from her hands.

Seconds later, there was a loud clatter on the outside of the container as the seal was cut and the locking bars swung aside.

When the door swung open from the outside, there was Paul. He knocked on the other, still latched door as if asking permission to enter.

Kate had rarely been so glad to see her twin.

18

———

PAUL DANGLED ON THE END OF A WINCH LINE FROM THE HOVERING helo. Though he'd worn a full harness, he figured that they didn't have time to harness up Kate and Harold. They had to get gone before the North Koreans snapped-to.

He and Sam had attached a pair of lifting rings to the same line.

"Super cozy, Katydid!" he shouted at Kate over the roar of the hovering helo to hide how damn glad he was to find her. As usual, she looked completely put together, despite spending over a day inside a shipping container with the handsome hunk of a man who stood protectively behind her.

Beneath Harold's open chef jacket, Paul could see that he'd mis-buttoned his shirt. Well, proved the man wasn't stupid. Locked in a shipping container with someone who looked like his sister and not going for it would indicate a severe mental deficiency. But that he'd convinced Kate to participate was the impressive part. He must be an okay guy to get past Kate's blast-door shields.

Kate helped the guy stick his arms and head through the

padded ring, then pulled his arms to his sides over and outside the ring.

"Keep your arms down and you're fine," Paul shouted. "Raise your arms and we'll be leaving behind a puddle of Harold on the deck below." He'd heard the *wanted by the police* bulletin plenty of times to know the man's name.

In the meantime, Kate had slid into her own rescue collar.

"You didn't want that, did you?"

Kate narrowed her eyes at him and then turned to look where Paul indicated with his flashlight. From under one edge of the mattress peeked a swatch of frilled, fire-red fabric.

Harold had done more than alright. He'd not only gotten them both out of their shirts, but he'd also managed to finagle Kate out of her bra. Paul bet that was hard-won ground and saw no reason to take away the man's advantage.

Before she could snag one of the straps, Paul called over the radio headset to have them lifted out of there.

Kate wasn't much given to blushing, but she sure wasn't meeting his eyes as they were whisked aloft.

19

———

Sam ran the winch and hauled the three of them upward to the lowered rear ramp of the hovering CH-53 Super Stallion helicopter.

As soon as they were clear of the containers, the ramp gunner called over the headset to his buddies flying the helo. "Get gone!"

The five-man crew didn't need any more invitation than that. When Sam had called, they'd been preparing for a run from Marine Corps Air Facility Quantico, Virginia, to Hurlburt Field in western Florida for joint training with the Air Force. He'd barely had to pull in any favors to have them take a run at a North Korean ghost ship steaming south along the eastern seaboard.

And, as he'd planned, the great mass of the Super Stallion had daunted the North Koreans into inaction for the crucial sixty seconds they needed for Search and Rescue operations.

Sam eased the speed of the winch and reached out to steady Paul until he was clipped into the helo's interior safety line. His purported rock-climbing skills appeared real; Paul looked comfortable in the harness. But the *grand adventure* of dangling on the end of a wire had left him looking as only Paul Stark could, like he was now ready for a deep insertion behind enemy lines. Sam kept waiting for someone to wipe the smug off that man's face.

He presently had his money on Erika Albert.

They'd kept sniping at each other the whole flight, and damn but that woman could hold her own.

Second aboard. Wimpy guy who looked like he'd suffered a surprise attack by a rabid Chihuahua by how wide his eyes were. Gym workout muscles, but no skills. He flailed clumsily when the ramp gunner grabbed him by the lifting ring and swung him into the cargo bay; it was clear he'd had zero days in the military and would survive zero plus two minutes if dropped into a zone.

Third aboard, was...shit! He knew it was her, but seeing Kate Stark brought back enough bitter memories to gut a man. She stepped aboard as casually and neatly as if climbing a stairway. Drop her in a zone and it was everyone else who had better look out.

Her jacket swung open as she shifted out of the lifting collar. Her sheer blouse revealed that the woman, despite how she was built, wasn't wearing a bra.

Women shouldn't be allowed. Definitely not on military aircraft, probably not in public. At least not if the woman in question was Kate Stark.

He focused on getting the damn rear ramp closed.

Three hours to Hurlburt Field.

Sam waited a beat. Now one hundred and seventy-nine minutes and fifty-nine seconds...fifty-eight...

20

"WHAT'S THAT?" KATE STARED UP AT THE MASSIVE PIECE OF armament that filled most of the spacious helicopter's bay.

Sam Fierro ignored her.

The man could hold a grudge like no one else she knew. Hell, he was even worse about that than she was.

So, she turned to the ramp gunner as he stowed the winch and lifting belts. She shouted her question over the roar of the helo's three turbine engines and the massive seven-blade rotor.

They'd come aboard over the lowered rear loading ramp, that folded upward behind them, sealing out the night. She managed only a brief glimpse of the *Chong Chon Gang's* lights as the bulk carrier with its atypical stack of containers fell rapidly behind.

Everything about the Super Stallion was enormous by rotorcraft standards. The cargo bay stretched thirty feet long, seven wide, and six-and-a-half high. And yet there was little room for their small party. Dominating the bay, a tracked vehicle carried three massive missiles mounted on a rack. They were what missiles were supposed to look like: twenty feet long, a foot through, with a pointy nose on this end and rocket fins on the other.

"Museum loaner," the gunner responded cheerfully. "Sam wasn't the only one who heard we were heading south empty. It's a retired MIM-23 HAWK system, that stands for Homing All the Way Killer. Marines kick ass."

Kate felt more dwarfed by the wholly daunting piece of hardware than the massive helicopter. "Does it work?"

"Thinking of shooting up that crappy Korean merchant rust bucket? Fifty kilos of blast-frag warhead on each, that's a tenth of a Mark 48 torpedo. Marginal at best. Maybe if you were to punch 'em in the waterline at the same point or hit the fuel stores. Be worth a try to see if it worked, but these are decommissioned. Display only now. So, nope. Sorry."

Kate stared up at them.

Paul had mentioned there were warrants for her and Harold's arrests waiting back in New York. She had to get back there to start figuring out what happened. However, her best guess was that New York's finest would not be impressed by her unverifiable cockamamie story about being kidnapped onto and rescued from a North Korean spy ship.

She wouldn't believe Paul if he came home with that piece of crap. Well, she would believe him, but only because he was always landing in the most ludicrous situations. Though *his* problems usually had to do with diamond-clad heiresses, often married. He honestly believed he was the modern-day incarnation of Cary Grant in *To Catch a Thief*—without the theft part, thankfully.

Kate occasionally threatened to track him down and catch him in the act, but even when they were younger, she'd never managed to trip him up—when his plans worked. Though she'd certainly had to rush to his rescue any number of times when they didn't.

"I need answers," she spoke to herself. The ramp gunner

had returned forward with his buddies. The others near her were...

She turned and looked at the others sitting on the deck plating at the back of the roaring helicopter, directly beneath the Army-green, pointed nose cones of the watchful HAWK missile system. Paul—as tall and handsome as Harold, but fair where Harold was dark—busy interrogating the man who had managed to remove half of Kate's clothes.

Harold, rebuttoning his shirt properly, revealed momentarily glimpses of that nice chest but held his own. Another point in his favor. *Go Harold.*

Rikka twitched. With neither a laptop nor something to slice into bits, *and* being wholly ignored by Paul, she was rapidly dissolving toward nutsoid. She'd be certifiable by the time they landed.

Only Sam remained standing, his feet planted like tree trunks as he leaned against the inside of the helo's hull. His blond crew cut almost brushing the six-foot-six ceiling, he stood as silent as a stone. He looked and acted like Midwest farmer stock, not third-generation Brooklyn butcher and third-generation US Marine. His dark eyes missing nothing, his expression as unreadable as ever. Until he noticed Kate watching him, then a scowl surfaced.

This is what she had to work with. The chef in her considered going back to New York and testing her luck with the NYPD to get this straightened out. Chance of success? *Zero minus infinity* as Paul would say.

So, she let her inner persona as former member of the Vice President's Secret Service Protection Detail take control instead. Whenever this happened inside her, Kate felt torn two ways. One—the chef in her felt a harsh chill slap around her like slamming into a Kevlar vest when the crisis was already well advanced. Two—the Secret Service Special Agent in her felt a homecoming to where she truly belonged.

This time she let the second one come forward instead of shrugging it off as she normally would.

"We need to go back," Kate said it loudly enough to be heard over the engine noise.

"That's where—"

"No!" Kate cut off her brother. "Back to the ship."

Harold smiled and pretended to be afraid until he saw she was serious. After that, the blood drained from his face and he fell silent.

Paul looked at her like she was an idiot.

Rikka stopped twitching.

Only Sam didn't shift his stance or expression.

"We go back to New York and I'm going to jail. Not my first choice. Harold, your ass will be parked in the next cell block over from mine."

"Do not pass go," Rikka agreed. "Do not collect two hundred dollars."

"And it's such a pretty ass, Harold," Paul teased him. "You'll be the new star of D-Block."

Kate considered telling Paul to shut the hell up, but it only ever encouraged him.

"I have questions for the captain of that boat."

"Hello, Sis. Insane North Koreans. How are you going to not end up back in your cozy shipping container? Unless that's your intent." He waggled his eyebrows at her and slapped Harold's shoulder hard enough to stagger the man if he hadn't been sitting on steel plate.

Kate ignored him and watched Sam carefully, "I had an idea or two on that."

Sam's dark gaze remained steady on hers. For a mere second, his line of sight flickered over her head, then returned to her.

She wasn't sure if he sighed before heading up to the cockpit to send them back the way they'd come.

"So, who here speaks Korean?"

21

———————

Captain Rang Jin-ho of the *Chong Chon Gang* knew he was lost to a ship-sized whirlpool of cascading disasters.

It was three a.m., deep in the night watch, and his leg hurt like hell because he hadn't had time to strap the prosthetic on properly. His right foot pointed awkwardly northeast, not true north.

Physical discomfort is of no— He knew that. Hard to believe Su-jin was lecturing him now. His wife was half a world away.

This was supposed to be the quiet time, steaming south on the open ocean.

But first there'd been the discovery Kyung's body, apparently he'd fallen while trying to rob a shipping container. Served him right.

None of the nine secret containers' seals were broken. He'd verified that from the ground. P'yo had returned after the other crew were gone to climb to each and double-check for tampering. There was none. Rang had sighed with relief; there lay one disaster diverted.

Then the helicopter's arrival.

After that had come Comrade Ro's absolute fit worse than a five-year-old's temper tantrum.

Supreme Leader Kim Jong-un's man had revealed himself by his arrogance months ago. If this was the Party's idea of an undercover agent, the Democratic People's Republic of Korea Worker's Party was in worse shape than Rang thought.

But any possible doubt of Comrade Ro's identity was removed by how he had threatened to kill every officer aboard after the Americans had taken whatever had been in that now unsealed and empty container.

Rang found it interesting that Ro didn't know what the contents had been, he'd simply been sent to guard them. Was Supreme Leader Kim Jong-un so hot for his Tesla car that he'd sent a pompous idiot to safeguard it? It wouldn't surprise him.

That meant the other unknown containers were Office 39 business, which meant he himself as Senior Captain should have known what was in there. Something deep had happened here, and he knew that he'd need to tread carefully if he wanted to continue as senior patriarch of the Rang clan.

He'd sent his trusted first officer P'yo up to inspect the container now that the seal was broken. He had reported that there was a mattress, the remains of a meal, and a waste bucket in the container. Someone had been stowed away on his ship and now the Americans had taken them.

Not stowed away.

Been locked behind a diplomatic seal and now they were gone, whisked away by a US military helicopter.

He didn't need Su-jin here to tell him that this could be ultimately useful information. But he must set that aside for the moment.

The helicopter was his concern now. He'd never seen such a massive one before. Its rotors reached wider than his ship—more than twenty meters across.

No!

He'd flatly refused Comrade Ro's order to shoot at it with a piece of Type 58 Kalashnikov knock-off crap as likely to explode in his hands from old age as to effectively fire.

Then the averted maelstrom returned!

Out of the darkness, the massive helicopter had appeared without warning by lights or radar until it was upon them. The machine roared like the ghost of an angry ancestor as it circled his ship at close quarters.

It finally swung around to hover with its stern directly over his bridge's starboard wing. He checked the helm's controls; his ship was moving forward at twelve knots.

Yet aimed directly off his starboard side, the helicopter hovered with its rear end facing him as if preparing to shit on his command bridge. That meant they were flying sideways at exactly the same speed as his ship was moving. Good pilots. Better than his brother who was one of the best in the entire Korean People's Army.

He rubbed at his eyes and wished he'd taken time to pull on his uniform. Instead, he stood barefoot and wore the tattered pants and sleeveless t-shirt of a common sailor.

Ro, the martinet—dressed perfectly of course—rushed onto Rang's command bridge without asking permission.

The rear ramp crashed onto his wing deck crushing a whole section of deck railing as if it was kindling for the fire. He could feel the impact through his feet.

Four people stepped off the ramp, walked through the starboard doors, and entered his command bridge as if they owned it. The helicopter rotor's wind and roar arrived through the open doors with them as if the people embodied the helicopter's power themselves. Perhaps they were ghosts of the helicopter's breath.

Perhaps they were his death.

Several of the officers rushed onto the bridge. Others were moving in the opposite direction. Two of those he didn't like or trust and would have to consider how to cleanse from his crew later.

The intruders stopped three steps onto his bridge. A massive man, a tall man and woman who looked enough alike to be related, and between them stood—

Comrade Ro hissed out a breath of displeasure.

—a tiny Japanese woman.

Rang's training told him that *such* wasn't even human and deserved no more than the Japanese had done to the Korean women during World War II—death or incarceration as a sexual slave.

Ro, such an animal of the Party, would certainly recommend both.

Rang believed that the Japanese nation deserved a simple death under the rain of superior North Korean weaponry...at least that's what he'd tell anyone who asked for his patriotic opinion.

Personally, he could think of a few other uses for the woman, both the women if he was being honest. Especially the tall one with the strange light-blue eyes. Though the large revolver she wore tucked into her belt, right where a man should be, could make him think twice before attempting to go there.

Who was in the container that they emptied?

Ah, Su-jin. You were always the wise one.

By the look of her fury, this woman had been prisoner on his ship.

At least ten centimeters taller than he was—with a massive weapon jammed into the front of her trousers and a chest no Korean woman had ever boasted—was about the most arousing image he'd ever seen. Power, danger, and a strange beauty made him want to jump her and bring her to her proverbial knees. Oh, there was an image that made him hard despite the madness of what was happening.

The huge man stood a step behind the trio. He was the only other one armed, a holstered sidearm and a truly massive machine gun comfortably slung in his arms. The kind usually mounted on a helicopter, not the kind one carried around. Rang doubted if his strongest crewman could lift it.

Comrade Ro pulled out his revolver.

As if on cue, a bright light flashed on inside the helicopter's cargo bay that opened directly outside the ship's bridge wing door.

Even Ro stumbled backwards as the light shone on the three massive missiles staring directly at them out of the helicopter's belly. They were aimed straight into the heart of the command bridge.

The center one pointed directly at Rang's chest. He tried shifting to the side, but its evil eye followed him.

22

THE KOREAN IN AN IMMACULATE UNIFORM RECOVERED FIRST, again brandishing his sidearm and now shouting.

Kate watched him as Rikka began interpreting, "You are every person under arrest. You criminals have invaded a sovereign ship of the Democratic Peop—"

He stopped waving his gun and aimed it at Rikka.

Kate grabbed for her weapon, but she was far too slow.

Sam's sidearm spit quietly twice.

The posturing officer dropped his gun, which clattered onto the deck and spun to rest by another's foot—and stared at his legs in horror as they collapsed.

Sam had knee-capped him in both legs.

His screams shattered the momentary silence.

"Anyone else feeling stupid?" Kate kept her weapon drawn and scanning.

Rikka interpreted for her automatically.

There were eight others on the bridge. One wore his radio headphones, one stood at the helm, most cowered. Only two faced her and one of those stood a pace behind the man who had *not* reached down to gather up the gun that rested by his foot.

By his oddly pointing...fake foot.

"P'yo," he called to the man close behind him, raising his voice to be heard over the knee-capped official's cries. "Help Comrade Ro. His screams are distracting."

As Rikka interpreted, this P'yo quickly dragged the injured man into the darkness of the port-side bridge wing.

Moments later, P'yo returned, though Ro's screams were no longer audible.

The captain, for that's who she assumed the fake-footed man to be, didn't look upset that the injured man had been dumped into the sea. Instead, he looked at his second in command as if saying, *You will have to invent the paperwork on that one.*

P'yo shrugged in reply.

The look made Kate like the man... a touch.

He turned back to them and spoke. Rikka interpreted simultaneously.

"Your, uh, my," Rikka stumbled over that one. "He says my accent is very good. Kaesong. Which makes sense because my teacher escaped from there by sea on a fishing—"

"Rikka," Kate cut her off.

"Right. Sorry Kate. He says that Kaesong is his own homeland which bears the brunt of the South's aggressions on its fragile shores. I am much better to listen to than Comrade Ro—I think that's the guy Sam shot—who was a Pyongyang city boy."

23

Rang hadn't meant that the man should be thrown overboard, but Ro had not made many friends aboard. What was it about members of the Ro clan, they always caused more paperwork. Rang sighed, yet another thing to explain, if the Americans let him live.

A glance at his radioman showed he was busy gawking at the giant missiles pointed right at them instead of transmitting as he should be—though perhaps not. If he tried the radio, he might have to be buried alongside Ro with more American bullets in him. So, if the Americans sank them here and now, no one would ever know what happened. He'd thought his troubles were over when Kyung was found dead in the night from looking through the containers for something to steal.

Then again after the Americans had robbed his ship.

Now...this night kept getting worse.

The tall woman with the strange eyes and a uniform jacket the dark red of a roaring fire spoke English to the Japanese women. Rang knew enough English to recognize it, but not sufficient to understand. His wife Su-jin had told him many times that he should learn, but he didn't have a good ear for such a harsh language. By now he should know to always do what she said, for Su-jin was never wrong.

"Who here knows," the Japanese woman interpreted in her small voice, "why two Americans were being held against their will aboard your ship?"

Two? He only had evidence of one. Had it been the two women and he hadn't known? Such an opportunity lost.

No. None other of these were captive.

Right. Because none of them looked at him with such anger. But neither did they show fear. Though the Japanese woman looked so angry on the tall woman's behalf...maybe she had been—

Again, the taller American woman spoke and the Japanese servant interpreted. He didn't recognize the red uniform, but she was clearly in charge. His foolish body thought that made her an even more exciting conquest. He hoped he still had a living body by the time the sun rose again.

"Speak unless you wish to you have your ship turned into a floating hulk. You have ten seconds to respond." And she began counting backwards. "*Yeol. Ahop. Yeodoel. Ilgop. Yeoseot...*"

The tall American hypnotized him with those sea-foam blue eyes, making it impossible to answer.

At *daseot* the big man lowered his massive machine gun.

Rang finally shook off his lethargy at *net.*

24

"I did not know," Kate listened as Rikka interpreted the man's words.

Kate had picked him out of the crowd for he was the one who remained steady. Others had run or gawked or cowered. Then he was the one who had ordered the disposal of the uniformed officer with the gun.

She hadn't cared about the ineffectual brandishing of his weapon, not until he'd pointed it at the innocent Rikka. It was amazing how fast Sam had been; drawn, two shots, and reholstered before she'd fully drawn. The man was amazing.

Now he shifted the massive maw of eighty pounds worth of GAU-18/A machine gun until it centered on the speaker's chest.

The man was breathing over-rapidly, but did not move.

"You are the captain?" His clothes were worn but serviceable. His artificial foot was turned oddly, and he was doing his best to keep his weight off it.

"Yes, I am Captain Rang Jin-ho," he took an awkward step forward in what looked to be a conciliatory gesture.

Rikka started to explain that she had not inverted his given and family names because that's how Korean's, like the Chinese—

Kate cut her off with, "Interpret only please. You can explain it later."

For a change, Rikka nodded without an argument.

Captain Rang tugged at a tattered pant leg, "I was called from my bed by your helicopter's arrival."

"So, who knows why I was kidnapped?"

He shrugged.

Sam raised his gun from the captain's chest to aim at his face. His paled, but he remained steadfast.

"I too would like the answer to that question," he managed to keep his voice steady despite Sam's threat.

Kate could get to like this man. So, neither of them knew. It was a puzzling problem. Then she recalled a chance comment by the jailor.

"Ask the cook."

Rikka interpreted.

The captain roared out for the cook to be fetched.

"Bok is the cook's name," Rikka told her. "Doesn't he look ticked enough to strangle the man himself?"

He did.

They waited while the man who had disposed of the screaming uniformed officer went running.

Kate felt as if she stood in the middle square of a chess match: in a terrible and bizarre setting.

The bridge's dim light, set for nighttime operations, was barely sufficient to see everyone. The bright lights they'd rigged on the missiles didn't flood into the area.

Only one member of the crew actually saw to his job, the man standing at the helm. Others were doing their best to observe what was happening yet remain behind substantial metal consoles.

By agreement, they had entered through the double bridge

wing door that had been chocked open in the sultry air of the mid-Atlantic in summer.

The helo's exhaust and the downwash of its rotors roared in through the door behind them and blasted out the far doors. The temperature in the room climbed rapidly, but no one moved.

25

RANG HAD TO SQUINT AGAINST THE BLAZING-HOT WIND FROM THE helicopter and the bright light that made the four Americans into partial silhouettes.

The helicopter continued to hold its position aloft over the starboard bridge wing as if parked there. He was half tempted to order the ship turned to test how good they were. Then he looked again at the three massive missiles and the maw of the giant machine gun centered on his face and could feel his balls shrivel. No testing.

He didn't know if the missiles could be fired without destroying the helicopter. He knew ships, not helicopters. But he'd heard enough stories regarding crazy Americans to believe them capable of anything.

Destroy a helicopter worth tens of millions US and kill everyone aboard to have vengeance on the *Chong Chon Gang?* Certainly possible. He'd rather not find out the true extent of their madness.

Not crazy. They are opportunity.

There are many, far more rational types of opportunity, Su-jin. But it was a new way to look at it.

For one, he wouldn't mind learning more about American women. He had certainly heard stories of their ways. The two women standing before him stirred images that not even the whores in the many ports of the world could cause anymore. The Japanese might make for good sport, but to bed the tall American woman…wouldn't that be something?

Perhaps there were other opportunities here. More realistic ones. But he could not see—

The cook's arrival was announced by his babbling terror before he entered the bridge. "Kyung say he had girlfriends. He pay me for food. Times two for food. Promised to introduce me to number two girl when we reach home. All I know. All I know." Bok dug into a pocket and pulled forth a wad of pitifully small *won* notes that tumbled to the deck from his nerveless fingers only to be stirred and scattered by the hot wind from the hovering helicopter.

Rang had extracted, with no one the wiser, a roll containing far more *won* than that from where the dead Kyung had tucked it in his sock. A year's income for a man like Kyung, in a single roll of bills.

He'd given a third of it to his senior lieutenant P'yo and pocketed the rest.

The woman with the blue eyes cursed.

"*Goja!*" the Japanese woman interpreted then blinked in surprise.

Had the American woman actually just called him dickless? Or… He could feel the commanding woman's unhappiness.

Again the situation felt on the brink of collapse.

He was a trained ship's captain of Office 39. He had spent three years facing the harshest taskmasters of the Democratic People's Republic of Korea counter-intelligence community for so-called *advanced* training and had served two decades since. The punishment for any failure in training or service of Office 39 was terminal, yet he had survived.

This was no different.

He doubted that there was a way to get the woman alone. And even less chance that he would survive if he did, so he needed to get them off his ship.

"I am sorry that we can be of no more help."

It was the first time the unarmed man with the eyes that matched the tall woman's spoke.

Again the Japanese woman interpreted.

"Ship's manifest? The record of that container."

Rang slapped his hands together and P'yo hurried over to the desk.

The blue-eyed man spoke, and the big man shifted his machine gun that spat a single round so close beside Rang's ear that his eardrum stung from the sharp crack of the supersonic round. He felt the lingering heat of its passage. Somewhere behind him a window shattered. He didn't turn to see which one.

"The *real* manifest," the Japanese woman interpreted quietly.

P'yo didn't even look at him before changing direction and reaching under a stack of marine charts. He extracted the binder of real manifests.

It only took him moments to find the correct one.

P'yo handed it to him.

He glanced at the sheet. *Farm Supplies.* He knew that the two containers of RPGs in his hold and the containers of the disassembled black market Bell Cobra helicopters were also labeled as farm equipment. The Supreme Leader's new Tesla roadster was labeled as sugar. He didn't know what lay in the other three containers. Now that one had been revealed to hold a woman, a highly dangerous woman, he hoped that the others merely held UN-sanctioned goods.

He and P'yo would discreetly inspect them at their earliest opportunity whether or not they were sealed.

Rang edged forward until his forehead was close against the tip of the big man's rifle barrel and held out the paper.

The Japanese woman took it, read with disgust, then folded it into her pocket, saying something to the tall woman.

This close, Rang managed a good look at the tall American woman. Despite the strangeness of her eyes and the pale skin, he knew he would cherish this memory in his most private thoughts. The memory of her truly amazing chest would be imprinted indelibly. Not that it was overwhelmingly large, but rather that the shape of the generous curve was so different and so suited her great height.

The massive revolver, once more tucked into her belt, lay against her flat belly.

Kyung's revolver he realized. The idiot. He'd spent a year's wages to purchase it and look what it had bought him, a broken neck in a container alley.

Rang looked back up into the woman's eyes. They were hard to read because of their color, but he thought he saw death there.

No. That is male thinking. Su-jin had taught him as much of reading women as reading men. *From this woman, you have earned respect.*

Rang didn't think that would matter, but who was he to unravel the strange workings of the universe?

He nodded back a respect of his own which was easy to such a formidable foe.

He waited unmoving as they retreated back aboard the helicopter, the big man departing last. Moments later the helo disappeared into the night as if it had never been here.

Rang slipped his hand into his pocket, once again sliding his fingers into the finest red silk he'd ever touched. P'yo had retrieved it from the container. It must have so recently been wrapped around those ever so glorious breasts that he could imagine its warmth.

Had Kyung felt that silk before he died? Rang thought not.

Had the Japanese woman been the second prisoner and had she run her fine fingers over the red silk and nuzzled what lay beneath? The image jolted his body hot once more with need and he cursed to himself. The nearest relief was a week's sail away.

26

———————

"Farm Supplies?!"

Harold had been called a lot of things in his life, but that was a new one.

He was so glad to be done with it. He'd spent the last two hours trying to sleep on the Marine Corps helicopter. Instead, his body felt as if it had been run through a blender; the hard steel decking had vibrated his body until he'd lost any sense of feeling except for a constant body-enveloping buzz.

It wasn't the buzz of good sex. It had started to be, in the few moments they'd had. He'd thought to show Kate Stark a thing or two about what he could do other than cook. When she'd laid that amazing body of hers upon him, he'd been more than impressed. Few women ever achieved such a level of fitness. And the ones who did, were typically too far into the lean category; often painfully lean, as in sharp knees and elbows.

Kate Stark was lush in every way a woman should be lush and strong in ways that promised a good tussle. But the mileage to get there was not worth the cost.

He'd been drugged, locked away in a shipping container on a Korean cargo ship—a North Korean one to make it even more

98

bizarre—and made to huddle out of sight aboard the helicopter while everyone else walked back onto the same ship they'd only just escaped.

He was so done, Kate's amazing body or not.

Even his feet buzzed as he staggered off the Super Stallion's rear cargo ramp and stood on the smooth tarmac at Hurlburt Field—Florida panhandle someone had told him as if shocked that he didn't know where every lousy Air Force base lay. He hadn't even heard of it, but that didn't abate his desire to kneel and kiss the tarmac. However, with the way his knees felt, he might not be able to stand again.

Instead, he relished the cloying pre-dawn heat of a spring morning on the Gulf Coast which was already oppressive. At least the smell was familiar, a couple of spring break road trips that were evocative to recall. Near sunrise on a warm beach with a coed curled—

He peeled off his chef's jacket.

He'd thought the perk of receiving a *Kate's Kitchen from Hell* judge's jacket was a nice bonus, but now he wanted to burn the damn thing—stinking of old fish and a steel coffin.

Paul indicated an especially neat Gulfstream G280 business jet parked on the tarmac and Harold gratefully began boarding. He looked forward to a glass of something cold, a meal of something warm that didn't taste like fermented Korean cabbage, and several hours of good sleep in a soft seat.

"Wait," Kate's hand on his arm stopped him halfway up the stairs. "You can't go."

"Watch me," he started again and then Kate showed another way she was strong; he moved forward but his hand remained pinned in place on the handrail. He collapsed to sit on the stairs to avoid falling off them backwards.

"You like going to jail? Fine, go." She released him, but he didn't move.

Jail? He'd bet that jails had glasses of something tepid and that a lot of the meals would be wholly indistinguishable from fermented Korean cabbage. "What *are* you talking about, Kate?"

They'd gathered at the base of the airplane's stairs by that point: Sam looming over the petite Rikka, Paul on the other side of his sister.

A small tractor appeared, was hitched to the massive helicopter, and towed it into a hangar leaving their group alone on the tarmac.

Kate tapped the hull of the airplane close beside where he sat at the top of the four steps that led into the cabin.

He could feel the luxury within calling to him. The gentle waft of air conditioning slid invitingly along the nape of his neck.

"This is our plane, not the network's. Paul's and mine. We land it back in New York and I'll give you one guess who will be waiting outside for us."

"The New York police?"

"I should have given you two guesses."

Harold didn't have a clue. He was now a wanted man by the police and... All he'd wanted to do was judge a cooking show and maybe enjoy their co-chef time. Harold had also had his eye on the competitor Marianne Rimaldi for some time. He always watching her shows because she was so...*had been so*— oh crap!

On the other hand, he'd never imagined that play time would be with the food icon Kate Stark. The thing with Kate was that she genuinely became more fearsome as he learned more about her. She handled guns as easily as she handled nearly *being* killed. It was attractive and scary as shit at the same time.

"FBI," Rikka reached out to pat his knee in sympathy.

"The FBI?"

"They're your second guess. That would be the Federal

Bureau of Investigation and not the Full-Blooded Italians wrestling tag team for the WWE."

Harold felt as if he'd eaten a double McDonald's Bacon Habanero Ranch burger. With extra grease and a side of hot sauce.

"When jerk-face," Rikka hooked a thumb toward Kate's brother, "sent the plane here to wait for you, it made you fugitives across state lines. The FBI will now be so involved; they love this kind of thing. I'm kinda surprised they aren't here yet to arrest your behind. Sorry Kate. I'd have stopped him if I knew that's what Mr. Brain Dead was planning."

"Hey!" Paul protested but no one bothered to turn to look at him.

"'Sorry, Kate'?" Harold's exclamation echoed off the tall side of the nearby hangar. "'*Sorry, Kate*'? What the hell? The FBI?" His voice was climbing out of his control as he tried to process it all.

The roiling in his gut grew until it now felt like a *triple* Habanero cheeseburger swirled there. He felt greasier and more nauseous than when he'd discovered he was trapped in a North Korean cargo container.

27

———————

Kate felt sorry for Harold, the poor man had gone practically fetal there on the steps of the Gulfstream. She rested her hand on his arm. She could feel the strength there. The rest of him was merely gym-level fit, but she could feel the chef's muscles in his forearm. This was a man who used his hands constantly for a dozen or more hours a day. He wasn't an executive chef who gave orders in his kitchen and let others do the work; Harold Merritt truly cooked for a living.

It was one of the things she liked about him. So few chefs at his level worked the line anymore. She made a point of spending an hour or so a day in the Cooks Network kitchens doing prep work or even feeding the staff to keep her hand in.

Harold's hands, it wasn't often she took a chef to her bed, but he had wonderful hands: both gentle and strong, sensitive to the significance of the slightest touch or motion. He'd felt wonderful and under any other circumstances... Well, if she had her way, she'd be arranging those circumstances at the earliest opportunity.

"I'd bet that they're negotiating with the Air Force right now to get permission to come on base," Kate told him. "We need to think before we act here, but we need to do it fast."

"C'mon, Kate. I'm not a complete idiot," her brother sounded like a twelve-year-old boy, freshly grounded and trying to find a way out of it. Somehow he always skated his way clear, a skill Kate had never learned on her own behalf. When she screwed up, she'd invariably been caught, judged, and lost privileges for it.

Rikka scoffed her assessment of Paul's idiocy.

"If the FBI are anywhere," he cut off the impending broadside Rikka was sure to be preparing, "they're three hundred miles away, sitting in good-old-boy Everglades country, just waiting at Collier County's Immokalee uncontrolled air strip. At least that's where they are if they followed our filed flight plan."

"That's such an improvement," Rikka sneered. "Falsifying a flight plan with the FAA. I'm sorry, Harold."

"For what? For the way you're making my head spin? Or the way I'm about to barf on everyone's sneakers?"

Everyone took a judicious step back.

Kate tried to laugh comfortingly at his joke—but remained poised to move fast if it wasn't.

"I should have given you three guesses," Rikka said as an aside.

Kate didn't turn her attention from her brother.

He squirmed beneath her inspection.

"And what's going to happen when we pull back into the hangar at Teterboro?" Kate asked him rhetorically.

"Ticked-off police, FBI, *and* FAA," Rikka answered for him. She sounded positively cheerful at having something to ram down Paul's throat while Paul tried to deny such a thing in universally ignored mumbles.

Harold moaned and clenched his stomach as if she'd kicked

him again. Now she *was* worried he might be sick and took a sidling step.

She had to wonder what her brother had done to Rikka back when they first met. Kate knew that of all the women she'd ever met, Erika Albert was one who definitely needed no one else's protection—except occasionally from herself. She certainly had Paul's number and could make him twitch on command, something Kate had never managed with her twin.

It was kind of cool.

Rikka continued sniping at Paul, Paul blustered in response, and Kate considered why she hadn't appreciated the silence of her cargo container more.

"Enough!" Harold cut them off with a shout loud enough to ricochet off the tall sides of the nearby Air Force hangar.

When Paul opened his mouth to speak, Harold stood up and held out his hand, palm out, "No, you don't." He stood several steps above them on the plane's stairway which gave him a commanding height.

Kate eyed him with one eyebrow raised.

"You least of all," he turned on her. "Be quiet a moment."

Kate had to bite her lip hard not to smile.

Sam stood in the background. Five feet away but it might have been fifty for how little of the dim airport lighting reached this obscure corner of the field.

Kate knew he'd just been waiting.

"So, if we go back to New York, we're screwed?" Harold asked.

"Way!" Rikka nodded and jabbed an elbow at Paul. Their height difference was enough that it was would have been a shot below the belt, but he managed to twist in time to take it on his hip.

"But you're sure that whatever is going on, the answer isn't aboard a black ops North Korean ship," Kate could see Harold continuing to put the pieces together. "Even if we, literally, were."

"You couldn't see the captain's face," Kate had been watching both the captain and chief officer carefully. "He hadn't known there were two of us in there. His Second in Command knew less, and anything their political officer knew is at the bottom of the Atlantic."

"It's where? Never mind." Harold went pale in the pre-dawn darkness. The only real light was from a security lamp at the back of the hangar.

Kate had stowed Harold safely behind the missiles inside the helicopter while they'd been boarding the Office 39 ship. He'd probably not seen much and heard nothing. She'd managed to protect him from the worst of it.

"That means that to figure out what in the world is going on, we have to go back to New York," his voice was steadier. Harold was catching up fast.

"Duh!" Erika nodded and elbowed Paul again. This time she faked him out and caught him in the kidney by coming around high the other direction.

Paul grunted.

Harold looked at Kate and for the first time since their rescue she saw the man who had kissed her in the dark. His smile had turned a bit wicked; it definitely reached those nice dark eyes of his. He nodded slightly for her to explain the obvious conclusion that he'd managed to reach on his own without any hint from her. Smart too. Nice.

He sat on the Gulfstream's steps. Kate returned to stand beside him. They were effectively the same height as she turned to face the others and leaned against him through the single piece railing.

"What do you do…" Kate had to catch her breath. Out of sight of the others he ran a hand possessively along her back, a slight sideways rub right where the bra strap normally chafed

—a tiny acknowledgement that he'd enjoyed removing it and wanted to get back to it. Another idea she was all in favor of.

She attempted to continue as if his hand wasn't tracing ever lower over her back.

"...when someone is cooking with the same ingredients you are, like in *Kate's Kitchen from Hell?*"

Harold was smiling at her. She could feel it in the half pat and half caress he gave her butt.

Paul and Rikka looked at her blank faced. Sam remained unreadable.

"You use the ingredients in ways they aren't expecting," Harold finally answered her question for them.

"But—"

"Shut up, Paul," Kate cut him off. "Harold's right. We're changing the role of the ingredients we have. You and Rikka are flying back in our place."

Kate saw that Paul was dumb enough to be pleased at the prospect and that Rikka's foul expression indicated Paul was a naïve idiot as usual. Then something registered.

"Hey, wait," her brother finally figured out the downside and clearly didn't like it. "You want us to go face the angry NYPD in your stead?"

"There might be FBI and FAA, too," Rikka teased him. "Could be fun. Maybe we can take in a show while they figure out who gets to arrest us first." Rikka turned and shot her a thumbs-up, "I'm in, Kate."

"Sam," Kate turned to the big man. "We'll need your help finding another route home for Harold and me."

She watched the muscle on his jaw ripple and clench like someone had dumped a rotten salmon on his plate.

Kate suddenly felt like shit.

Sam would never forgive her for the Vice President's death. Ever. He'd led the VP's protection detail back when the man was a Senator visiting the heart of the Afghanistan war zone.

Sam and his team had kept him alive through firefights and three IEDs. Secret Service liaison to the Marine Recon protection team had been her first overseas assignment. That's how she and Sam had met, and how she'd eventually ended up heading the VP-elect's protection detail.

Except, unlike Sam's team, she'd let him die at the corner of Connecticut and N Street on his way to get a Reuben sandwich at DGS deli. Safe in the heart of DC the day after he'd been elected. He hadn't survived a single day as VP-elect.

She had no other option at the moment and tried to show she was sorry for asking.

The grinding of Sam's teeth might well be the loudest sound as the first of dawn's light hit the airfield like a jackhammer, turning the Florida Gulf Coast air from muggy to oven blast.

28

───────

Rikka clambered onto the Gulfstream jet and reminded herself that she'd have to thank Harold Merritt for his dumb-ass suggestion. Four hours with Paul Stark in the confines of a jet the size of a fat knitting needle with wings. At least it was a comfortable, fast knitting needle. Hard to make a sweater with it though—even if she could knit.

She quickly discovered that the Starks' jet had several nice features that made it not quite so awful. One was that the galley was stocked by Kate personally, Rikka recognized the handwriting on the packages. The meals were frozen, but the tiny microwave was powerful. Rikka zapped a mac and cheese with smoked ham and sun-dried tomato while the pilots were starting the plane and talking to the tower. It was Kate-level awesome.

A second nice feature was the seating. In the front part of the cabin was a group of four seats, either side of the aisle in facing pairs. In the after-cabin were a pair of couches long enough to stretch out on and watch a movie. Maybe an Angelina Jolie one that would illustrate creative ways to kill off obnoxious men. How many men had she toasted in her movies? The body count in *Mr. & Mrs. Smith* alone was pretty awesome.

The third advantage was no cabin attendant. No one hovering around who might raise a stink if she found it necessary to simply knife Paul Stark and dump his body down the toilet in tiny pieces.

She'd tried to argue for letting Paul return to New York on his own and let her travel with them or Sam or perhaps one of the nasty North Koreans, but Kate sounded as if having both Paul and Rikka aboard was necessary to the plan. Worse, she was right.

Maybe someone, in their eagerness to find Kate and Harold, combined with having a male and a female aboard when the jet returned to Teterboro, would lead to a degree of confusion when they landed. If it was NYPD or the FAA, they might pull it off. FBI? Not so much.

"This reminds me of last winter when I was playing in Cancun," Paul started out as he dropped into one of the four-seat group.

Maybe whoever met the plane would shoot Paul for her.

"I don't want to learn about your latest Latina conquest." Rikka wanted to stretch out on one of the couches and watch a baseball game, BoSox would be awesome; she'd become a fan two incarnations ago and saw no reason to change her loyalties along with her identity. But she was afraid that Paul would think it was an invitation. Rikka had long since learned that Paul thought women, by their merest existence, were an invitation. So, she sat across the aisle from him.

"Consuela and I were working this dive."

His idea of a dive was a three-star hotel with only a two-star restaurant. And his idea of working... Rikka should not have left her knives in the safe back in New York. Angelina would never approve.

"I had a trio of Florida widows on the real estate hook. And

Consuela had a pair of banker bravoes, well, on the hook. If you saw Consuela, you'd understand," he held out his cupped hands excessively far in front of his chest. The woman would have to be a mutant to fit his story.

What Rikka didn't understand was why so many women were thrilled by Paul's misinterpretation about the purpose of their existence. Had she been such a gullible mark when they first met? A tasty treat that he'd toyed with, tried to take home, and become bored with when she'd wised up fast enough to refuse? God damn it. She suspected that she had been.

At least she was smarter now, despite her body's reactions. Actually, something had chilled. She didn't feel the desperate urge to jump him that Paul Stark pheromones always invoked. Something had taken their place, though she had no idea who or what.

Paul wandered off to the galley in mid-story and returned with a bottle champagne and two flutes.

"It's not even sunrise, Paul." Rikka waved out the plane's window as they took off.

"It's okay," he continued opening the bottle, unconcerned. "We also have orange juice. Besides, you're eating mac and cheese."

"It's Kate's. I'll eat her food every chance I get."

Paul brightened at that. No matter what else he did, he loved his sister and was so proud of her. It made him—

No! That was another of his ways in, appearing decent. No matter what, she was *not* falling for his charms. It had been the right choice then, as it was now. She hadn't needed Kate's warning to know what Paul was: grifter, con artist, thief, and most of all womanizer with the emotional depth of an evaporating rain puddle. The smart, handsome, thoughtful gazillionaire was merely a mirage.

On his second trip to the galley, he fetched the orange juice and a pink box from Levain Bakery on West 74th, which was simply cruel and downright unfair bribery.

For Levain's prosciutto, arugula, and parmesan on a country baguette served alongside a Barons de Rothschild mimosa for breakfast she'd do anything. With her metabolism, the fact that she'd just eaten a mac and cheese didn't matter, much. Besides, she'd missed two meals yesterday and been awake the whole night. For a Levain's breakfast she'd...

She sighed.

Okay.

Not that.

Not with Paul Stark.

Not even if the world was coming to an end.

But she would give in...a tad.

"Okay. Tell me your tale of widows, bankers, and the seriously endowed Consuela."

29

"I'm not traveling FedEx!"

Kate Stark looked at Sam looming up behind Harold. They stood inside a small door at the side of the hangar. The low indoor worklights lit up the massive helicopter now parked behind Sam, making him appear bigger and angrier.

She closed her eyes for a moment then refocused on Harold.

"Look, Harold. It has been a day and a half since we were drugged..." A day and a half going on two.

She didn't have time for this. Kate waved at the small side door that opened directly into the large shipping crate that FedEx had backed up against the outside of the building.

"Harold. It's not a fish-ridden North Korean Conex; it's FedEx White Glove Service. We travel Custom Critical which means secure, environmentally controlled, and you can buy a small country for what it costs." It was against their rules to FedEx people, but she wasn't going to be telling them what they carried. Another advantage of strictly domestic White Glove Service, no customs forms.

"I'm not—"

Kate held up a hand to stop him. "Listen. I need us back in New York to start tracing what happened. You aren't safe out here without me."

"I'll buy a ticket and—"

"You don't have a wallet. Or any ID. They're in the locker at the studio changing room...which you can bet the police have long since cleaned out. And if you did, the moment you tried to buy a ticket to anywhere they'd arrest your sorry self. I can guarantee there are alarms set on every one of our IDs. You have to stay with me, and we'll figure this out."

"I am *not*," he was over-articulating as if she was an idiot, "going to be shipped like Farm Supplies in yet another—" he waved a hand at the large cargo box waiting through the door.

Kate looked up at Sam who reached around from behind Harold and snapped a drug capsule under Harold's nose as he inhaled to continue his tirade. She shifted back as Sam caught the collapsing man and then waved a hand through the air to disperse any of the residual drug.

"Man," Kate was not looking forward to this. "Is he going to be angry when he wakes up or what?"

Sam didn't answer. Instead, he hoisted Harold over his shoulder as if the man were Rikka's size and not a nicely muscled six-foot. He turned around and loaded Harold gently into the box in the back of the FedEx Custom Critical truck. He patted the man on the shoulder as if reassuring him he'd be okay.

The FedEx drivers remained outside the hangar's personnel door that the truck had been backed up against. When Kate checked, the drivers' faces matched those in the secure and bonded transmission from FedEx she'd ordered sent to Sam's phone.

Kate looked at the unconscious Harold and tried not to sigh.

Mattress in a box... Again.

This time their bed was built out of a stack of scratchy wool Marine Corps blankets Sam had scared up from the back of the hangar that no one would miss for a while.

Kate sighed and climbed in beside Harold. She was not looking forward to this. The box was six feet wide, six high, and ten long: half the size of their last prison. At this rate, the next size smaller would be a coffin which was an image she definitely didn't need right now.

At least there would be no dead-fish smell this time. On the top of the box was mounted a temperature control unit and on the front was an air pressure system to maintain fresh air inside the box for the four-hour flight.

Sam closed and locked the doors himself. He would be traveling with them to New York.

At least she hoped so. If it were only her, she'd worry that Sam would toss the key and walk away, but that didn't seem terribly likely under the circumstances.

Did it?

30

FBI AGENT MARCUS REYNOLDS WATCHED THE SLEEK JET LAND and pull off the taxiway to turn toward the Starks' hangar at Teterboro Airport. He ignored that his stomach was growling, his cup of coffee and Egg McMuffin were way past gone, but he hadn't wanted to risk missing the plane. It was now one in the afternoon.

"They clean?" he asked Leona.

She was on the phone with the control tower and held up one long finger for him to hold his damn horses. He kept his attention divided between the Gulfstream G280 and her. Then he imagined her *in* that Gulfstream G280 and cursed his overactive libido for the thousandth time.

She snapped her phone into its holster at her hip, *do* not *think about Leona's hips,* and came up beside him. She wore a subtle perfume. It didn't punch you in the face and make your eyes water; it slid quietly around, tapped you on the other shoulder, and then wasn't there when you turned. It left behind the absolute knowledge of missing a major looker by half a moment.

He needed to get himself a new fantasy life. The one starring his FBI partner was not a good thing.

"Transit time," she reported in that deeply sexy voice that had started the whole Leona-fantasy problem in the first place, "from Hurlburt Field is in keeping with the Gulfstream's cruise speed and wind conditions. Unlikely they had time to stop. On top of that, they used flight following the whole way. Tower and taxiway control report no unusual deceleration since their landing."

"Flight following, huh? Like they wanted us to be sure they hadn't stopped." It meant that they'd been passed from one air traffic control center to another with active tracking all the way up the coast; something they definitely hadn't used on the way down when they'd marooned their Florida FBI team at Immokalee Field. He knew how to pronounce it now, after the team had called to rant about no one showing up.

"The Everglades, at night," Leona shared a smile with him. They'd have no problem thinking of a couple teams here in New York to do *that* to.

Marcus focused on the jet. One thing he was sure of, whatever they found on the Starks' jet, they weren't going to like it.

"Sweet machine. Could give a girl ideas..." Leona trailed it off. As usual she was messing with him and, as usual, it worked way too well.

He focused on the sleek jet as it pulled up in front of the hangar and did a neat dancer's turn. The tail number checked: definitely the Starks' machine. Money must be nice.

The murders had been forty-eight hours ago. But it wasn't until the flag went up on their jet's flight plan twelve hours ago that he'd started digging into Kate Stark's past, and now her brother's.

She and Paul had two very rich but dead parents who had owned three television stations and twelve radio networks.

Paul Kato Stark had a list of a hundred brushes with the law, always in countries with questionable to non-existent law enforcement, and nothing ever sticking to his Teflon tux—not once. Jet-set playboy who lived high, and might be an international thief and con man, though there was no proof.

Kate Pauline Stark—parents too cutesy for words in the naming of their fraternal twins—the exact opposite record of her brother. Started cooking on television at twelve. After college—valedictorian at Duke University, BA and MA, for crying out loud—went Secret Service for five years. Enough service awards to prove she was professional and intelligent. Right up until the VP died on her watch. Fully exonerated from what reports weren't too classified for him to see.

Quit and went to work for one of her parents' TV stations and turned Cooks Network from a piddling property worth only a couple hundred million into a major international success. She was a consummate showman, and her photo said she was more jaw-droppingly stunning than her brother. They both always posted in the single digits on annual most-eligible bachelor lists.

Shit!

They could fly anywhere, why were they rolling right up to their own hangar where they had to know someone was waiting? He hadn't had time to finish the background check, but something wasn't adding up. Well, he'd get answers as soon as the engines stopped.

When her parents were killed under an avalanche at Courchevel ski resort in the French Alps, she and her brother had become overnight billionaires. Other than taking over the board seats of the Stark Management Company and moving into the top three floors of the Chrysler Building, there hadn't been much change in their habits.

Murder performed by Kate Stark and the guest judge Merritt didn't make sense.

More likely? Victims.

But the blackout time on the tape during the deaths of Marianne Rimaldi and Zania, birth name Gretel Berkowski, had been so short—eleven seconds—that it was hard to imagine anyone having time to overpower both her and her solid guest judge Harold Merritt and whisk them away. Not even their chairs were out of place. That they'd avoided every surveillance camera both in the building and on the street on their way out only made it that much more unlikely.

Until this morning's alert, he'd expected them to turn up as bodies if they turned up at all. With them alive, it now bore the earmarks of a carefully planned, professional job with Kate and Harold as primary players.

Still didn't make any sense.

A quick scan, no newsies had picked up on this landing yet. Someone had dropped the ball. This was high profile, and folks loved to watch when the mighty fell.

The door swung open as he and Leona approached. At a slight nod, Leona hung back to make sure no one else departed the plane from the emergency exit on the other side without them noticing.

The first one out of the plane was a Stark, but it was the wrong one. Paul was as handsome as the photos and looked as suave and cool as when they'd visited him at his apartment yesterday. The collarless Armani shirt was open enough to show that he worked out. The white island pants and soft leather loafers made him look like a young Jimmy Buffett returned from an island full of half-naked women and margaritas.

His smile shone bright against tanned skin. But it was a shade too smooth and too sure of itself; a look Marcus had seen across the interrogation table many times moments before the fall.

He decided that the labels thief *and* con man would rest comfortably on this man's shoulders.

"Hi. Well, you're too well dressed to be NYPD detectives, means you're FBI or FAA."

If he thought his charm was going to be disarming, he was fooling no one but himself.

A petite Asian woman with a long fall of dark hair and the greenest eyes he'd ever seen—who didn't come up to Paul's shoulder—clambered down the stairs wearing garish red-and-yellow sneakers in sharp contrast to her otherwise black attire. She shoved him aside when he blocked the last step.

Also definitely not Kate Stark.

"They're FBI, you idiot. Or they would have a radio instead of a phone to get their tower report, and also a lot less weaponry. In addition to that, do you see any NYPD hanging around? No? Means the Feds have clearly taken over the case." She looked at Leona. "Feel free to check the plane."

Marcus watched her carefully, though her tight black clothes left no room for weaponry. She had a confidence and an amused smile that also looked too sure of itself.

The woman held out a hand, "I'm Erika Albert, most folks call me Rikka."

He introduced himself and Leona. Her hand was tiny in his, but her grip was strong. Not a victim's stance, yet not a fighter's either. If she had any training, it was well hidden. There'd been nothing regarding her in any of Kate or Paul's files.

"You don't look like an Erika Albert," Leona asked the question for him.

"You know Albert Einstein?"

"I've heard of him," Leona said cautiously, detecting an obvious trap.

"No relation," Rikka said cheerfully as if that answered Leona's observation. She also sounded as if they were newly met friends at a bar, not people about to be arrested by the FBI as accomplices in whatever was going on. Too comfortable in what was happening to merely be a girl toy for Paul Stark. Perhaps his girlfriend. That didn't quite fit. Secretary? Absolutely not.

The pilots started down the steps, but Paul unwittingly blocked their passage until the small woman shoved him aside, hard enough to send him stumbling into the wing where he landed with a grunt.

The pilots handed over their IDs without being asked. Pilots liked following rules and regulations; it would be suspicious if they hadn't.

"Who do you work for?"

"The Starks," one replied.

"Not the Stark Management Company or Cooks Network?"

"No sir."

Personal plane. Personal pilots. Must be nice, but money did not equal privilege before the law. He'd leave these two for Leona to question and directed them to wait off to the side.

Leona had moved rapidly around the plane, opening both cargo and inspection hatches before touring inside the plane itself.

She returned with a slight shake of her head. She now stood behind Paul and the woman not related to Albert Einstein. From there, she took the opportunity to arch her eyebrows in a way that indicated the luxury inside was more than they'd guessed. Shit.

"Didn't find what you were looking for?" Paul Stark's smile at Leona as she came up beside Marcus looked positively predatory.

Marcus considered how a billionaire might look after a fist had messed up his pretty face.

Leona sashayed up close and personal to Stark until their bodies were millimeters from brushing.

Marcus braced himself to leap.

"Will you," Leona asked in a breathy voice, "be so cocky if I accidentally scrub your face back and forth on the tarmac after I pin and handcuff you?"

Marcus eased back onto his heels. Damn but he liked having her for a partner.

"Yes," Erika Albert answered before Stark could speak. "It's like this disease he has. Incurable, though lord knows we've tried."

Paul's smile looked less certain at her words as Leona moved to check in with the waiting pilots.

"Despite the casual threat," Stark rolled back to his earlier smile proving he was incurable, "I'm glad to tell you where you can find Kate Stark and Harold Merritt."

The Asian woman rolled her eyes at Paul's back.

Here comes the con man's lie, Marcus told himself.

"As a matter of fact, I left my car in the city. If you want to give us a ride back to our apartment in midtown, I'd be glad to introduce you to them."

Albert Einstein's non-relation's shock was so complete that agent Marcus Reynolds actually believed him.

31

KATE WISHED THAT SAM FIERRO'S KNOCK-OUT CAPSULE HAD BEEN either more or less effective.

Had it been less effective, Harold would have woken during the flight and Kate might not have been bored out of her skull. Next time she was locked in a small dark box with a drugged man for five hours she'd make sure she brought along her e-reader.

Had it been more effective, Harold would not have been woken up by the bump of the FedEx plane hitting the tarmac and the roar of reversing engines.

First Harold had been groggy.

Then furious.

Then she was tempted to hit him again to keep his voice soft.

Kate decided that ticking off FedEx was the least of her worries at the moment, but it wasn't a battle she wanted to fight while confined in a small box with no light.

The ride in the back of the truck through the streets of Manhattan had been stonily silent and distinctly uncomfortable.

The unloading, which couldn't have lasted more than five minutes, took forever. Through the steel box, she could hear the bright beep of the Custom Critical FedEx truck backing up into the Chrysler Building loading dock on 43rd Street. Then the box had jostled onto a set of dolly wheels and been trundled along a hall with uncomfortable seams in the concrete that jolted a headache into being which had been brewing since Harold had awoken.

Sam unlocked their crate from the outside. Light blinded her. Fluorescent light. Harold made his first sound in half an hour, a low steady stream of invective that she did her best to ignore.

When her eyes finally could focus, she stumbled forward into the waiting stainless steel of a freight elevator; her third box of the day—thankfully not that much smaller than the container they'd just escaped. Definitely better than coffin-sized. Not a mattress or scratchy blanket in sight.

Sam didn't touch her, but he helped Harold to his feet and guided him into the elevator where he immediately moved to the corner farthest from Kate. Sam gathered up the pile of Marine Corps blankets and stood silently with them draped them over one arm, like a posh waiter at a slumber party. One who looked like he could kick your ass if the mood struck him.

He gave the side of the box a double-slap to acknowledge he was done with it. The White Glove Services container started on its trip along the hallway, through the bowels of the Chrysler Building. Sam stepped back into the corridor as the elevator doors began to close.

Kate raised a hand in thanks, but Sam had already turned to follow the container on its return to the truck.

The doors snicked closed and Kate keyed in her floor's security code. She tried not to sigh as they shot upward. Damn Sam for constantly reminding her she'd lost the Vice President. It had been years, wasn't he ever going to give her a break?

Simple answer? No.

The doors didn't open for sixty-six floors.

"First priority is a shower and fresh clothes. Anyone who stops me is toast."

32

———

Harold continued to shield his eyes as they slowly adapted to the fluorescent lights inside the elevator. His eyes felt as if they'd been sandpapered. Whether it was a hangover from being drugged twice in the last two days, spending the bulk of that time inside a steel box, or that he and Kate reeked badly enough from their multiple incarcerations to make his eyes water, he didn't know.

The door pinged a cheerful welcome at the sixty-sixth floor.

"Where are we?" His throat was so dry it came out as a croak.

"My apartment. Top of the Chrysler Building. It was Paul's idea. Floors sixty-six through sixty-eight used to be the Cloud Club. It was the most exclusive men's club in the thirties and forties. Now we own it, long-term lease."

The elevator opened into the reception hall of the apartment. Harold was stunned enough that Kate had to guide him forward out of the elevator before the door closed him back in.

"Paul recreated the old Cloud Club appointments as well as he could."

It was beautiful and rich and grand. The pegged pine flooring was a warm welcome. Mortise-and-tenon oak paneling added depth to the walls. Kate's brother had installed Art Deco leaded-glass doors to define the smaller nooks and crannies. Harold could see the curving arcs of the sharply triangular windows that gave the building its distinctive skyline shape.

"I told him this was utterly ridiculous, but I've come to like it. We've thrown truly spectacular parties here, live bands, room to boogie, and quiet corners to do, well, quieter things. We hold the annual Cooks Network Christmas party here too."

Kate headed for the broad marble stairs that led up to the next story. He followed, appreciating what her thin slacks revealed as she took the steps. Damn, as grimy as he felt, the woman screamed sex appeal. Zania's energy had been weird; great to look at, but not attractive. Marianne, poor Marianne, had looked to be kick-ass fun. But Kate Stark was somewhere between a plunge in a cool ocean and a briny slap in the face.

The second floor was far cozier than the lofty-ceilinged and muraled main level. This area was vast as well, though a third smaller than the floor below and the top of the building narrowed with the roof line taper.

"This is the level we live on."

It boasted several comfortable seating areas; the one with a couple of couches and several chairs was clearly the favored one. The kitchen and dining area took up most of one wall. Six chefs could work there. It was magnificent and clearly set up by a professional to be her own kitchen. It was easy to forget that in addition to personally running several of the most popular cooking shows on television, managing the network, and being a knockout—Harold wished he hadn't thought that particular phrase—Kate Stark was also an exceptional chef.

She led him up a near-normal sized mahogany staircase to the third floor. It was half the size of the floor below and had been partitioned off into rooms.

"Paul's room is that way. There's a shower and his clothes should fit you."

Harold looked toward the open door. He could see a bedroom appointed in black-and-chrome furnishings.

Kate moved forward into a quite different room. It had soft pastel curtains, light wood floor with cheerful throw rugs, and several vases. Feminine, welcoming, and a surprising side of Kate Stark.

She was already stripping off her clothes, shedding the red show jacket and her shoes in the same motion.

Harold stood mesmerized as she shed the blouse and revealed a bare back that was pure, undiluted woman. Slim waist and powerful muscle definition on a slender frame. A slight turn to the side was enough to remind him that she was generous in all the right places. At the door that must lead to the bathroom, she steadied herself on the door frame while she shed her slacks.

He had to swallow hard. Any number of pretty women had graced his bed, but...damn!

He should already be in Paul's room and in the shower himself, but he couldn't tear his eyes away.

Then Kate glanced back over her shoulder at him. Not coy, not teasing. A frank gaze with a small smile at his absolute paralysis. Then she moved into the bath and turned out of his line of sight without closing the door.

He heard the water start running and the shower door open and close before he was able to shake it off. His anger and frustration at the insanities of the day sloughed off him like an old skin.

He finally broke free and started peeling off his own jacket. He dropped it on top of where she'd dropped hers. His clothes continued to join hers piece by matching piece in the trail across the middle of her bedroom.

33

Kate felt absolutely glorious as she pulled on a light silk robe after drying her hair. Harold had been exactly what she needed. The things that man could do with soap and a washcloth had left her shuddering all the way to her very core, more than once.

She was also glad she'd kept a small stash of protection in the drawer she could reach without leaving the shower, because Harold was as well-endowed as his charisma implied.

If he was up to it, she'd take him again right now on the bathroom mat, but apparently twice in the duration of a long shower was his limit. For now.

She'd sent him to Paul's room for fresh clothes. He came back wearing khakis and a blue Armani shirt that was deliciously tight across his chest.

"Holy hell, Kate!" his eyes took their time scanning her body, eliciting a fresh heat. He didn't bother wasting time on any other compliments, simply dragged her into his arms, brushed the silk robe open, and laid a toe-curler of a kiss on her.

He did have exceptionally good hands.

Finally she broke away, "Hungry?"

"Yes!" His smile spoke of one kind of hunger; the rumble of his stomach spoke of another.

He proved himself an appreciative lover as she dressed; it had never taken her so long nor had she ever so enjoyed the simple act of donning clothes. Many men had helped undress her; he was the first to do the opposite. He took his time about it in ways she deeply appreciated.

They finally headed downstairs to hit the kitchen.

As she entered the living room with Harold close behind her, she spotted Paul and Rikka.

"Made good time," she greeted them. She was disappointed that she wouldn't be dragging Harold into her bed after they ate, but it was time to start figuring out what had happened.

Then a couple—man and woman in dark suits—rose from where they'd been sitting on the couch.

One held two pairs of handcuffs.

The other had her hand inches from a holstered FN Herstal semi-auto handgun.

34

Captain Rang Jin-ho stared aghast at the latest radio signal.

This morning he'd been ordered to detour to Havana. He would be passing within a few hundred kilometers of Cuba anyway, so stopping to pick up four thousand tons of sugar on the way wasn't a problem.

Maybe one of the Latina dockside doxies would want to model a red silk bra. There were those who would fill it out nicely, though their skin would be too dark; it might ruin the image in his head.

Maybe not.

Looking at the rest of the signal, he wondered if he should have jumped ship when they were still back in New York. But he was fifty years old and had been in the service of Office 39 for nineteen years. Nowhere else would he have the privileges of a Senior Captain of the Office. Aboard he ate three meals a day as opposed to most of the country who ate only two *Patriotic Austerity* meals. And that was what most ate in the good years. In the bad years the peasants were lucky to get one.

He'd spent most of the 1990s at sea when one in ten

children had died of malnutrition, so he had only gone hungry when he'd been in his home port. He'd had to be careful not to look too well fed, but with the active life at sea that hadn't been overly difficult.

The encoded private radio signal from his wife that came in as they were pulling up to the dock in Havana?

Bad news.

Very bad news.

One of Office 39's Council of Five members, Park Yeong-suk, would be meeting his ship in Cuba.

The Park family was powerful and Yeong-suk was the most dangerous of them all.

Linking such a visit to the, ah, accidental loss overboard of Comrade Ro seemed unlikely. No, an *accident* wouldn't work for there'd been too many witnesses. As Ro couldn't be resurrected from the depths of the Atlantic Ocean, a plausible reason would have to be created and documented.

His loss truly was an improvement to the world. As one of the few North Koreans trusted to sample the outside world, Rang saw that there were things worth wanting no matter what the men of the state's propaganda machine touted. But hope had been only a false tease that Swiss-educated Supreme Leader Kim Jong-un had dangled until he had consolidated his new position.

Then it had evaporated like a sea mist that had never been, and Rang had been more glad of the protection afforded him by Office 39 and his own seafaring existence. More than once, he'd returned home and been surprised to find that his wife and their daughter were yet among the living.

But Su-jin's news ranked at least as dangerous as the Supreme Leader's brutal consolidation of power.

A surprise official visit from one of Office 39's Council of Five? Park could act with impunity and in one moment Rang and his family could cease to exist, and no one would ever dare to say a word.

He would prepare in case Park's visit was regarding the death of the Party lackey, but he suspected it had to do with the four unexplained containers.

Please let it not be about the one that now stood empty.

This is going to be bad. He wished his wife's memory would tell him something he didn't already know.

As a precaution, Rang replaced the container's shipping manifest that the Japanese woman had taken with her, creating a fake that said the same thing, *Farm Supplies.* He had the mattress thrown overboard and ordered five hundred bags of rice loaded in its place.

He didn't have a replacement for the official seal, so the cut one went overboard.

Then Rang settled in to wait, hoping he had time ashore before Council of Five member Park showed up and ruined his comfortable existence.

35

"KATE PAULINE STARK—"

"Don't use that name!" Kate snapped out at the FBI agent standing in the middle of her living room.

He blinked once at the peremptory command.

"That middle name. Don't! I'm warning you." It was bad enough having Paul for a brother, but what complete mental aberration had caused Mom to give her the middle name of Pauline had always eluded her.

"Kate. Stark." He started again, making her name two carefully distinct words. "I am Federal Agent Marcus Reynolds. You are wanted for—"

"Paul!"

Kate brushed by him. She veered close to the female agent, slapped aside her wrist and grabbed the Glock 17 out of her shoulder holster. She dumped the magazine, cleared the chamber, and tossed them on the couch.

Marcus reached for his weapon, but holding the handcuffs made him slow enough for her to beat him to it. She cleared and dumped his weapon.

They both braced for a fight. Instead, she shoved hard

133

enough at the center of their chests for them to tumble back onto the couch they'd been occupying when she'd entered.

The woman was grabbing for her ankle piece, but Kate figured she'd made her point. She turned her back on them and stalked across the floor to face Paul.

"What the hell, Paul?" She got right up in his face. "I need a decent meal and then time to solve what's going on. Not this shit. Your only job was to make sure this exact scene didn't happen. Couldn't you even do that?"

Kate glanced at Rikka's eyes to see if the agents were going to be a problem. But the angle of Rikka's sightline said that the agents had opted to remain seated…for the moment.

She turned her full attention back on her brother.

"You took," Kate remained toe-to-toe with Paul, their noses practically touching as she yelled at him, "the Medellin drug cartel for eighteen million in untraceable bearer bonds."

The female agent grunted with surprise then whispered, "Always wondered who did that."

Kate ignored her.

"And you couldn't keep away *two* goddamned FBI agents when I ask you to? What is wrong with your screwed-up brain?"

Harold moved up close beside her in obvious support.

Last thing she needed at the moment, but she'd already hit the man twice. Now they were lovers and hitting him a third time wouldn't be appropriate.

Sometimes simple relationships that were only about sex weren't worth the trouble. She ignored him.

Paul looked unconscionably pleased with himself.

She balled a fist.

Her fury had finally found the proper target.

36

———————

"Do you want me to kill him for you?" Rikka shouldered Harold out of the way and moved up beside Kate to glare at Paul. "Please!"

Kate had rocked back on her heels, ready to pound Paul square in his smug expression. But that wouldn't achieve what she needed. Two seconds later she'd be tackled from behind by the two FBI agents and dragged off for questioning.

Let Rikka kill Paul?

"You'd have to hide the body," she used the moment to recover at least some semblance of composure.

Paul gaped at her.

"Already figured it out. Carve him up like a slab of tuna. No one to miss him. I'd never be able to use the knife again, not with Paul-ick on it." Rikka flapped her hands in disgust. "I wouldn't use my good *yanagi* knife, that's totally for sure."

"I'll replace it for you," she kept her tone matter-of-fact, which was keeping Paul off balance. Paul was never off balance, except around Rikka Albert.

"Deal," Rikka crossed her arms and mirrored Kate's stance.

"I—" Paul tried to get a word in edgewise.

135

"I wouldn't do it here, of course," Rikka plowed right over him. "Blood is messy if you aren't set up for it. I'll take his body over to Sam's and borrow his bone grinder for the leftover bits."

"Bone grinder?" Agent Marcus Reynolds asked from where he had wisely remained on the sofa. Kate had heard them reassemble their weapons; one reholstered, one not. She'd wager the woman had hers at the ready.

She could see Paul's eyes shifting toward equal parts cute puppy dog and older brother. Kate knew that in a minute she'd be forgiving him, because that's what people did for Paul.

It pissed her off more, if that was possible.

"Our pal Sam," Rikka answered the FBI guy, "who helped us rescue Kate and Harold, owns Fierro's Meats."

"That's the best salami I've ever had. Wait. What rescue?"

"Sure. Sam is awesome. And he'd like to hear that you appreciate his product."

Sounded like Rikka was going to make best friends of the Feds. The fact that her, or at least her exploits, had been on FBI's most wanted for several years before Kate finally caught her would certainly be news to them.

Rikka turned back to her.

"What do you think, Kate? Can I finally get rid of him? The women of the world would celebrate. They'd throw one hell of a party in your honor. Sam and I would be glad to cater it for you."

"I'll help," Harold added from somewhere behind her, "as long as I get to keep his clothes. Nice threads, Paul."

"Thanks. I—"

"Shut up!" Kate snapped at him.

It was too goddamn much. The whole room was reshaping around Paul. His smile was a millimeter from smug. Again.

Well, she wasn't going to fall for it.

"Do it, Rikka! Get him out of here and chop him up before I

kill him myself," she turned her back on Paul and headed for the kitchen. "I'm going to get something to eat."

"Hey!" Paul grabbed her arm.

Rikka moved to fend him off.

Kate shoved Rikka out of the way. She landed in Kate's IKEA chair, which skidded back several feet across the hardwood floor. She hadn't meant to shove her so hard.

Grabbing Paul's hand, she flipped it up, eliciting a satisfying cry as he folded to his knees.

With a crash, she had her brother face down on the floor with his arm twisted up behind his back.

Then she sat on his back hard enough to drive the air out of him.

37

——————

Kate leaned close until her mouth was inches from Paul's ear.

"This is not one of your goddamn games, Kato." She ground out his middle name and felt ill.

He'd always loved that name. As a kid he'd been totally into pretending he was Bruce Lee helping out the Green Hornet. It had led them both into many near disasters, for which she always received the blame. One of these days she was going to let him dangle at the end of his own rope. Maybe this was the day.

"There are people dead. At least four, maybe more. As in lost their lives."

"Four?" one of the FBI agents stumbled to his feet, Marcus. "Who are the other two you killed?"

"Shut up!" she snarled at him.

His female partner wisely pulled him back onto the couch.

Kate turned her attention back to Paul. "I have absolutely no way to prove that it wasn't us if Harold and I are behind bars, so what the *hell* were you thinking?"

When he started to speak in one of his soothing tones, she wrenched his arm higher, right on the edge of dislocating it.

He yelped.

"*Why* did you bring them here?" she eased off enough that he could speak, but only in short gaspy breaths.

"Because...I have...proof."

She let him go feeling like she'd been burned. His arm flapped free out of control and his knuckles banged hard on a nearby and distinctly stout coffee table.

She'd never literally hurt him before. Not really.

"Ow! Shit, sis! What is your problem?"

She didn't bother answering. "You have proof? Show me, now! Or so help me I *will* let Rikka slice you up and be done with you once and for all. Better yet, I'll stuff you in a North Korean cargo container and see how you like it."

He sat up and began massaging his arm, "When did I ever let you down?"

"Wrong question, Paul."

And yet it wasn't.

He always did come through for her, at least when it mattered. He made her totally crazy most of the time, caused her no end of troubles, but he did take his big-brother-by-thirteen-minutes role seriously when the shit hit the fan.

She let herself sag into a chair and rubbed at her face. Everyone was looking at her horrified. Rikka, despite her teasing talk, wouldn't hurt a fly. Bluster and threaten? Sure. Hurt beyond a poke and a prod? Never.

Neither Harold nor the two agents had a clue what was happening.

Paul clambered slowly to his feet and stared at her as if she'd totally lost it.

Right at the moment Kate wasn't so sure she hadn't.

Paul moved over to open the entertainment center. A ten-foot wall of paneling slid silently to the side.

"Cool!" Rikka moved up to the electronics array beside the massive hundred-inch television like a fly to a Louisiana porch light bulb. "Oh," she ran her fingers over the gear. "This totally rocks!"

Paul handed her a USB flash drive.

In moments Rikka had it plugged in, and the screen flickered to life.

Kate studied the image that came up on the screen: a long shot of a container ship by infrared night vision. In a thousand shades of poison-apple green, the *Chong Chon Gang* cargo ship revealed itself. In night vision, it looked like an aging, rusty crank of a ship. The high rounded stern bore the name in dark lettering, both English and ideogrammatic characters. Hard to believe it was one of the most successful smuggling ships plying the oceans for any country.

The funnel, bright with heat, glowed above the five-story amidships crew's quarters, topped by the command bridge.

Clearly shot from the helicopter, the video circled in. There, on the screen, was the rescue. Paul had apparently been wearing a shoulder cam.

Stacks of containers. The opening of the door.

Two disheveled humans and one mattress.

Kate was thankful that the angle was such that her body had blocked him from videoing her bra peeking out from under the mattress. Or had he planned that too?

The video then cut-jumped to the scene on the bridge. He'd kept his wits about him enough to stop and restart the camera.

The agents twitched and Harold moaned when Sam shot the guy with his silenced handgun.

"That's Sam," Rikka informed the FBI agents proudly who had paled as they watched the images unfold.

Kate considered and decided that Sam and Rikka would make an interesting couple. Maybe there'd be a time she could ask Rikka why she hadn't gone there. He'd be far better for her than Paul, that was for certain. What kind of woman would be right for her brother? Other than yet another rich, blonde bimbo? Nope, an absolute mystery.

In the scene that continued on the huge screen—that Paul had insisted on installing, *so that it will feel like we're actually there*—they could see with the infrared what the night had hidden beyond the bridge wing door. The man who the captain called P'yo frisked the uniformed man Sam had knee-capped, taking his gun and wallet. He'd emptied the wallet then flicked it overboard. Its owner followed it into the waves only moments later.

"Not seeing a whole lot of love there," Paul commented drily.

"Communist Party political officer," Kate told him. "Not a smart one. I was watching the captain's face when Sam shot him. The man genuinely looked relieved. Here," she stepped up to the television screen to tap the captain's face as P'yo walked back in alone. "You can see the captain shake his head in disgust, probably due to the paperwork he'd need to fabricate, rather than that P'yo did anything inappropriate in killing the man."

They watched the rest of it in silence, right up to the taking of the manifest page and Rikka folding it into her pocket.

"Hey, do you still have that?"

Rikka slapped her pockets, then smiled and pulled it forth.

"Anything useful?"

"Other than classifying us as Farm Supplies?" Harold spoke for the first time in a while. His tone said that he'd accepted their situation. But that small detail bothered him.

He mouthed a *sorry* to Kate, she presumed for the whole mess and the way they'd both been acting and reacting.

Me too, she sent back and received a nod and half a smile.

"Yeah!" Rikka smoothed out the manifest, set it to one side, and attacked the keyboard. "Farming, here I come."

38

"Rice?!" Council of Five member Park turned on Rang so fast that he'd nearly lost the balance of his artificial leg. Not the least respect for a senior captain.

They were standing in the narrow alleyway between containers in the Number Three hatch of the *Chong Chon Gang.*

At Park's orders, Rang had sent Senior Lieutenant P'yo up in the harness to the container that was causing them such problems. He had called out what the contents were though he had already known, as P'yo had overseen the covert reloading personally.

Rang was reaching the limits of his patience despite Park being on the Council of Five.

Keep your face calm, especially when your heart is so angry, Sujin had taught him. Rang's wife had chased him around the house for three days with a switch of bamboo to teach him the lesson. She was always right and so, once again, he kept his face impassive despite his irritation.

Park had been waiting on the pier in Havana for the arrival of the *Chong Chon Gang.* There hadn't been enough time to go ashore, touch Cuban soil, or purchase a fresh bottle of rum before facing Park.

Park had no official rank, no one did within Office 39. Out in the world, Rang had the rank of Senior Captain so that foreigners knew who they were to deal with on ship matters. But inside Office 39, while there was no rank—and Party affiliation was the least important factor—there was a definite hierarchy.

The Council of Five sat at the pinnacle of that tree. *Best be careful, Park, the branches grow thin up there.*

Rang, though the most senior naval officer working for Office 39, was not a member of the controlling Council of Five. Park had been on the Council for six years. The Council members were impervious to external events, including Kim Jong-un's notorious housecleaning by disgrace. Execution had not touched a single member of the Office 39 Council nor a single member of their extended families.

Having one of the Council of Five raging at him made him physically ill.

"Perhaps there was a mix-up, Park-ssi." Rang used the peer-to-peer honorific to remind him that he wasn't dealing with an idiot.

Park seethed but then recalled that they had an audience of fifteen of the ship's thirty-man crew watching them.

"Every container, Rang-ssi," he hissed out the honorific in turn, making it sound more like a threat than an acknowledgement. "You will have every single container inspected."

"There are a few containers that are not to be opened before arrival in Pyongyang." The Supreme Leader's Tesla car came to mind. Rang had to be careful and remind himself that to have reached the Council of Five, Park must be snake-dangerous. And Rang worried what he would find in the three unknown containers. Those that had their inspection ports sealed.

"Then cut the goddamn seals!" Park roared.

"And what are we looking for, Comrade Park?"

"A woman, Rang. A woman with black hair and the bluest eyes." Then he lowered his voice to the barest whisper, "And if you don't find her, it will mean both our deaths."

Nothing that would be found by any inspection or seal cutting.

Any comfort Rang had obtained in recalling the tall American well enough to imagine her features evaporated. He couldn't think of what he might have done differently. He remembered the way Ro's kneecaps had exploded into sprays of blood and felt sympathetic twinges in both his real and artificial knees as if it was his own that had been shot.

Being as close to the blue-eyed woman as he now stood to the raging Park, he knew that he was lucky to still be alive to remember it.

At least he wasn't going to be the sole man to blame.

And that gave him an idea.

If a woman was the problem, perhaps a woman could be the answer.

39

Leona Edwards watched Erika, the tiny Asian woman, work the keyboard of the Starks' computer system.

"It says on the manifest that they were loaded at the Brooklyn Red Hook Container Terminal," Rikka continued to study the crumpled shipping manifest she'd pulled from her pocket. "Pretty quiet place compared to the rest of the port terminals."

Leona was getting tired of her and Marcus' lack of control of this situation. She foolishly underestimated Kate Stark's training until she was too close. Time to become a player.

"We can check the camera feeds at the dock," Leona stood in order to increase her presence in the room.

She glanced at Marcus and caught his nod. It was obvious there was something deeper going on around Kate Stark and they were going to pursue that. She enjoyed the instant simpatico she'd had with Marcus Reynolds, beginning on their first day as partners.

As much as she'd been shaken by the loss of Jake, Marcus turned out to be so much better qualified that it was hard to feel bad for long. Jake was old and jaundiced about making a difference, Marcus still believed in the good fight as she did. They rarely needed to discuss next steps, yet he valued her opinions when they were hashing out a case.

Sometimes Marcus would go glassy eyed about her body, which she'd finally decided was sweet. After all, it was a good body, and she enjoyed using it when the opportunity arose. She'd been irritated at his staring at first but had come to find it amusing as she saw him struggle time and again to be decent. The problem was, he'd turned decent into a permanent habit.

Maybe it was time to fix that.

Rikka stood at a computer built into the electronics setup, and as Leona reached for her phone to call in for a warrant, the woman continued working at the keyboard.

Leona was a field agent and not a dedicated geek, but she was way better than average on digging information out of the Internet. She hadn't yet hit speed dial for the office before several blocks of code scrolled up the television screen too fast to read. On the giant screen the letters were as big as Leona's hand. She had to step back to read them and still couldn't make sense of it.

"There it is," Rikka mumbled to herself, and the screen abruptly divided into twenty-four images. The Red Hook Container Yard was laid out before them. The images were from active cameras: on cranes, overlooking yard entries, and multiple views of each of the three ship-docking slips—two were presently filled.

Rikka had hacked the Port of New York and New Jersey without a warrant—in under thirty seconds. Leona wasn't sure she could have *found* the port's site that fast. Maybe she was less useful than she'd hoped.

"Crap!" More rattling of keys. "Aww, that totally sucks!" Rikka slapped at the keys and then raised her hands in disgust. "Sorry, Kate. I can see that they archive the images, but they don't keep their recordings online. We're going to have to go to their terminal and sit at the damned security station to see the back video."

"Well," Leona managed to keep most of the frustration out of her voice. "So, the FBI can serve a purpose here."

It was the first time Leona saw Kate Stark smile.

Damn, no wonder the woman was primetime. If Leona learned to smile like that, maybe Marcus Reynolds wouldn't be so awkward and strictly business around her.

"Why are you here, anyway?" Rikka had moved to stand right in front of her, well inside confrontational space.

Leona looked at the narrowed green eyes.

"We have questions for Ms. Stark regarding a case she worked on several years ago. Then we arrived at the television studio within minutes of the murders of Ms. Rimaldi and Zania. When your jet crossed state lines, we stepped in to assist on that case as well."

Kate came up behind Rikka, "What questions?"

Marcus rose beside Leona, moved close enough that she could feel his body heat, but didn't speak. So she had his support to continue.

How much to tell? More than she would have twenty minutes ago. She'd go with her gut on this one.

"Our Data Intercept Technology Unit's database was hacked by someone with a unique signature. A hacker that you, Ms. Stark, took out of circulation approximately ten years ago. And now—"

Kate, who stood close behind Rikka, looked down at the top of her head.

"What were you up to this time, Albert?"

Leona gasped. This woman was the hacker who had busted into— There was a major arrest warrant out for her. A couple of them.

"I was checking up on the old gang. You know, seeing who'd

been caught and who remained on the loose. Stuff like that. Just catching up on the news."

Marcus managed to find words before Leona could. "You hacked the FBI's DITU system like you were checking their online profiles?"

"Sure. You guys gather all their private noise: e-mails, phone calls, credit cards, and that sort of stuff. Easier to go where it's already in one place and distilled for me." Rikka strolled back to the computer console. "You guys need a new database."

"One you can't hack?" Leona managed.

"No, duh! Good luck with that. You need one named R2. Then you'd have R2 and D2. By the way, is Rafe the guy you two are so wound up about?"

"How—" she couldn't finish the question.

"His records had your names all over them." Rikka shut down the Starks' system and returned the jump drive to Paul.

Leona simply nodded, not trusting herself to speak.

"Ralph Feldman. R-a-F-e. His real name is nowhere in your records. He may look and act like a sinister Chinese man, but he was adopted at birth and is Jewish Mob to the core. Always goes home and squats in his mom's basement out in Flatbush for a couple weeks after he's screwed up; though killing a Fed is pretty extreme, even for him." Rikka handed her a small piece of paper she'd been scribbling on. "Here's her address. Use the storm cellar entrance against the back of the house; she gets very upset if you track dirt on her carpets. You don't want to be ticking off Ma Feldman."

Marcus took the bit of paper as carefully as a snake, looked wide-eyed at Leona, then yanked out his phone to call it in.

Leona stared at the programmer.

"I don't know whether to thank you, arrest you, or shoot you on the spot."

Kate Stark put an arm around the smaller woman's

shoulders to give her a sideways hug. She flashed another of those radiant smiles.

"We all feel that way about Rikka."

40

THEY HAD TO SPLIT UP VEHICLES. MARCUS MADE SURE THAT KATE Stark and Harold Merritt were with him and Leona.

Paul Stark and Erika Albert followed the FBI's car in Paul's 458 Italia Ferrari—in sunshine yellow with a blue racing stripe and red interior—which made Marcus totally envious. The damn thing shone in the mid-afternoon Manhattan light like a second sun and looked like it was going sixty standing still… maybe a hundred. It also made him pray for a couple of good New York-scale potholes to rip the bottom out of the man's car.

"He usually drives a Mazda Miata in the city. He's driving the Ferrari to make you and Rikka nuts," Kate informed him. Leona had opted for the back seat beside Harold in the standard-issue black Ford Taurus. From there, she could offer him cover in case these two were only playing at being rational.

"Well, it's working! Count me as one hundred percent envious." Marcus wanted to try that machine so badly it hurt. More, he wanted to be able to afford the damned thing but that was never ever going to happen. "Why is it making Rikka nuts?"

"Put that woman in a three-hundred-thousand-dollar car and then don't let her drive it. But my bet is on Rikka. There's bound to be a ticket or two by the end of the day. Or if Paul holds out on her, I may have a death in the family."

Marcus kept his eye on the rearview mirror, could feel Paul teasing him from three car lengths back. Abruptly, in the mid-span of the Brooklyn Bridge, the Ferrari jerked to a halt. Since Paul was blocking the right lane behind him, Marcus felt no guilt stopping in the same lane to see what was happening.

Horns began blaring from the other two lanes as everyone squeezed over.

The car sat motionless for thirty seconds, then the driver's door popped open and narrowly missed being torn off by a passing cabbie who barely slammed on his brakes in time, which now blocked the middle lane.

Paul climbed out of the driver's side and stomped around the back of the car. Before he reached the passenger side, the car roared forward, slamming the driver's door closed with its own momentum. Rikka must have crossed to the driver's seat over the center console.

She stopped only inches from Marcus' bumper and raced the engine so that it sounded like a panther ready to leap. He could hear Paul shouting as he sprinted after his own car. Stark grabbed the passenger side door handle and dove into the Ferrari's seat as if it was the last lifeboat off the *Titanic*.

Marcus could practically hear Rikka laughing. He shared a smile with Kate. Well, the woman certainly knew her people. He started forward.

The moment there was space, the Ferrari whipped around him. Then, because the lane they'd been blocking was mostly empty, the car launched ahead in a streak of yellow.

When she hit traffic, the car disappeared in a quick volley across three lanes of New York mid-afternoon madness that he wasn't sure if he could follow no matter what he was driving, despite his FBI training.

"Damn, she's good."

"Used to do a lot of car racing video games. Maybe she still does."

"What's her past?"

"She doesn't have one." Kate's tone slammed that door, hard. He could feel her glare boring twin holes into the side of his head though he kept watching the road.

"I'm not a goddamned idiot. You took down a Tong hacker during a counterfeiting bust. Last week that hacker resurfaced in our database and, now, here she is at your side. Explain that, Ms. Stark." He'd thought they were building a rapport. He'd, cautiously, started to believe that she might be innocent of the double murder on her TV show. So much for the first idea anyway, which cast a haze over the latter one.

"I'll answer another question if I can, but not that one."

"I will—"

"And then my lawyers will— Don't go there, Agent Reynolds. Trust me on that. You're now on the wrong side of the Witness Security Program. She turned State's evidence years ago and hasn't done a harmful thing since."

"Harmful?" He pounded a fist against the steering wheel. "She hacked out DITU database and—"

"Did she damage anything?"

"How the hell can we tell if she did?"

Kate smiled at him. "Because she'd tell me. Now leave it at that."

"And I assume your rescuer Mr. Sam Fierro is equally without a history?" he snapped it back with enough vehemence for Leona to eye him oddly in the rearview mirror.

"Marine Corps," Kate's tone was conciliatory.

Well, that was something.

He took the exit ramp off the bridge. There were plenty of ex-Marines in the FBI. Not many that could tote around a massive GAU-18/A machine gun. None he knew of that could kneecap a guy at forty feet so fast that Marcus hadn't been able to see it happen despite the big man being in the picture's frame when he did so.

Kate apparently read his silence as well as you'd expect from a former Secret Service agent. "Twenty years in. Most of that as Marine Force Recon. Just out two years ago."

"Recon?" No wonder. Though not classified as a US Military Tier 1 asset like Delta, the DEVGRU Seal Team Six guys, and the Air Force's 24th Special Tactical Squadron, they were right up there. But Marine Force Recon's focus was reconnaissance not attack. Though he'd heard they were plenty extreme when it hit the fan. And a twenty-year man? That meant he was one of the best and most highly trained warriors on the planet.

"And he's actually a butcher?"

"Yep."

He eyed Kate Stark as they pulled up to the Red Hook security gate and flashed his badge to gain admittance.

Then who was she—behind that beautiful face and awesome bio?

41

Captain Rang Jin-ho considered his options as he led Council of Five member Park into his private ship's cabin on Fourth Deck of the crew quarters, one level below the command bridge.

He hated the long climb, even when he'd had time to put his leg on correctly. Park had followed behind him, acting superior and condescending to the poor cripple.

Well, there wasn't a damn thing wrong with Rang's mind. Park must be aware that he wasn't the only dangerous man aboard this ship.

Do nothing to remind him of that.

He wouldn't.

Rang led the way into his quarters.

They were well aired out and the sheets on the generous bunk were clean, because he knew women preferred that and wouldn't be in such a hurry to leave. He also had a private toilet and shower, one of only two on the ship. The women liked that as well. He saw that it was kept well stocked with amenities they wouldn't have in their shore-based hovels.

A desk and several chairs dominated the space. A row of file cabinets that were rarely used. His bed graced the opposite corner. Beside it were several smuggling cavities that were difficult to discover and used far more often than the filing cabinets. Exotic travel posters brightened the walls, and a single photo of his wife graced his desk. Though fifty, her great beauty shone through as it had in her youth.

His first option included offing a member of the Office 39 Council, but that would be a dangerous choice. Too many had seen Park come aboard, both North Korean and Cuban. Besides, that was the easy way out of his current dilemma. Experience had taught him that the easy way was rarely the best way.

His second choice would be to plead for mercy. He knew that looking weak stroked a certain type of man's ego. The lost and unlamented Comrade Ro had responded well to that, thinking he was in control though Rang never listened to a word he said.

The third choice—

I already know the right choice! Su-jin had always told him that the first choice was the one everyone thought of and the second was the one smart people thought of. The third choice was the one used by people wise enough to discard the obvious. (Occasionally it was necessary to seek the elusive fourth choice, but not yet.)

His third choice was to treat Park as an equal. They both worked outside the law, both the Party's and the Supreme Leader's. As long as they didn't cross either too obviously, Office 39 remained a rule unto itself.

So, he closed the door to his private cabin, moved behind his desk, and dug into a drawer.

Park stiffened, his hand near his holstered CZ-82. Rang envied him the Czech weapon, issued only to senior officials. His own Type 68, a North Korean knock-off of the Soviet TT-33, was even less reliable and impressive than the original. A .44

magnum like Kyung's would be too ridiculous. The woman hadn't offered to return it and he hadn't asked; Kyung had simply been asking to have it taken.

Rang idly wondered how much bigger a wad of bills he'd have found in Kyung's possession if not for the purchase of that ridiculous weapon.

Rang left the Type 68 handgun in his desk drawer, though he'd wager he could outdraw Park, and pulled out a bottle he'd had smuggled aboard in America.

He set it in the center of the desk and faced Park whose hand still hovered uncertainly by his weapon.

"Jack Daniels Tennessee Sour Mash Whiskey. The Black Label. I think we need to take the time to talk."

42

———————

"WHAT TOOK YOU SO LONG, MY FRIEND?" KATE ASKED RIKKA AS the Ferrari whipped into the parking spot beside the FBI's black Taurus and she climbed out from the driver's side. Despite Rikka's significant head start, she'd arrived ten minutes later than Kate with her FBI escort in tow.

Leona and Harold had gone into the Red Hook Container Terminal's offices to see about getting access to the security videos.

Kate and Marcus had remained outside and waited in the warm afternoon sunshine, leaning back against the agent's car and chosen every New Yorker's first topic. He wasn't a big foodie, but they were both lifetime New Yorkers and shared favorite restaurants.

Discussion of Sam Fierro's deli had led them to Katz's. The pizza man in the photo district, though he belonged to their youth and was decades gone, and the hotdog cart vendor near St. Patty's cathedral. It might have been the first peaceful ten minutes she'd had since the start of filming on the fatal episode of *Kate's Kitchen from Hell*.

She also expected that these moments had been her last peace until this was done.

Rikka flashed a big smile at her, "Took a detour. Oh man, I want one of those cars."

"No ticket?"

"They never had a chance, though I think I gave one cop whiplash." She leaned in close, "Paul actually whimpered. It was excellent!"

Kate traded a high-five slap with her then led them into the front office of the Terminal.

Paul tried to sweet talk his way into the port's security office, but it was Marcus Reynolds' FBI badge that did the trick much to her brother's chagrin. The old dock hand turned security guard had cut up stiff on Leona as well, not wanting to accept that she was an FBI agent. A point that Marcus had picked up on and nearly rammed down the guy's throat.

The port's inner security room looked little different from a television studio control booth. Though, unlike a studio, the two operators that slouched at their computers looked bored out of their skulls. The wall was covered with flat-screen TVs, each chopped up into four views. Consoles offered control of individual cameras.

Kate watched for a moment as cranes trundled back-and-forth loading containers onto ships. Trucks arrived and departed. Longshoreman did longshore things, whatever those might be. After two minutes, she felt that she too had seen everything there was to see or ever would be.

It took Rikka significantly less time than that to become frustrated with the bewildered surveillance operator and nudge him out of his chair.

In moments they were watching the last three days roll backwards from four different angles. She slowed slightly when the *Chong Chon Gang* was pushed backward against the wharf by a pair of tugboats on longlines. The ship settled into place;

fore and aft lines were unhauled and retied by dock hands moving in reverse.

Two of the towering dock cranes rolled sideways into position and began *unloading* containers.

"They only took on a hundred containers here," Rikka was querying the system on a side screen. "What are the North Koreans doing in an American port? That doesn't seem right to me. Does that seem right to you?"

No one answered Rikka as she continued her monologue and her investigation with a buzz of the keyboard so fast it was hard to credit.

One of the surveillance operators tried to protest but ran into the wall of two determined FBI agents and subsided quickly.

Rikka began accessing other records as the video continued to roll backwards across the main security screens on the wall. "Most of these are moving as part of the UN World Food Programme. But these are shipping containers, not bulk cargo like wheat or rice."

"Maybe we're sending them Rice Krispies," Paul leaned in close to look over Rikka's shoulder. Close enough that she paused typing long enough to slap his face. Hard. He backed off and massaged the red marks on his cheek.

Kate managed not to laugh too loudly at her brother. Was he truly her twin? Seriously, there had to be untold major differences twisting around in their DNA, way more than simply gender and hair color.

"And maybe they're flour or something that can't be exposed—" Harold started.

"What's with those containers?" Kate interrupted him. She'd been letting her eyes linger on the screen and had spotted a pattern shift like when a chef rethinks their dish halfway through a competition. She could see the shift in flow before she knew what caused it.

"Which ones?" Rikka let the images run forward in real time. "I'm not seeing it."

"Roll back again and watch these here," she stepped forward to tap the area of the screen that had snagged her attention.

Rikka rolled the image back and forth. Going backward in time, the containers were being *unloaded* into the same stack. Except a group of nine containers were *unloaded* onto a line of trucks that rolled backwards toward the gate.

"No US Customs inspector. No nothing. They simply appeared. That one is you," Rikka pausing long enough from her typing to tap the screen with a bright click of her fingernail.

Kate leaned in to inspect the container in the frozen image. She felt a hand land gently on her back, a comforting touch. Harold leaning in to look with her.

"That was us?"

"Around this time two days ago, a few hours before sunset."

It was a bit surreal to see, like stepping into a time warp. The same sensation as when she would catch the airing of a show that she'd recorded months before. She never became used to the feeling.

Agent Reynolds came up on Kate's other side, "That was really you?"

"The two of us, Harold and I, yes. I saw Zania and Marianne Rimaldi get poisoned. Then lights out, we were shot with darts, and woke up somewhere off the Virginia coast in that container."

"Container number matches, Mr. Secret Agent Man." Rikka handed over the manifest form she'd taken from the ship.

Kate read out the number on the screen as Marcus confirmed it on the manifest.

"Hey," Harold pointed to another container. "What's wrong with that one?" One container came back out of the hold as quickly as it went in, and they placed it back on the truck.

"Same ID number," Leona observed.

Rikka kept working.

"Ooo! Catch this. That one they rejected, wasn't a rejection. Same make, model and color, and same registration ID painted on the side, but check this out."

She ran the video segment again, but at a different camera angle, one from the very tip of the crane's boom that looked down and back into the hold where the crane operator could not have seen.

The container in question was lowered into the hold.

Four men, poised for action, unlatched one container and attached the lifting harness to the one beside it. They dove clear as the new container was pulled back out.

"Where did that container go?"

More keyboard rattles then a low whistle by Rikka.

"Holy shit!" Rikka wasn't watching the video. She sat back and turned to look at them.

"Well, we now know why there were no Customs inspectors. These nine containers, including the one you were in and the one they did the old switcheroo on, moved as part of a special diplomatic pouch under the auspices of the People's Republic of China."

43

—————

FRANCO LAMAR GENERALLY DIDN'T TAKE JOBS LIKE THIS ONE, BUT the pay was good for a couple hours work—two hundred thousand in nicely worn, non-consecutive banknotes. Pre-paid.

US Senator for New York State Mel McAuley should not have answered the door. He also shouldn't have called the escort service that he had, but his tastes were known and that was his own problem. Never be predictable.

Franco had personally delivered the twin thirteen-year-old Chinese girls who said they were actually twenty and looked like they were ten, even shaved below to keep selling it.

One of them left the door off the latch after entering the hotel room.

By the time Franco and Jason rolled in with cameras, they were doing interesting things with leather straps and nothing else on.

Not tied up, but the twins sure made it look like they were.

Not afraid, but the *terror* shone white on their faces when the cameras clicked.

Senator Mel McAuley would be hearing from the head of

his banking committee shortly and Franco could guarantee his newfound desire to cooperate.

After the photo shoot, they'd emptied Mel's wallet for the girls—he'd clearly come bankrolled for a busy week in the city —and shoved the senator out into the hall along with his clothes. The girls proved appreciative of the massive bonus, though the one Jason had used would take a while for the bruises to fade. She could afford it. Hell, she'd market it.

Franco's phone rang twice as they were leaving the hotel.

He ignored it.

Fifteen seconds later it rang again, and he answered.

"I may have another job for you, are you available?"

"Yes."

The line disconnected.

The last one from this client had been two-and-a-half million on direct deposit in his Cayman account for grabbing Kate Stark in her studio.

Now *that* was his kind of job.

44

"HEY, YOU GUYS HAVE GREAT BANDWIDTH HERE," RIKKA WAS punching out through the Red Hook Container Terminal's router and then reached the Port Authority of New York and New Jersey's firewall.

The Port Authority surveillance guys didn't look happy, but that was the FBI's problem.

For once the Feds were watching benevolently over her shoulder in lieu of busting through her door. Which was kind of cool, though she didn't plan on making a habit of it.

The firewall was busy.

Fifty thousand or so tasks were cycling through the servers at the moment. Requests for e-mails, files-sharing, end-of-shift porn, whatever. With a couple of keystrokes, she bought herself serious bandwidth by breaking all pending requests and temporarily killing the password service so no one could get back in. Access denied. The loading cranes out in the yard trundled to a halt. On the security cameras, nothing was going on in the yard.

What she was looking for had to be buried in the data somewhere.

Nine containers had arrived by truck and been pre-cleared through Customs. They were tagged with *No Inspection* orders.

"The trucks," Kate said softly from over her shoulder. Then Rikka saw it. Damn but Kate was so good. First, she'd spotted the anomaly of the containers' arrival and now this.

Every truck had the same logo on its door—Express Truck of the Five Boroughs.

"Hey," Mr. Agent Man spoke up. "I was nearly clipped by one of those trucks."

"Shit!" Ms. Agent Girl knew how to lay down a curse so you *felt* how pissed she was.

"What?"

"Marcus was almost clipped by an Express Truck climbing out of the Rockefeller Center loading dock only minutes after you were allegedly kidnapped."

"Well, that's helpful. Maybe if you'd stopped them, huh?" Rikka couldn't resist the chance to needle the FBI.

"Focus, Rikka," Kate cut off her next volley. So, she turned to the screens again.

"Express Truck of the Five Boroughs," she punched through the shipping company's firewall using the paired truck and containers' ID numbers and the time it had entered the gate at the Port Authority. She intercepted their server's password validation request with a simple response that mimicked the *yes* of a valid password.

"Come on, guys," she spoke to the non-present Express Truck security operators. "That trick has been around since 1983 when Heath Zenith designed the first hundred percent IBM-compatible PC. That hole should be dead and closed by now. You need to get out of twentieth-century code, guys." She punched into the detailed manifests. "They did make a *freight* pickup at Cooks Network. No. Yes. That's odd."

"What's odd?"

Rikka blinked and looked up at Kate. She wasn't used to

having people around her when she was hacking, so she didn't often grasp that she spoke her questions aloud as she worked.

Well, if anyone had a right to ask, it was Kate.

Rikka might ignore the rest of them, but she answered the woman who had twice saved her life. And also, she'd called Rikka *her friend*. Rikka knew she was being dumb; Kate was merely a kind woman she hadn't seen in two years. It was ridiculous and sappy, but Rikka would do anything to hear it again. Both pitiful and true.

"What's odd is, according to their records, the container you were in was empty: it arrived at Cooks Network on that truck, then after backing into the loading dock, the driver was told to take it away empty to the Red Hook Container Terminal. It's here on the copy of the driver's report; they keep extra good records. You should use them in the future. They didn't give him time to get out of his cab. According to this, nothing was ever loaded into that container."

"But they shipped us to North Korea," Harold protested.

"Pansy! Who am I supposed to believe, you or the truck driver who delivered you? Besides, we got you back, so what are you whining about, Stud Muffin?" Rikka waited a beat for him to respond, but he missed his chance. She didn't bother turning. "Hey, Mr. Muffin. You want a woman like Kate, you're gonna have to sharpen up your act or she'll dust you something fierce."

"What," Kate cut off Rikka's next salvo to protect her Mr. Muffin, "can you tell me about the other eight containers? Were we maybe in one of those?"

"Nope. That one was the container we pulled you out of. They loaded you so fast and slick that the driver never noticed it." Maybe Studly had done better than Rikka thought if Kate was defending him. They had both looked pretty relaxed coming down the stairs of the Stark's condo. She'd thought it was simply a shower and fresh clothes. But what if...

Rikka dove deeper into the records, "Ugh! These guys aren't as good as the guy who drove you, sloppy records. Stick with driver 735 if you ever need anything; his name is Fred Smith, believe it or not. All nine containers were moved by Express Truck. All from different points of origin spread across the five boroughs but timed to arrive at the same moment for loading. Three came off a coastal trader over at Howland Hook on Staten Island. Two out of JFK, a Bronx furniture manufacturer, and, huh, two down the street from where I *used* to have a kitchen. Our mysterious Switcheroo container went back there."

She looked up at Paul and mouthed, *Asshole.* She had liked that warehouse locale and couldn't believe he'd found her there. Now she would have to bug out. As soon as she had a moment, she was going to trace Paul's contact at the NSA or wherever who had done *The Find* on her shut-off phone. She'd pre-built tracers that captured the fingerprints off his code blocks. Rikka was gonna hack back his ass so hard he would never dare to cut code again in his life. Much more satisfying than getting a new phone.

"You could have shipped yourselves out of the country," Ms. Agent Woman Leona said slowly.

"What is wrong with your brain, wo—"

Kate's hand on her shoulder stopped her.

"But for the moment," the Mr. Agent Man finished, "let's say that seems unlikely."

Rikka kinda liked the way the two FeeBee's worked together, despite pissing her off. It made her think for maybe the first time in her life that there could be a way to make things happen other than doing them totally by herself.

Paul managed to shift himself incredibly close beside the shapely Ms. Agent Woman and was staring distractedly into her shirt collar.

Rikka returned her attention to the keyboard. Maybe the

phone-tracer guy wasn't the only asshole she was gonna hack off at the neck.

"Can you trace what happened to that switched container from the cargo ship?"

Ten minutes later, Rikka was unable to answer Kate's question.

But one minute more and she found the container. It was being towed back to the yard from the Mott Haven drop off in the Bronx.

Empty.

45

RANG KNEW THAT HIS PAYOFF TO PURCHASE THE WHISKEY WASN'T of any matter compared with the container of a quarter of a billion dollars in supernotes that was now pumping through the Chinese Tongs in the Bronx. But it felt good that he'd paid for the whiskey with a full gram bag of heroin. His dealer at the dock thought he was nuts, but Rang knew that the devil drug would hit the American streets.

It's the little things that add up more than the big ones. Su-jin had taught him that one the first time she'd let him into her bed.

The *Chong Chon Gang* had offloaded four hundred and fifty kilos of heroin in France on this trip and received payment in nice fat bricks of euros, thirty million worth—wholesale. They also came in denominations of five hundred, making them far more portable, and were as valuable as American currency. The fact that Office 39 wasn't counterfeiting those made them much safer to accept.

He set the whiskey on his desk and deliberately turned his back to fetch two clean glasses. By the time he turned once more, Park had not shot him in the back. Instead, he had settled into the chair across the desk, though his hand yet hovered near his weapon.

Rang smiled to himself. Park had not reached the Council of Five by being an incautious man.

Well, neither had he himself risen to Senior Captain by being a fool. Killing Park outright? A fool's choice.

His onshore contact—for Rang hadn't dared leave the ship during the three hours they'd been in the US dock—had thrown in a couple of Jack Daniels souvenir shot glasses.

Rang made a show of opening the bottle and pouring them each a glass.

He clasped his right forearm with his left hand to show the respect due a host as he raised his glass, "To business."

Park nodded, also clasping his right forearm, "To business."

This was good. They understood each other. Nothing else mattered except what was good for Office 39.

They each knocked back the shot and thumped the glasses on the desk as the whiskey burned and took his breath away. It was so strong that it made his eyes water, yet so smooth that he didn't have to cough near to choking like with the poor quality *munbeaju* that was all one could get anymore in the DPRK.

He topped up the glasses.

"I will tell you what I know of Comrade Ro's—"

"To hell with him," Park dismissed the topic, "stupid man. If he crossed into your path, he received whatever he deserved. We only let him on board as a favor to his mother-in-law who wanted him out of the country. No one will complain if he does not return. Especially not his wife, apparently his prick and his intelligence were of the same size."

Rang acknowledged the topic closed with a sip of his drink. The burn was smoother this time.

"Then I will tell you what I know of this woman," always offer something first. "And after you tell me why she is so important, we will work together and save both our heads."

"To do that, we will have to get her back," Park knocked back his second glass and thumped it on the desk.

Rang shrugged his acceptance. If that's what they had to do, so be it. He'd certainly done worse over the years. So maybe he would get to see her in the red bra yet, nothing but the red bra.

46

____

Much to Kate's surprise, Rikka couldn't hack the Cooks Network security cameras from here. After all, she'd had Rikka set up that security system.

"Didn't you insert a backdoor code or one of those things you do?"

Rikka grimaced as she reenabled the Port's system and let the employees log in again to return to their workday.

"What?" Kate could see that the work orders were again flowing out to the cranes and the yard. Everything slowly regained its momentum.

"I didn't leave any backdoors in your system, Kate. I locked it down hard, like you asked, and clean, like I, well, haven't done before or since. Yours had to be done right. I owed you."

Kate couldn't help herself. She leaned down and kissed Rikka atop her hair where she sat at the Port Authority's computer. "Next time, Rikka. Don't be so goddamn anal. Okay?"

"Okay," she sounded breathless.

Kate wondered how alone Rikka was. Twice Kate had ripped her from everything she knew, once to turn her State's evidence against the Chinese gangs and once more to save her life with a second churn through the Witness Protection Program. Did she even have a friend?

Did Kate? She had a lot of close acquaintances, but actual friends... Well, if she had to start with one, she'd be hard pressed to find one better than Erika Albert.

"Next stop is the Cooks Network offices," Kate turned to the FBI agents. "You up for it?"

"We're with you the whole way, Ms. Stark. There are outstanding warrants and I'm violating orders by not bringing you in immediately, though I have a degree of discretionary latitude there. We're keeping you under escort and will follow your lead, *for the moment.*"

Kate nodded her thanks and headed for the door. She wouldn't mind driving Paul's car, but she didn't think the FBI would appreciate it and she didn't want to deprive Rikka of another opportunity to bait her brother.

47

———

Building security at Cooks Network was easy to bypass. Kate had the FBI park in her private spot under Rockefeller Center and Paul parked in his. Or rather Rikka did, as she had again commandeered the Ferrari. The executive elevator went directly to her office twenty stories above the New York City streets and one story above the main studios. She liked to stay close to the heart of her business.

"Thief in the night," Paul whispered as the elevator whisked them upward.

"It's not a goddamn game, Paul. And it's late afternoon." She pointed at the sun shining in from the southwest as they entered her office.

She hated the feeling of sneaking into a place where she'd felt such joy. Yet one story below her, a pair of women had met untimely deaths, and she wouldn't rest until she had that solved. And preferably the solution wouldn't include her and Harold in adjacent jail cells.

Kate stumbled to a halt and began cursing roundly. The others pushed in behind her until they were lined up against the wall on either side of the doorway. None of them moved further in.

Instead of a tasteful set of fine furniture, careful décor, and personal mementos to enhance the sweeping corner office view of midtown including the Rockefeller Plaza with its Atlas statue, the seasonal views of the ice rink and Christmas tree, and St. Patty's cathedral, her office was a disaster area.

The chairs and sofas had the cushions slashed open and removed, been flipped on their backs, and the bottom cloth hacked off looking for secret compartments. How distressed had they been to find only springs?

On the walls, every framed photo was askew; someone had searched behind each one. The shot from her first-ever show—fourteen years old and cooking alongside the great Julia Child—now had cracked glass.

The only reason her desk hadn't been disassembled was because there was nothing to take apart. A sheet of glass with a dual-screen computer on it. She ran a paperless office. The screens remained, but the computer was gone.

The police hadn't made the least effort to be careful or put anything back together. Or had it been—

"Did your people do this?" she rounded on the two FBI agents.

"No, ma'am," Marcus Reynolds raised his hands. "We haven't been here yet."

"And your other teams?"

"Other than the two chaps you led on a wild goose chase in Florida, you're looking at the team. Until a few hours ago, we thought it was a simple murder case with the fugitives crossing state lines. Until we met Ms. Albert, there was no real indication that there was any connection between you and our case."

Connection? Kate hoped not. Two murdered chefs, two

kidnapped chefs, the same computer hacker, and the North Koreans? Crap! They were way past coincidence.

She didn't have enough information for any of it to make sense, but she'd now know what she was looking for when she finally saw it. She turned back to face the disaster that was her office.

Had someone other than the police torn up her office? If so, who and why? She couldn't imagine.

"No computer, no answers here," Rikka observed.

That finally broke Kate's attention loose. Later. This would have to be fixed later.

"Nothing on the machine anyway except software. As you trained me, everything except the generic software is on the servers and the key passwords are only here," she tapped her temple.

"Well done, you," Rikka looked pleased.

As Kate had learned in the Secret Service, grinding through the information-gathering phase without becoming snarled in dumb-ass, second-guessed theories, was a major challenge. So without another word, she led everyone out of her office, down the flight of stairs, and into the main studio.

She swung open the door that led directly to the control booth and was confronted by a bright yellow streamer of plastic tape across the width of the door, *Crime Scene Do Not Cross.*

Managing not to give in to the desire to yank it off, shred it, and murder someone (a bad choice, considering)—Kate detached one end of the tape, let it flutter to the floor, and walked in.

At least the control room was intact. She struggled not to look, the main studio was far more important to her than her office, but she couldn't resist.

The window to the left side of the room looked out over the production floor. It was intact. Everything had been opened, but nothing destroyed. The work here had been done by a forensic team not a band of junior detective hooligans doing a joy ride through her lovely—

Calm.

Take a breath.

The studio looked okay.

She would remain calm.

People had died there. She could still see them, though the bodies were long gone.

Kate forced herself to turn away.

She waved Rikka toward the technical director's position at the control desk. It was at the center of the console next to the production director's position. This was her network's main studio and equipped with the best that money could buy.

It was only as Rikka excitedly sat where she was surrounded by computers and faced the monitor wall that Kate understood what she'd done.

She'd unleashed a monster.

48

─────────

"The idiots," Park seethed as he poured himself a fresh whiskey, "were supposed to grab four people, not two. Though only the one was named a top priority target. You had her. And you lost her! How could you let Kate Stark get away?"

Captain Rang Jin-ho described the helicopter with its missiles—the Americans were crazy enough to use them too—and the massive man with the silenced Markov and the giant machine gun.

"Should have let that idiot Ro take a shot at them," Park said though privately he agreed with the captain's choice to let them go. He wouldn't have wanted to experience the same fate that had found the officious Party observer.

"That's how he was kneecapped. He had waved his pistol around, but no one seemed to care. But when he aimed it directly at their interpreter, that was when the big man shot Ro. And he was fast. Very, very fast. P'yo too was stunned, and he is my best shooter."

Park drank another shot of the American bourbon whiskey. He could feel it coursing through his blood. Making it so that his ulcer complained more, but what was left of his liver no

178

longer cared. This had been his idea, his plan. It had turned to ruin and if the Council found out how badly, it would be the end of him.

What he had told the Council was simple.

"Like Choi Eun-hee," he had said. "The greatest actress in the history of the decadent South Korea that the Americans manage to keep from us. We, Office 39, were the ones who freed her and her director husband and took them north. For eight glorious years they made the most sublime films to ever be created in the Democratic People's Republic."

By unspoken mutual consent, everyone at the table had ignored that the couple's first five years had been spent in re-education camps and that they eventually escaped due to Kim Jong-il's supreme arrogance. The aged Supreme Leader, in believing that it was finally safe to allow the couple to travel to promote their films in Europe, had offered them a way out. Since then, couples never left the DPRK together.

"But films are dead," one of the Council had whined and others nodded.

"But not television." He had promised them he would build a television station by *convincing* America's best stars to work for them. "They so love their decadent cooking shows. It will be the perfect propaganda vehicle."

That and their own fantasies had made them buy into the lie. While they imagined themselves bedding Kate Stark or Zania, or even the Rimaldi woman, Park had been planning for so much more.

Of everyone on the Council, only he had discovered Kate Stark's true identity.

49

Rikka had installed Kate's personal computer system and done the security-side work for Cooks Network.

She'd had nothing to do with setting up the studio, so this was way cool. Tapping keyboards—she had three of them— woke the monitors on her desk.

Agent Woman Leona sat beside her, which was fine as long as she kept her fingers to herself. Kate stood close by her shoulder. Harold looked through the window to the studio with Mr. Agent Man, describing what he remembered.

Sounded gruesome; she tuned it out.

Paul fluttered about near his sister's side, the opposite side from Rikka. She still couldn't believe she'd finally smacked him. Lara Croft, here I come. Whoo-hoo!

"I can't log in as you, Kate," Rikka muttered mostly to herself.

Kate set a couple of energy bars and a bottle of orange juice close beside her. Rikka took a quick bite and swallow knowing that her blood sugar would crash soon if she didn't; she'd go snarky and then goofy brain dead. It was nice that Kate remembered that about her. To be taken care of a bit was kind of cool.

"If the cops have any brains, they inserted a security flag on your account in case it's accessed."

"Uh, you can use my account," Paul volunteered. "Let me key in my password."

"Too little. Too late," Rikka had already done that while he was talking. "Lame-o password, Paul. Your initials scrambled and your birthday."

"The initials aren't scramble—" he bit his tongue and slid a glance in Kate's direction.

"Aww," Rikka cooed at him. "Ain't that too sweet! Now don't get all sniffly on us, Kate, just because big brother used your initials. Maybe he just thought he was being clever."

A quick glance revealed that Kate was indeed touched as she gave her brother a quick hug. Paul blushed. He actually was an okay guy, as long as you weren't an unattached female. Maybe if you weren't female at all.

"There," Rikka declared. "I've reset your password to something serious that I can't guess on my second try."

"What is it?"

"Not telling," Rikka continued to pound the keys. *YourFerrari458IsMine!* sounded like a good password to her. She resisted the urge to lock it so that it could never be changed, then he'd have to type that message forever. Not a good security practice, so she locked it in for only ninety days.

Paul growled in exasperation.

"It'll cost you. I'm thinking a road trip in your Ferrari after this is done." She wasn't above giving him a hint at least.

"I think I could—" Rikka heard the smooth honey enter his tone.

Kate sputtered in surprise that she'd suggest such a thing with her brother.

Rikka wasn't that stupid.

"You aren't invited," she told Paul. "Only me. I mean what a cool pickup machine is that? I'll find me a uber-stud of a guy *easy* with that hotrod. Uber awesome!" Her fingers didn't stop racing across the keys through the whole conversation. Sometimes her brain was connected to them, but a lot of the easy stuff was sort of automatic and she didn't need to think about it much.

"No! You can't have my Ferrari to pick up a guy who isn't me." He sounded quite offended at the idea.

Kate turned her face away from her brother to protect his feelings, but Rikka could see her struggling not to laugh in his face.

Her work here was done for the moment.

Rikka returned her attention to the triple screens.

Let's snoop at the admin level to see what we can see.

Paul with admin privileges. Scary thought.

Make my own superuser account, change logon, and drop Paul's access to standard.

"Hey!" Paul complained somewhere in the background, but she ignored him.

Rikka needed to learn to not talk aloud while she worked.

Security systems are...there. History server for the security cameras...got it. She needed a way to manage all of the feeds at once.

Scanning through the locally installed software, this was a television studio console after all, revealed something called *Avid Media Composer* which looked interesting.

Way interesting!

"This seriously rocks!"

"We call it 'The Avid'," Kate told her.

She pumped the security camera feeds into the front end and suddenly had control of everything at once. People were starting to lean in around her, so she took a moment to figure out the links to the monitor wall and splashed the results up there. That won her back her breathing space.

"Here are the camera feeds from the studio security cams." Everyone watched but learned nothing new. Two dead—one chef and eye candy babe, blackout, and eleven seconds later, lights on but no Kate and no Harold. Exactly as Kate had told the story.

"That's it then," Kate sounded disappointed.

"Ah, that is what the police must have thought, but their Kung-fu is not strong." Nothing like a good hacker quote from *The Core*. There was a dead silence, no one in the room got it, not even Ms. Agent Lady who she'd been starting to like. Sad.

She made a mental note to make sure Kate watched that movie sometime soon.

"Now we start prowling." A glance at the studio.

Two possible doors Kate and Harold could have been taken through from the judges' table. She brought up those much grainier security feeds. Then began tracing the next ones along each hall, each branching. Hallways, stairwells, elevators. The loading dock had three cameras...

50

Kate wondered if her head was going to explode. Rikka had multiple images moving and shifting so fast across the screens of the control room's monitor wall that Kate couldn't keep up.

At first it hurt her eyes, then it started hurting her brain as she tried to make sense of the shifting images.

Only two people weren't rubbing their eyes or looking away, Rikka and Leona Edwards.

"You have a rolling blackout moving through the building," the FBI agent noted.

She did? Kate squinted her eyes at the dazzling screens to try and see what was happening.

Rikka was rearranging cameras in sequence and suddenly they were in order and Kate's eyes stopped hurting. Each image had small white numerals in the corner that she knew to be time stamps. They showed the same numbers, and they were moving forward in real time.

Starting at the top left screen was a view inside the studio of Zania's then Marianne's deaths.

Blackout.

Ten seconds later, a blackout in the back hall beyond the studio's rear exit. By the time the lights came up in the studio, she and Harold were gone.

Nine seconds after that the next stretch of hall blacked out, but only for six seconds this time.

Then the freight elevator, thirty-two seconds.

Loading dock for fourteen.

And then the back of the Truck Express of the Five Boroughs pulling out into the sunlight with a container on its bed. It bore an identification number that she was coming to know far too well. A couple in black suits could be seen dodging around the nose of the truck as it reached the street— Marcus and Leona.

"That was incredible timing." Kate wondered how she would plan an operation that precise and didn't think she could, regardless it being in her own building.

"Not so much as an emergency exit light," Rikka noted. "That takes someone with access to your building systems."

"It would require people posted at several key breakers on the electrical panels," Leona offered carefully.

"Nope," Kate pointed at the bottom row of cameras that hadn't been blacked out. She managed to identify those images once everything else stopped moving. "Each area's main electrical panels. Well done, Rikka. No one there. So, someone hacked in."

"No way!" Rikka protested. "I made this system bullet-proof. Why else did we have to come here to look at this? I can't get in here. It makes the FBI's stuff look like a cakewalk. Uh...I didn't just say that."

Marcus and Leona shared a worried glance but didn't say anything.

"That means they had help on the inside." Harold's statement silenced the room.

51

———

Park stared glumly at the glass of whiskey Rang Jin-ho had poured for him. The light was failing outside, yet neither of them were sober enough to notice the growing darkness of Rang's cabin.

Rang had slumped back in his chair and might have passed out.

When it interfered with his drinking, only then would Park care.

Kate Stark had taken down the DPRK's greatest hacker and shredded the most lucrative operation in Office 39's entire roster.

He knew if he brought her to the Supreme Leader and then revealed that she was the Secret Service agent who had shattered so much of their counterfeit distribution system in America five years ago, it would be a triumph. Office 39 would have not only the agent but also, by the time they were done with her, the deep knowledge of her methodologies and contacts.

He would become the greatest power on the Council.

It would reveal the failure of the Council's aging leader, the dickless old pussy, who had risked and lost an entire year's printing of supernotes to that single moment.

Park also knew that if he came back without her, this toady across from him could well be the one taking his Council seat. For the Council was dreaming of stupid television shows and bedding beautiful American actresses. And would now toss him, Park Yeong-suk, aside if they didn't get to live their fantasy.

No, Park blinked against the level of alcohol rising in his brain. If he went down, so would Rang. Park took no comfort that his life was somehow tied to such an underling's.

But he couldn't show those thoughts to Senior Captain Rang Jin-ho, of course.

He'd known Rang for years.

Slept with Rang's wife whenever her husband was at sea, but that didn't make Rang any less of a man to be cautious around. He had worked his way to Senior Captain not only through competence. Rang possessed a deep ruthlessness that Park had to admire.

Right now, he needed Rang.

He also needed him to stay alive for the foreseeable future. For as long as he lived, Rang's wife would not want more than Park gave her between the sheets.

Su-jin knew her own power, married to Office 39's highest ranked sailor. She would not hound Park to leave his own wife for her, as long as she had Rang's position to tend.

Had Rang taught his wife tricks that he had learned from whores in foreign ports, or had his wife learned them herself? Park would wager his next allotment of foreign magazines on the latter. If so, who had she learned them from? He'd like to shake the man's hand...then he'd execute the man to guard those secrets.

Now that he thought of it, he understood that she was the true reason behind her husband's success.

Su-jin wasn't only a fantastically skilled lover—especially

when compared to his own serviceable but uninspiring Mi-sook—able to draw more out of an orgasm than any woman he'd ever been with. She was also a smart and dangerous woman herself. A true asset.

So, what questions would Su-jin ask him about this hostage situation, or rather this lack-of-hostage situation, if he were at this moment buried deep within her, spent with his own release, and her muscles working him ever so gently inside her? She did often ask him questions then and, Park had to acknowledge, he often answered them when he was in that state.

Including the questions he shouldn't have.

If he wasn't more careful in the future, he'd have to name Rang to the Council of Five the next time there was an opening simply to ensure his wife's silence. He idly wondered if he was already past that decision point.

He'd have to ask Su-jin, she'd know, as it was her doing anyway.

52

———

Leona watched as Kate Stark shifted the direction of her pacing the length of the monitor wall to return beside Rikka and stare at the same display Rikka was. Leona leaned in to see what they were looking at.

She wondered why the FBI hadn't recruited this programmer. Because Kate Stark had. It didn't make any sense despite Leona's conviction of its accuracy—there was no questioning the absolute loyalty.

The camera images were segmented off on the two side screens. Her central screen was filled with the code of her hacking.

Code.

Leona laughed and everyone looked at her. She waited, but no one else got the joke. Including Rikka Albert. Which made Leona feel pretty damned pleased with herself.

"You were right, Mr. Merritt. It was an inside job. There was no blackout. What's the last thing you remember?"

"Zania licking the plate like a porn star licking...uh, sorry. But she was." He squinted his eyes to concentrate. "Then, her collapsing forward." Another hesitation. "Poor Marianne sitting on the floor and then falling over sideways. I saw Kate collapse onto the table. I may have seen the dart in her neck. Or I might be imagining it. Then a stab of pain here," he tapped his neck, "as I was hit. Then…nothing else."

"Give me the last few seconds of the studio images, Ms. Albert. Run them slowly."

Rikka zoomed in on the two studio security cameras as well as the television show footage shot by the two camera operators.

Zania fell in slow motion. One of the cameras caught the escape of her breast. A look of surprise on Kate's face as she turned to Marianne Rimaldi. The other camera picked up what Kate would be seeing.

Marianne drooping to sit as slowly as a feather.

A different look on Kate's face, as if she knew what was happening in that moment.

Marianne falling over sideways. And blackout.

"That's wrong," Kate said softly. "I saw her head hit the floor. I saw her eyes pop open as she hit."

Rikka stopped exactly on the frame that transitioned from the image to the blackout.

"It's too clean," Kate studied the image. "The studio lights don't fade that fast no matter what you do."

"Someone overwrote the recorded images with black," Leona informed them. "And they didn't miss a single camera."

"That's not quite right," Rikka announced. "I synchronized the clocks on the cameras. Cool software by the way, Kate."

"You're welcome." If Ms. Albert heard the dryness of Kate Stark's tone, she didn't show it.

"The blackouts," Rikka continued, "are deleted segments of the recording. If the NYPD looked at these camera feeds without synchronizing them, and I'm betting that's what they did, they wouldn't notice the missing chunks of time by merely watching them. There wouldn't be black. They'd only see an empty hall remaining empty and miss the small jump in the recording times imprinted on the image's lower corner."

"I don't get it," Paul and Harold were both staring intently at the screens with furrowed brows as if they were twins.

Marcus got it though and was nodding his thanks to her. Damn but Leona liked working with the man.

"They didn't overwrite the camera images with black," Leona explained. "The inside man simply deleted the sections they didn't want anyone to see. It would attract less attention to their getaway route."

"But that's not what happened in the studio. Even the NYPD would have noticed a time jump there."

Marcus was watching her, "But if Ms. Stark and Mr. Merritt saw more—"

"It means they did the studio cameras differently," the man was practically inside her brain when they were working like this, a very good feeling. A very good one. "Play the end of the studio blackout again, please, Ms. Albert."

The black image remained for a few moments, with the timer showing in the lower right corner. Then the studio lights faded back up to normal lighting.

Ms. Albert quickly ran through the other transitions. All of the others were false.

Then she ran the exact beginning of the studio blackout. It was an abrupt cutoff.

"The studio lights *were* blacked out," Leona turned to inform the others, "because we can see it fading back up. But the timing was off on the initial blackout, so they overwrote the last bit of the filming with black."

Everyone was nodding, they understood it now.

"There was something they didn't want us to see during the fadeout. So, they overwrote the actual fade to black. We need to know what that was."

53

Kate had Paul locate Mac Olson, Cooks Network's senior floor director, and have him come up to the studio control room. He'd been the one working the taping of *Kate's Kitchen from Hell.*

Thankfully, Mac was in the building and arrived quickly. It saved her from contemplating quite how appropriate that show title was at the moment.

Paul led him into the control room.

Mac froze on seeing Kate. She was watching his round face carefully and saw shock, but no dismay. Instead, the instant he recovered, Mac rushed up to her all aflutter and hugged her three separate times, as if hating to let go.

"Katie? Honey? You're alive?" Mac's words stumbled over each other in their rush to get out as he gave her yet another effusive hug. "God, I feared the worst. But if anyone was going to survive, I knew it would be you. I kept hoping that, oh I can't tell you how I hoped. We have such a total mess going on in programming. No one knows if we should keep shooting, or if it's safe to enter our kitchens. The whole filming schedule for

Good, Better, Best Chef is blown, and I don't know what to do. I've put it on hold at the moment. But the contracts... Lawyers. Oh God, honey, spare me from lawyers. Such a total mess. I'm so stressed that I can't eat a thing. You must tell me what to do, sweetheart."

He'd be comical if he wasn't also one of the best directors in the business. The Food Channel still hadn't forgiven her for stealing him away.

She led him by the hand he wouldn't release to a pair of the open console chairs, making sure he sat beside Rikka in the one that would normally be his. Kate sat to his other side.

Paul leaned against the closed door; Marcus rested easy in a position Kate recognized as looking casual, but wholly prepared to act if needed.

Harold sat in the chair next to Kate.

Rikka faced her and mouthed, "Cute!"

Kate ignored her.

Rikka made a pout for the failure.

Kate turned her attention to Mac.

"Mac, I'm sorry to leave you in the lurch, but you're going to have to keep dealing with it for the moment. I have a few other problems to resolve first."

His quick glance around the room had him instantly focusing on the FBI agents. "Honey, I'm so sorry. Feds. By the way, you two need to loosen up on your clothing design; it's so passé that it couldn't even pass as post-ironic." He turned back to Kate, "Okay, honey, you take care of your mess, and I'll make sure you have a network to come back to."

"You're the best, Mac. Get Tommy to—"

"Already done," he cut her off. "I've been looking for a chance to work closer with him anyway, you know." He winked.

She knew. "What I need from you now, Mac, is—what did you see before the lights went out?"

"You mean other than Zania and Marianne looking as if they died?"

Her own gasp was echoed around the room.

54

"'Looking'? 'As if'?" Kate managed to choke out. "They're not—" She tried to stand to look through the studio window, as if she might see them out there flirting with each other.

Mac's gentle hand on her arm was all that kept her in place.

"Oh no," he placed his other hand over his heart. "They're dead now. Sorry, honey, I guess you wouldn't know. They were poisoned with a paralytic of some sort. It paralyzed everything, including their diaphragms, hearts, you name it. They couldn't breathe or blink. Doctors told us if they'd been given an antidote in the first three minutes, they'd have been fine, though maybe not because they both had such big doses, but we didn't know that and didn't have the antidote regardless of if we had known it. They said it was something like... Wait, I noted it down." He pulled out his phone and poked around for a moment.

Kate looked wide-eyed at Harold. So that was what had happened to them. They'd dropped as fast as the others after they'd been poisoned. But they'd been given the antidote once they were bundled into the container.

"Ve-cur-on-ium or maybe Vec-u-ron-ium," Mac squinted at

the word as if it might leap out of his phone and attack him, "with a kind of an accelerant so it hit their nervous systems ever so horribly fast instead of the normal sixty seconds. Apparently, it's used to paralyze muscles for when they do surgery on people. In big doses, it paralyzes *all* of the body's muscles. I didn't get the name of the antidote, it's this long," Mac gestured wildly to the side and, without noticing, missed punching Leona's nose only because she ducked in time.

Mac then put his phone away. "ACH something. It gives me the shivers thinking about it."

Gave her the shivers too. How long had Marianne remained conscious with her eyes open and her heart not beating? When Kate found out who did that, they were going to be in a world of hurt.

She and Harold had been hit with the same drug, but they'd been given the antidote immediately and then a knockout drug that had kept them asleep until they were well out to sea.

Why had two of them been taken and not the others?

55

"Why," Park mused aloud over the question, pretending he was whispering it to Su-jin while buried deep inside her, "did the United States Marines come to rescue a television actress?"

"Maybe they didn't," Rang slouched lower in his chair, propping his feet on the desk. He wasn't asleep. "The tall woman with the blue eyes was clearly in command of the team that came onto my command bridge. She wore a red jacket the color of flames, I don't think that is normal US military."

Park shook his head. He didn't think it was either; wasn't it the English who wore red? He held his breath for a few moments as the room kept spinning though he was no longer moving his head.

"It had writing stitched over her left breast, but none of us could read what it said. One of the men had the same blue eyes but with blond hair, the other man was huge. Only he and the Stark woman were armed. The fourth was a tiny Japanese woman who spoke Korean like a native."

"Japanese?" Park hissed with displeasure. He was one-quarter Japanese, though he'd never let anyone know. He would not have been allowed into Office 39 if anyone ever knew, never mind the Council of Five. His father's mother had been one of the Japanese soldiers' unwilling *comfort women* during World War II and his father had been the result. Grandmother had the good sense to use her beauty to marry a particularly malleable high Party official with narrow cheekbones immediately after the war and provide him with many more sons and daughters, so Father looked to be a pure Korean when viewed with his family. He had always passed as one.

Rang started humming an old ballad about a cuckold, his wife, and a handsome farmhand. How much did the man know? Was he making a threat or was it merely an idle tune?

"You let her live?"

"Who? Oh, the Japanese one," Rang shrugged. "I did not have many options."

Park was half tempted to kill the man right here and now. Extremely tempted. But that meant he'd have to purge Su-jin as well on his return to Pyongyang. He could never trust her in his bed if he killed her husband. He sighed. Once again, everything was more complicated than it should be.

"I am thinking," Rang had slipped lower in his chair and was staring up at the steel beams of the room's ceiling as he sipped more of Mr. Jack Daniel's bourbon. "I am thinking that there is no method for our agents to get near the Stark woman again."

"There must be a way, or we are finished." At least he was, and he'd make sure he didn't go down alone.

"Perhaps it doesn't matter," Rang closed his eyes and leaned his head back.

Park realized he was in no better condition himself. If the desk was not there to stop his knees, he might well slide to the floor.

Rang sipped his drink without opening his eyes, proving he remained conscious.

"What is your idea, Rang?" Maybe if he arranged for his

own wife to have an accident. Rang too. Maybe then he could have both Su-jin's talented body and her dangerous mind for his own. Maybe then she could help him survive the results of returning without the Stark woman.

Or maybe she'd make sure it landed on Park's own shoulders and take his place herself.

Women were always trouble.

"They were," Rang sighed, his voice merely a mumble, "protective of the little Japanese."

Park blinked his eyes to refocus them on Rang. "Really?"

Rang nodded without opening his eyes.

Park considered the problem. Then he decided that allowing Rang to live was not such a bad idea. For now.

56

———

"I don't know what I saw that could be of any help," Mac hurried over to a mini fridge at the back of the control booth, found a bottle of water for himself. Before he opened it, he offered it to Paul, pulled out more and handed them out around the room before returning to his chair and forgetting to get one himself.

Kate smiled as Rikka rolled her eyes and crossed to the fridge to fetch one for him.

"I mean, Marianne and I, we were such good friends. Our mothers were close, too; they did so many films together."

"I didn't know that." Kate was always amazed at what she didn't know about the people around her, including the people she thought she knew well. "What did your mother act in? Anything I might have seen?"

"Honey. You wouldn't have. Our mothers were," he pressed fingertips to his mouth for a moment before whispering, "in adult films."

"*Two Tramps in...* wherever," Paul said. "I think that was their most popular series. The travel context added something that most of those movies set in nameless rooms lacked.

Though I personally liked them better in the *Being Wild in...*series. They had a real life to them, fun to watch."

Kate prepared to smack her brother. She knew he'd watched a lot of porn in his teens, and was relieved that as far as she knew, that was in his past. But he wasn't helping the conversation.

Before she could act, Mac responded.

"You sweetheart, Paul! Mama and 'Jessica Anne,' that's Marianne's mom's screen name, had such a good time doing those. And they'd agree with you. I think Marianne and I were about twelve at the time and we'd travel everywhere with them. At night they'd take us out exploring: sightseeing in Italy, dancing at clubs in Brasília—all ages do that there, whatever. It was wonderful. When they were shooting, we'd be doing our homework together in a dressing-room trailer. Or as Marianne used to joke, 'an *un*dressing-room trailer.' Oh, I miss her so much. She was my first and only *woman*. I already knew my preferences, but we loved each other so much. I was so hoping she'd win and she's..." He wiped at his eyes and took a steadying breath. "I called Jessica Anne myself to tell her about Marianne...after making sure Mama was there first. Oh, it was horrible. Simply horrible."

Kate gave him a moment but was starting to worry about the clock. An itch between her shoulder blades that had kept her alive many times over the years, warned her that time was growing short. The NYPD might be en route right now.

"Mac, I'm sorry, but..."

"Yes, of course," he wiped his eyes again and gave a loud sniff. "They are such natural women. Not brazen hussies like Zania's mother and her 38HH implants and three face lifts."

"Ewww!" Paul agreed with a straight face. Which was apparently enough to satisfy Mac's sense of honor and get him back on track.

Mac switched to director mode.

He led them out into the studio. Kate didn't like to follow, but Harold's sympathetic smile encouraged her, at least she wasn't alone in that feeling. The set wasn't due for a major refresh before next season, but she was certainly going to redo the judges' platform and table before she sat there again.

The kitchen had been cleared of food, taken away for testing. The air was air-conditioner fresh, and the lighting looked terribly dim without the floods and spots she was used to. There were a few work lights turned on above the overhead pipe grid from which floods, spots, microphones, and a pair of remote-controlled camera travelers were hung. It cast eerie shadows over every surface.

Mac's speech patterns didn't change, but the information was immensely detailed and his intensely organized brain—that could track four camera angles and anticipate every move of multiple show participants from moment to moment—was able to recreate which direction he was facing and everything he saw as he worked his way through those last crucial seconds.

Paul and Harold were quickly recruited to stand in for the camera men. Kate herself became floor director. Rikka became the unfortunate Marianne, an image that unnerved Kate more than it did Rikka.

Marcus Reynolds was discreetly holding out a micro-recorder and Leona Edwards was taking notes, allowing Kate to focus on the details.

Mac rushed from one person to the next, adjusting their positions as he told the story of what he had witnessed.

For the most part he'd seen the same things. But he continued after the camera blackout. He saw Kate and then Harold collapse forward.

"I was so shocked, I couldn't breathe, I can tell you. I understood right away that the chocolate ganache was poisoned, but neither of you had touched it, you simply jerked and then collapsed. Both cameras were focused on the victims, so I think I'm the only one who saw your collapse. Then I saw the four men moving forward."

Kate wanted a description of the men but managed to restrain herself until he'd finished his story.

"That's when the lights blacked out. In the glow as they faded, I could see them pulling on those night-vision cyborg goggle thingies over their faces and reach for your necks. They seemed to pull something out."

"Darts, maybe?" Harold prompted from where he stood at the camera position with the perfect angle to see Zania's escaped breast. Paul's camera position had captured Marianne Rimaldi's demise.

Prompting a witness wasn't proper questioning technique, but Kate let it go without interruption.

"Could be," Mac acknowledged. "Yes, it could be. Then, it went fully dark. By the time the lights came back up, you were both gone."

"Why didn't you tell the police?" Harold protested. "Then they might have looked for us before—"

Kate held up a hand to cut him off.

"But I did," Mac's protest rang close to a whine of agony. "Then they started checking the videos and held me for twenty-four hours assuming I was an accomplice making up a story to protect you. They decided that I had ordered the studio blacked out to hide your escape. They took copies," he turned his attention back to Kate. "That horrible piece on the Internet and the news didn't come from us, Katie. I promise. It was leaked by someone at the police."

Mac was the only one ever allowed to call her Katie. And she forced herself not to think how they would treat a gentle man like Mac in a New York holding cell.

"The men," she prompted him, "the ones who took us. Can you describe them?"

"They were big. All over six foot and three had big shoulders. One was thinner, but he was the tallest of them."

"That lets out our Koreans," Paul remarked. "The biggest guy on that boat didn't come up to my armpit. It had to be someone else they hired to grab you."

"Koreans?"

"Ignore him for the moment, Mac," Kate's itch was worsening. They had to hurry. "Anything else?"

"Black masks, black turtlenecks, black pants. They had gloves too."

"Damn it!" Nothing useful. Kate heard the elevator ding down the hall. They only had seconds. She grabbed Harold by the arm and gave the two agents a quick nod back toward the control room that had the advantage of a rear exit, which opened close beside the stairwell. She knew she didn't have time to waste with the police.

Mac rose and took her arm for a moment, "I remember one had rolled up his sleeves, it was just so awfully warm in the studio that day. He had strange tattoos running up his arms. One was of a skull. The other had words: 'Swift, Silent,' and something that started with a D."

Kate felt a deep chill run up her spine, then the four of them bolted for the control room door, signaling for Paul and Rikka to stay and run interference.

57

Sam sighed. He'd thought he was done with Kate and company. They were getting awfully predictable. Ten p.m. and once again no visit from Devlin.

They were here.

Sam held the same long-handled lamb cleaver his grandfather had forged seventy years ago and considered. He waited for everyone to enter. Three trips to his alarm, but four entered.

None with the soft step of Erika Albert.

Kate. The only one other than Devlin well enough trained to spot and avoid the innermost alarm.

Shit!

He closed his eyes searching for strength. Not finding the kind of strength he sought, he slammed the curved blade down and neatly severed the lamb's head at the base of the neck. Then with a single stroke he split the lamb's belly from neck to hindquarters and left the blade buried there. That would give them a distraction in case he needed one.

Sam turned to face the intruders.

Harold, and two FBI marked plainly by their clothes and

stances. They'd both seen field time, at least a couple years' worth.

And goddamn Kate Stark.

The first three were indeed focused on the lamb and looking a touch green. Wasn't as if it was alive. They edged farther into the shadows cast by the sole work light hanging above his bench. Harold backed into one of the narrow windows, looked around, and jumped at his own reflection against the night's darkness beyond.

Hard to see why Kate was keeping him around. He was handsome in a city-boy way, treated her decently from what Sam had seen, and he was functioning despite being kidnapped. Is that what it took these days, being pretty and nice? Sam knew he failed on both counts there.

Not that he cared.

Of them all, only Kate stood unmoving. And for only the third time since he'd first met her six years ago, she looked trail-worn. It took a lot to wear down a woman like Kate Stark. Losing the Vice President three years ago had been the first one. Then shortly after that when she'd lost her parents.

This whole thing with the North Koreans wasn't hitting her quite that bad, but it also wasn't good. Normal mode? Seriously even-keeled. But behind that he could see in her eyes and her stance that she was exhausted and mad as a poked wasp's nest.

If anyone asked him, they should blow Pyongyang back to the Stone Age. He doubted if anyone outside the capital city would complain. Sam had spent two weeks on the ground there with three other Force Recons scoping out their sub-orbital launch facilities. He'd also spent a month in-country mapping the anti-aircraft placements at the height of one of Kim Jong-il's generated crises. They had more anti-aircraft around their capital than every other city on the planet—combined. Paranoia reigned supreme in the DPRK.

But no one had asked him, so their damned government

was ticking along, starving its own people who'd been so kind to him, and scaring the shit out of everybody in every nation.

The others had stopped focusing on the half-butchered lamb and were now staring at his folded arms. The FBI both grabbed for their weapons and shifted sideways to get two good angles on him. Not bad for Feds. The male had clearly fired his weapon at a perp before, though no hit. The woman—he checked her eyes—had shot one, but not two. There was a certainty in the male's motions that would never be there if he'd actually killed a man; a surety that wouldn't return until he'd killed many more. There was a tightness in the woman's eyes that spoke of the hard-learned lesson of taking a life.

He ignored them.

It was only Kate who mattered. Her gaze slowly raised to look into his eyes. First time in a long time she'd done that, but it was Harold who spoke first.

"Is that Latin? The third letter of your arm tattoo doesn't start with a 'D' like Mac said."

"*Mortalis* means Deadly," Kate didn't look aside as she spoke. Had more spine than he'd thought. "*Celer, Silens, Mortalis* —Swift, Silent, Deadly. Marine Force Recon's motto. Put your guns away, Sam didn't kidnap me."

The man lowered his weapon slowly, then holstered it. The woman raised her weapon to a two-handed ready position pointed at the ceiling and made no move to holster her sidearm.

Sam could get to like her.

He kept his attention on Kate.

"Harold and I were taken from the studios by four men, all over six feet tall, three big, one narrow. They were dressed in black including masks and had night-vision gear. One had rolled up his sleeves. Skull logo on one arm, 'Swift, Silent, Deadly' in English on the other."

That was not the best news Sam had heard lately.

"Not much of a clue," the female agent finally holstered her weapon. "But that mistake is the first lead we have."

"Not a mistake."

Kate knew her stuff. Sam nodded for her to continue.

"Marine Force Recon don't make mistakes. It was a message; one for Sam based on his reaction."

Everyone turned to look at him.

He ignored them, moved to the still open doorway, and stepped out onto the alleyway stoop. It was dark night in a Brooklyn back alley in Carroll Gardens. A faint light spilling from one end which faced the park—filled with tired moms and over-eager kids during the day. Now quiet, but safe.

It was safe because at the other end of the alley were the Carroll Gardens preservation blocks. A couple blocks of brownstones, most of which were filled with mafia families: grandmothers, aunts, and such. The buildings were over a century old, in a neighborhood that dated back over three, and were in beautiful condition. No burglar was dumb enough to mess with anything in that protected area. Ten blocks over on Atlantic Ave., well that was a whole other world.

He clicked his thumb and index fingernails together a couple times, a sound no one would notice or pay attention to —unless they were trained to do exactly that.

He then made three distinct clicks, one long, followed by two short. He waited five seconds, then repeated the Morse Code for the letter D.

Devlin slipped out of a doorway across and thirty yards along the alley, a shadowed corner darker than the night. He came up close and eyed the door uncertainly.

"You sure, Sam?"

Sam rested a hand on his back and led him inside. The FBI agents had shifted into deeper shadows in the shop, definite hope for them. Devlin obviously read exactly who they were and scooted around to his usual stool with more speed than Sam had seen in a while. Devlin liked that spot because his back was to the wall, and the exit door toward the front of Sam's shop was close to hand in case something bad came in the back door.

Ignoring everyone for the moment, Sam pulled out a small cutting board and a clean knife. He sliced the fresh-baked Ciabatta from the Italian bakery across the alley, spread on stone-ground mustard, and dug lettuce, tomatoes, and aged cheddar out of the low-boy fridge under the counter. Reaching up to a beam, he cut down a salami that he had hanging overhead and sliced off several thick pieces.

He set the cutting board with the sandwich and a big glass of water in front of Devlin. Sam stood so that he was clearly blocking the FBI agents' way, though not the sight lines to them; blocking what Devlin would interpret as lines of their possible attack.

When he'd calmed enough to take a hurried bite of his sandwich, Sam turned to Kate and nodded for her to repeat what she'd said.

Devlin stopped in mid-chew and studied her before looking back to Sam for confirmation. At his look of agreement that Kate was a credible source of intel, Devlin twisted his neck. Sam could hear the vertebrae crackling.

"Four guys?" His voice a bare whisper.

Kate confirmed that.

"One with tats like Sam's?" Devlin looked ready to bolt for the door.

Sam shifted enough to make it clear that wasn't going to happen, but it didn't change Devlin's readiness to run. He must be spooked.

Kate spoke again, her voice the right mixture of calm and certainty. "Same tattoos, except in English. Operating in Manhattan. At least they were two days ago."

Devlin was shaking his head, like an old dog trying to rid himself of a persistent hornet.

Sam leaned in close, casually resting a hand on Devlin's shoulder, with enough weight for it to be clear that he wasn't going anywhere until he'd told Sam what he knew.

Devlin's eyes were wide, panicked wide. Marine Force Recon didn't panic; it had been trained out of them. But Devlin was panicked.

Sam felt bad for him. To have fallen so far that—

"Franco," he whispered low and fast. "Upper West Side. Word is he's got Vince Tarello, Manuel Nogalo, and the thin man must be Jason Mann because he was always Franco's right hand. Also, by the twisted way some of the shit has gone down, it's definitely Jason. That guy always had a vicious streak. I mean shit, Sam. The street is saying they're heavy; nothing they won't do for the right price and it's sky high. Top-dollar shit. Heard they did a grab on a chef and left bodies behind. They had an inside man, police found him floating in the East River the next morning. Someone said he'd squeal; not anymore. Whoever messes with them is dead, Sam. You stay away from that shit. Most on the street won't even say their names."

Sam could feel Devlin's shoulder shaking beneath his grip. Okay, those four working together were enough that he'd forgive Devlin being spooked. That *was* bad news. He patted Devlin on the shoulder twice: partly in thanks, and partly as the universal military signal that he was safe to move.

The alcoholic slipped from the room so fast and smooth that it was like old times. Good to know he still had it in him, though motivated by fear.

Kate's eyes followed him. The others had blinked at the wrong moment or were looking off to the side a bit too much and missed his departure.

Sam glanced at the cutting board.

Devlin had left his sandwich with only two bites out of it.

Shit!

Next time he'd make Kate hold her questions until after Devlin had eaten.

Of course, with Franco *Slammer* Lamar in on it, then there was no guarantee there would be a next time.

If Kate was going to live through this, it meant they were now attached at the hip.

Definitely not his idea of a good time.

He'd also bet not hers.

58

Franco's phone rang twice then stopped.

Fifteen seconds later it rang again; he picked it up to listen.

"Associate of Kate Stark. Japanese. Female. One hundred and fifty centimeters. Fifty kilos maximum. Alive. No damage. If you stumble on Stark and can grab her again, do it, but not without the Japanese. She is the target. Delivery to dock thirty-four in the Galainela shipyard, Havana, within forty-eight hours. Usual fee on deposit. Image in normal Dropbox account."

"Done."

The man on the other end hung up the phone. No need to identify himself despite using a language that was native to neither of them, with a voice masker over that. After all, they'd done business on Kate Stark two days ago, neatly boxed and delivered.

The idiots hadn't been able to hold on to a pair of chefs? It didn't matter; Park's money was good. Nothing counterfeit. Although his supernotes always passed inspection, Franco Lamar insisted on electronic money for the payments.

Every now and then they sent him a bundle of a thousand

notes of the near-perfect US hundred-dollar bills as a bonus. He handed them to his crew to pass off, never messed with one himself. Why should he? They'd deposited a half mil in his Cayman account, and there'd be two more when he was done, so he wasn't hurting.

Franco Lamar immediately transferred the money to another bank so that they couldn't take it back, then logged onto the Dropbox account and downloaded the image. The resolution was crap. It was shot at night on a ship's command bridge with lousy lighting and a cheap camera.

He dumped it into a photo program and ran a contrast and brightness enhancement on it.

Four figures. Kate and Paul Stark. A tiny Japanese woman.

And...that had to be Sam Fierro.

Franco cracked his knuckles.

This job he'd do for free.

59

"Well, that was fun," Paul leaned over to whisper as they walked, taking advantage of the excuse to lean in especially close and totally invade Rikka's personal space.

She didn't hit him this time, but neither was she giving back his key to the Ferrari as they walked out the front doors of the New York Police Department's 17th Precinct building. When they were taken into custody, the key had been confiscated out of her pocket, therefore the properties officer had returned it to her. The car was parked at Rockefeller Center, so she could fetch it at her leisure. Maybe she'd take it to her bolt hole upstate. Paul would never find it there.

The sidewalk was half covered with NYPD cruisers and unmarked sedans backed up over the curb to park on the sidewalks. Whoever had designed the building, should have made the whole ground floor nose-out parking. As it was, the taxicab waiting area was a line of backed-in vehicles popped up onto the pedestrian portion of the sidewalk.

"Six hours of my life I'm never getting back," Rikka made her voice angrier than she felt to make Paul to back off a bit. If that helped Kate, great!

The arresting officers had been polite, and she'd managed to get through the whole interrogation without any lies; not a lot of truth either, but that didn't bother her. Cops were a good place to practice saying a whole lot while communicating next to nothing, a trick she'd learned while working with the street gangs who'd paid her to do their hacking work. The gangs themselves had offered her practice in the reverse skill, saying next to nothing and communicating everything they needed. A good game, until Kate Stark had caught her and thrown her in a Secret Service lockup—she hadn't enjoyed that one bit.

"It's nearly eleven," Paul looked up and down the street, well lit with blinking neon and taxicab headlights. The 17th Precinct was midtown on the East Side. "We should go out."

"We should find Kate," Rikka countered. No way was she going clubbing with Paul Stark.

"Maloney & Porcelli is only a block over. They have a Filet Oscar that's amazing."

"We should find Kate." She wondered if she spoke on an alien frequency that could only be heard by people not named Paul Stark.

"Or a nice veal saltimbocca for two."

"I'm going to find Kate!" She gritted her teeth.

"Kate already answered my text. She's at Sam's but won't be there much longer. She's already reserved a table for us at Maloney's."

In place of screaming aloud, she decided that she wasn't going to merely borrow his Ferrari.

She was keeping it.

60

IT WAS PAST MIDNIGHT WHEN THEY FINISHED THE MEAL. NOTHING remained but emptied plates of crème brûlées, apple tarts, red velvet cake, and a split of Sandeman Tawny Port.

Kate knew better than to hurry a meal at Maloney & Porcelli's. The maître d' had given them the back corner table in the Mahogany Room. The walls and ceiling were fully paneled, a floor-to-ceiling glass-fronted wine cabinet covered one of the shorter walls and a beautiful oak bar one of the long ones. The rest of the room had long since emptied, leaving the seven of them owning the space: Kate and Rikka as the brains, Sam and a pair of FBI agents for enforcers, leaving Paul and Harold as what, her molls? It made Kate feel like a mafia mob boss and that was kind of fun.

It was the only part of it that was fun; she itched to get to work.

"Shouldn't we be safe?" Harold sat close beside her, too close.

Kate enjoyed him as a lover, wanted to try on more of that for size, but there was a close-and-clingy thing that Harold seemed to think was endearing but just served to mess up her concentration. She knew she wasn't the easiest lover to have, but Harold needed to turn it down a couple notches.

Paul was being more than usually obnoxious to Rikka—who looked ready to pith him with a dessert fork. What Kate found interesting was that Sam was slowly rising to a boil in his own quiet way. If Paul wasn't careful, he was going to have far more attention than he bargained for.

The FBI agents were uncomfortable with Kate picking up the check, but the restaurant had been her choice, and the meal was probably five times their entire per diem allowance.

"They tried for us once and failed, right?" Harold swirled his cognac. "Are they stupid enough to try twice?"

"These are the people who killed Zania and Marianne," and Kate was damned if anyone was getting away with that on her watch. "Someone must have paid them a couple million dollars to grab me; that kind of work doesn't come cheap. They also caught, boxed, and shipped you; whether they planned that part or grabbing you counted as a bonus, we don't know. Are you willing to bet that whoever is behind this isn't going to pay the same again?" She sure wasn't.

Harold's hand jerked badly enough to slop a bit of the cognac out of his glass and over the back of his hand. She'd take that as an answer.

"What can we do now?" Kate asked the table.

"Sleep?" Harold suggested.

When everyone turned to glare at him, he winced. "Well, you've all been up for thirty-six to forty-eight hours. I would have been too except for someone drugging me out for four hours."

"If," Rikka pulled over the last of the crème brûlée that Kate had been unable to finish and began eating it, "I could get access to a system, I might be able to track these guys. Though if they're being smart, their data footprint is going to be pretty small."

"Where do you think they are now?"

Kate looked over at Paul; she couldn't begin to guess.

61

Franco Lamar sat two blocks from Fierro's Meats in a midnight-blue BMW 760Li sedan and watched the live feeds from his team's shoulder cameras on his tablet. Jason Mann sat at the wheel. Vince and the new guy, Nicky Basco, were working their way forward along the alley in back of Sam's place.

The front of the target site was not of interest. The storefront opened onto a busy street that had traffic even at midnight in Brooklyn. Up the back alley was the way of it. They'd bypassed two trip alarms that were so amateur it was ridiculous.

Old Sam was losing his touch.

They now had cameras mounted at either end of the alley, painted to blend in with the rusted fire escapes. Equally small motion detectors were mounted by each one to conserve time and battery power. Now they were working on a trio of cameras giving him a reliable view of the shop's back door and windows.

Manuel's task lay a block away, mounting a booster transmitter. He mounted it where no one would look, on top of the bathroom building in the kiddie park. It would pump the signal into a burner cell number and squirt any new data to them every five minutes.

"Camera One set," Nicky announced. A minute later he reported Camera Two in place directly opposite Sam's alley-side door. Another two minutes and Camera Three was in place, the same distance again past the door.

Nicky had been an S-6 comm specialist before being mustered out after only two tours. He told a sob story of an idiot commander who'd never liked him.

Franco had checked. Nicky had been caught selling provisions to a bunch of ragheads. That would have been bad enough in command's view, if he hadn't also been lacing them with strychnine, killing their families as well. That part was hushed up and he was booted.

Nicky had been tight with Vince, so Franco was working them as a team for a trial period. Which meant telling them squat except what to do, which was what he ever told him anyway.

Franco knew that staking out Sam's place was a long shot, but it was somewhere to begin. Next he'd wire up the Chrysler Building, but that would be trickier. To do that, they'd have to pose as a real security crew with fake IDs and work orders.

Getting back inside Rockefeller Center was gonna be the real bitch. For the hundredth time, he wished Jason had paid the Cooks Network programmer the extra twenty grand to keep his mouth shut. It wasn't like they were using real money. The North Korean's counterfeit crap was plenty good for payoffs.

But Jason had already fed the man his own balls while he bled out then dumped him in the East River. No time to get someone new inside the television station at this point.

"Door cam set," Vince reported from the other side of the alley.

Franco tapped his screen to bring up the feeds. The day/night cams showed both long and short views of the alley.

He thought he caught a glimpse of Nicky moving further along the alley, but only because he was looking for him. Kid was doing well.

Vince was in the doorway to Sam's shop. "No triggers. No sensors. No motion detectors or lasers. There is nothing on this door."

Franco waited for Vince to place the fourth and last camera up in a pinhole placement inside the small overhang that jutted out into the alley. That too came online.

"Going in."

Franco could see by the newest camera as Vince reached for the door handle.

"Shit," Vince sounded derisive. "Dude doesn't lock the place."

"No!" Franco shouted, knowing he was too late. "Don't! Blue One, abort op!"

62

———

Sam's phone buzzed.

Kate looked up from her cup of decaf and watched him pull it out and glance at the screen.

He swiped at the screen and looked at the message. He tapped it once and Kate could see that an image filled the small screen. One corner of Sam's mouth tilted up in a half smile, perhaps the first time she'd ever seen such an expression on his face.

Noticing her attention, he slid the phone across the white tablecloth of Maloney & Porcelli from where he sat to Rikka's other side. Kate blinked. Hadn't Paul been on Rikka's other side? She'd missed something. Maybe Harold was right, and sleep was in order.

Kate left the phone lying on the table in front of Rikka so that she and Sam could lean in from either side to look at it.

A video feed.

Paul continued regaling Harold and the FBI agents with stories of his prowess during a trip to Argentina. He'd divested an ex-Nazi's son—who kept the faith—of his trophy wife, her jewels, and his art collection. The wife—after a brief sojourn with Paul on a yacht in the Caribbean—along with her copious bank accounts had gone on to marry a Wall Street broker. The art collection had anonymously arrived at the *Staatliche Museum zu Berlin Gemäldegalerie* for return to any original owners they could find, and the jewels had been remounted and bestowed on various willing young women as trinkets; Ms. ex-Trophy Wife wanting nothing to do with them. The son apparently ran afoul of an Argentine street gang shortly after that, though Paul insisted he had no idea how that could have happened.

On the small screen of Sam's phone, a face peered around a doorframe. A set of night-vision gear with a single long lens that sprouted from the bridge of his nose led the way.

A blinding light flashed. It was clear that the man screamed in pain though there was no sound. He tore off the night-vision gear which would have turned the sudden light into a sun-bright blast.

Sam's software immediately snapped a photo and began running facial recognition. It flashed up a match incredibly quickly. Sam must have given it a small database.

Vince Tarello. Master Sergeant (ret.). Marine Force Recon.

The screen went white then black.

Kate looked up at Sam in question.

He reached across in front of Rikka and tapped the screen again.

A long view of the back alley behind Sam's butchery.

63

———

It happened so fast that Franco couldn't keep track of what happened.

Vince's feed—gone.

The three camera feeds across the alley from Sam's butcher shop's back door—gone.

The cameras they'd placed as backups at either end of the alley showed a tongue of flame reaching out of the shop door like a giant blowtorch, slashing against a massive steel dumpster that was well on its way to melting.

No wonder Vince's feed had cut off.

Nicky's shoulder-cam feed was hard to interpret at first. He appeared to be lying in the alley. There was an odd movement, as if he was flailing about. One of the long-shot cameras showed that he'd been blown fifty feet along the alley and landed close to the street. He lay mostly in deep shadow, making him hard to see.

"Let's go fetch him and then get out of here."

64

KATE SAW THAT PAUL HAD THE OTHERS LAUGHING AT THE END OF his story.

Rikka's attention was riveted on the screen with a ghoulish fascination.

Sam tapped the phone a couple of times and redirected Kate's attention there.

She watched Sam's homeless friend slip forward from a doorway. He was in such deep shadow that if they weren't watching on a night-vision camera, there would have been nothing to see.

Instead, they saw a green shadow stoop and pick up a piece of glass with a scrap of cloth, then ram it into the prone man's throat.

He melted back into the dark.

65

AT FRANCO'S ORDER, JASON STARTED THE CAR AND ROARED UP alongside the end of the alley that had just been blown to shit.

Franco popped the door, but didn't see Nicky at first.

He lay in deep shadow. Only his foot was sticking out into a splash of light from the street. The foot was twitching in a way that Franco knew only too well. He pulled the car door shut.

"He's done. We're out of here."

"Want me to be sure?" Jason looked up at him in the rearview mirror.

"No need. He's a goner. Doesn't know anything to spill if he wasn't."

Jason hit the gas and they were outta there.

Franco's locator on Manuel showed that he had finished up in the park and he too was leaving the area. The first police siren began ramping up.

66

KATE WATCHED RIKKA TURN TO SAM. "YOUR BEAUTIFUL SHOP, ever since your grandfather. It's gone." There were actually tears running down her face.

Kate smiled to herself. So, she wasn't wrong about how much Sam and Rikka cared for each other. Kate would bet that Sam knew it...and that Rikka didn't.

Again, Sam fussed with the phone.

The flames that had shot out of the shop like an explosion disappeared as if they'd never been.

Then he tapped to a new view and turned the phone to them a second time. It showed the inside of his shop, apparently intact, only the windows and door were gone. A precisely engineered and directed explosion and gas jet.

A last tap and he held up the phone once more.

Well. Wasn't that interesting.

Kate smiled at Sam.

She knew it was a grim smile, for his was much the same.

67

It was past three a.m. by the time the cops had cleared Nicky's corpse from the alley and taken pictures of the blown door and windows and an inexplicably melted dumpster. It looked as if the explosion had been outside the shop in the alley, exactly as an intruder's explosive gone bad might have done.

Kate, Harold, and Paul had waited in the car, not wanting to be recognized. The two FBI agents took turns sitting with them and overseeing the alley cleanup. They were being extra polite...yet keeping an eye on her. This scenario had long since lost its charm.

Sam, as the owner, had stood with arms crossed, unmoving, at the head of the alley with his back to the car through the entire thing. Rikka had stood silent and immobile at his side, a whole new aspect to her personality.

The NYPD clearly wanted to do more but, unnerved by Sam's steadfast gaze, moved off fairly quickly.

It was another thirty minutes before Sam indicated that the alley was secure. He and Devlin had cleared each of Franco's cameras as well as the transmitter the old man had pointed out in the park.

Sam scrounged up the lumber to block the windows and assembled a new door out of an old table, at least enough to make the place secure.

Once the temporary door was in place and they'd turned on the lights, Kate could see it.

There was a thin seam in the concrete floor making a four-by-four-foot square one step inside the doorway. Again, she and Sam traded grim smiles.

Devlin took a fresh sandwich and disappeared into the darkness. The rest of them descended the creaking wooden stairs into the basement whose walls were so old they were made of man-sized boulders.

Kate would have preferred to lose the FBI and Harold at the very least, and preferably her brother and Rikka. None of that was going to happen, so she'd better get used to it.

Sam's basement was what Kate would have expected beneath a century-old storefront. A massive oil-fired heater that looked more like a multi-armed evil alien than an appliance. A well-stocked workbench, including a couple of wheel grinders with successively finer stones for the sharpening of butchering tools. Old chairs, tables, a piece of countertop. The lighting was good and the floor was clean, if age-cracked, concrete.

There was also a hidden door in the wall behind rusty shelves loaded with ancient tools. It would be invisible to someone who didn't know it was there.

It lined up exactly beneath the seamed section of floor upstairs—a trapdoor to a concrete cell that opened into the basement. A trapdoor that had disappeared from below Vince's feet an instant before the blast of flame. Then it had resealed so tightly that there remained no sign of anything out of place.

Sam checked a peephole, then opened the door releasing the strong smell of burned hair. He hauled out a very alive

Vince Tarello. Vince wouldn't need to update his crew cut for a while—the timing of his drop into the hole and the blast of flame above his head must have been very close indeed.

Kate stood back and waited while Sam strip-searched him, uncovering an impressive array of weaponry and miscellany. Two guns—a Sig Sauer P226 and an M1911, which was stupid because they weren't different enough to serve two purposes and they couldn't share ammunition. Three knives—pocket, switchblade, and a military K-bar. A two-handled wire garrote made of two wine corks and a guitar's E-string. Several spy cams with mounting magnets and a shoulder cam that Sam had switched off before pulling Vince from the lead-lined trap. No signals out for Franco to intercept. He also had forty thousand in hundred-dollar bills.

"Here," Kate handed them to Agent Marcus Reynolds. "I can pretty much guarantee that these are counterfeit. North Korean, therefore high quality and hard to detect, but you'll be able to hold him on that charge alone if nothing else."

"I've been reluctant to ask, but you aren't going to be doing any torture here, are you? I can't allow that."

"Well," Kate looked him right in the eye. "I won't be reading him his rights, if that's what you're wondering. You can have that honor when I'm done. Are we going to have a problem here?"

The agents barely glanced at each other before the woman replied. "How about we decide that as we go?"

She nodded. She could work with that.

After an especially careful inspection of Vince's underwear, Sam had returned the garment before tying him to a stout chair.

Then he stepped back out of the way.

Kate began to step forward, when a hand rested on her arm. Harold.

She'd forgotten about him.

He was sheet white.

Kate led him aside.

"Can I go?"

"The police are still looking for us."

"But you're going to—" he blanched even whiter. She wondered if he really would be sick this time.

"No," she whispered, "I'm not. None of us are. But he doesn't know that."

Harold blew out a breath and a few shades of color returned. "You're the damnedest—and one of the scariest— women I've ever met, Kate Stark."

That wasn't quite the compliment she'd be hoping for from a lover. He must have sensed that as well for he blushed slightly and brushed a hand along her arm.

"You're also the strongest and sexiest woman I've ever been with."

And that easily, he made her feel wonderful. Well, wonderful considering the circumstances. "Please," she squeezed his hand, "try to remember that. For later. Right now, I need to—"

He nodded. Swallowed hard...but nodded again.

68

———————

Sam had never seen this side of Kate Stark in action before. They'd overlapped on a couple of planning assignments when she'd been in the Secret Service and one security-escort op in Iraq. After that he'd only ever seen her be the bright, charming, and beautiful television personality. Off screen she was charming, if more thoughtful. He'd come to doubt his memories of the quiet and efficient agent.

Now, as she moseyed across the basement ever so casually, a whole different level of her came to light. Harold trailed behind her, then peeled off and found a stool to sit on next to the FBI agents. A good place for him at the moment.

Kate didn't move to the narrow-eyed Vince who was busy doing that tough, evil, you-can't-get-to-me-bitch glare that made him look like a dangerous weasel, not the rabid dog he thought it did. Instead, Kate moved up to the workbench and began sorting through Vince's weapons as if she had not a worry in the world.

When she reached the shoulder cam, she picked it up, inspected it for a moment, then tossed it to Rikka.

Sam picked up the laptop he kept on the bench and passed it to Rikka which she accepted with a distracted nod—all she ever seemed to manage when she was in the gravitational pull of a computer. She would extract the data and, once she'd forced Rikka to let go of it, Kate would hand the camera off to the FBI agents.

In moments she sat cross-legged on the floor, the laptop across her jean-clad legs. Her long dark hair slid forward completely hiding her face and figure as she bent to her task. How could the woman be so damn intriguing and so damn beautiful at the same time? Like the purest blade. She had stood unmoving beside him while the police cleared the alley. Nicky's body hadn't made her flinch. She—

He forced his attention back to Kate and Vince.

Kate toyed with the big K-bar knife. Admiring the edge. Tapping the blade against the table and letting the steel ring a moment, high and true. Teasing Vince.

She set it aside.

Then she picked up the wire garrote.

It was an elegant choice and exactly what he'd expected. Kate Stark was an elegant woman.

Pulled slowly, it strangled.

Pulled sharply? It could slice right through a man's trachea before he could gurgle a warning.

Yanked hard, it would take out both jugular veins at the same time as the windpipe, though a full decapitation was difficult unless the wire happened to line up exactly between two vertebrae. There were tricks to making that happen, but Sam hoped, for her sake, that Kate didn't know those.

Kate wandered around behind Vince, stopping in his blind spot.

Vince tried to simultaneously tuck in his chin to block the wire from wrapping around his neck and twist to see behind him, but he was too nervous to do the former well and too well-tied to do the latter at all.

"Agent Edwards," Kate spoke in an absolutely casual tone, "you told me that a Cooks Network programmer was killed?"

Leona made a show of referring to her notepad. "Yes, Ephraim Yudin." She played her role perfectly without being told. No wonder Agent Marcus Reynolds was so nuts about her.

"And you say they found his chewed testes in his stomach?"

"That's correct. As well as most of his penis."

"How interesting."

She winked at the agent from behind Vince, who had given up on trying to protect his throat and was once again trying to twist around to see Kate.

"Sam," she could have been discussing one of her recipes. "I'm thinking this wire would have been ideal for such an operation. What do you think? One-inch sections should be the proper size to chew and swallow."

He gave a considered nod and Vince turned whiter than Harold Merritt after he'd seen his first-ever corpse in the back alley. Now he focused on keeping his knees together.

"Sam, would you mind removing Mr. Tarello's underwear?"

Sam picked up the K-bar field knife and began to move forward when Vince shouted at him.

"Wasn't me! Jason Mann did it! He wasn't even s'pposed to. Franco was so fuckin' pissed I thought he was going to tell me to do in Jason. No way. That fucker's way too dangerous. He's a cold-blooded psycho who's never more than inches from Franco. I'd be fuckin' dog meat if I tried to take on that bastard."

Sam looked up at Kate. She'd been such an amazing field agent. It wasn't her fault a shafted-over mistress got through the lines to kill the VP.

The bastard had deserved it anyway.

As a senator, the man had spent most of his tour in Iraq trying to bed female warriors; finally settled for a couple of local whores that Sam had paid to keep that slime off the military women who chose to fight for their country. He'd considered inviting the newsies in on it; now he wished he had.

To this day, he couldn't forgive Kate Stark for quitting the Service over that useless piece of trash's death.

69

KATE SAW SAM'S GLARE, KNEW HOW MUCH HE HATED HER FOR letting the VP die, but there wasn't a thing she could do about it right now. They needed information. A lousy confession wasn't going to help her, no matter how pleased the FBI were looking.

The man was squirming in his chair already.

Time to push. "I don't care about Ephraim. No idea who he was anyway." It was impossible to know all thousand employees in the Cooks corporation, but she'd find out and make sure his family was taken care of.

Vince squirmed around toward her, but she made sure to stay out of his line of vision. Made the wire that much scarier if you couldn't see it coming.

"I thought it was an interesting way to get rid of you. You are a problem, Vince Tarello. You already kidnapped me once. Did you poison the chocolate dish too?"

"No. No. Manuel did that one. Ducked in with the show's catering crew. Latino bastard fit right in. His mum's a cook. He doctored the bottle of liquor she was usin'. No one asked a thing. I was the one with the dart gun and the antidote. I gave you an' him," he nodded toward Harold, "the antidote before we stuffed you in that crate." He was so panicked that he didn't understand that bit hadn't earned him any good will.

He was starting to talk faster and faster. Sweating, he couldn't sit still as he spoke. She tapped a loop of the wire on the back of the chair—and he tried to leap out of it only to be slammed back by his restraints.

"Why save Harold and me, but not the other two?"

"Client was angry as hell. We were supposed to grab the four of you. But the overdose cut 'em down too far too fast. I didn't have that much antidote. No help for either of the bitches. We only had a few seconds to get away clean."

"Why did they want us?"

"You think they tell me shit? Swear to God, lady. I don't know. I don't know why they were after you before, or this time. Don't cut me. Oh please God don't cut me." Sweat was streaming down his face.

"Okay. One last question. Where do I find the others?"

He told her, practically shuddering in terror.

She believed him.

She nodded to Reynolds who nodded back, then stood and pulled a card from his pocket and began to read Vince his Miranda rights.

Kate returned to the workbench to drop off the garrote.

Sam moved up beside her and tapped the top of a small glass bottle that sat beside Vince's clothes. It was filled with a reddish powder and labeled with Sam's neat printing.

Kate didn't need to read the label to know what it was.

Sam was grinning at her. He was the most inscrutable man she'd ever met, and she'd met some strange ones.

Marcus and Leona had Vince untied, handcuffed, and were escorting him out.

She stopped Marcus.

"We're good," he assured her. "Got that on tape. We're going to raid that address."

"No, Agent Reynolds. Not unless you want a lot of dead people. They're going to have traps that make Sam's little firestorm look tame."

"Let's ask—" he started to haul Vince around.

"He won't know. This is Franco and Jason's show. Everyone else is merely hired muscle." Vince's expression said she'd nailed it.

"Well, at least we can pull the warrants—"

"No," she cut him off. "That will tip our hand. We're wanted. As a matter of fact, I need to ask you and Agent Edwards to continue to escort us as if we were criminals. Call in another team to pick up Vince."

"I did. They're already en route."

"Good." Kate glanced at Sam who was smiling at her. "They must not admit to Vince's arrest for at least forty-eight hours. Also tell them to get him a shower and fresh underwear as soon as they can."

She held out the bottle so that the two agents could read the label, but Vince couldn't.

Powdered Cayenne Pepper.

Marcus winced with sympathetic pain, but Leona Edwards' smile was vicious.

The more Vince had sweat, the more painful the burning in his crotch became, making it too easy to imagine how Kate's threats of chopping him up with the wire would feel.

70

AT KATE'S REQUEST, SAM CALLED IN A COUPLE FAVORS. SOON they were gathered in Kate's office on the floor above the Rockefeller Center studio. She thought it unlikely that the NYPD would raid her office again after their failure with Paul and Rikka.

She'd braced for the worst, but Mac must have sent someone in to clean it up. Everything was righted and put back together. They'd installed a new computer and put new glass over the photo of her with Julia, though there was now a crease across one corner. Beyond the windows it was two hours until dawn and the city slept, as much as it ever did.

They circled up couches and chairs in front of the sixty-inch screen that she used for reviewing the final edits of new shows. Rikka had disappeared into the new computer and was bound to have something for them momentarily.

In addition to what she was now thinking of as her regular crew, Devlin paced around them. He had tagged along from where he'd been lurking out in the dark alley outside the deli when they'd emerged with Vince Tarello in tow. Sam had given him a shower and fresh clothes.

Devlin was more complete than the other times Kate had seen him. As if his brain and nervous system had lacked only the adrenaline of a covert operation to return him to more than a shadow of his former self.

He accepted a shot of whiskey to keep his hands steady, but refused a second, *Two makes me sloppy.* He prowled her office as if seeking secret passages and hidden traps. She wondered how deep-seated the remaining Marine Recon identity was for him. She suspected that it was only a thin veneer that held the man together. Well, now was not the time to wonder if he'd survive when he went back out on the streets.

Sam had brought in two other Marines: Mick and Rio. Neither had offered their last names; both had balled their hands into fists at the mention of Jason Mann.

Rio explained that while Franco was merely a bucket of slime, at least he'd been a decent enough fighter. Though a piss-poor soldier—calling a Marine a soldier was a deep, deep insult. When things got hairy on a *deep run* in Russia, he'd sold out the team for his own safety. It was only Sam who had saved their sorry asses. It had taken them two months and three lives to hike out of central Russia. Franco had the good sense to transfer out of Recon, then resign from the Marines altogether and disappear before Sam's team had made it to the border.

Jason, on the other hand, had always been a vicious bastard who should have been aborted at birth. The fact that he'd been allowed into Recon, however briefly, they considered as a disgrace to the Corps. Kate gathered that there was no worse insult on the planet.

Her attempt to offer them payment had deeply pissed them off.

"It's not a goddamn insult," she knew that facing up to them was the only way to get their respect. "It's a thank you for helping out."

"We'd pay *you* for a shot at Jason."

"Then choose a goddamn charity."

"Wounded Warriors."

"Twenty grand apiece. Done."

The two guys had nodded at her to indicate that made everything good between them. Any insult—wiped away that easily. Thank God she'd learned guy-speak in the Secret Service.

Not trusting Vince Tarello's information, Rikka had remotely hacked Franco's Upper West Side condo's security cams and proved that he and his crew were indeed *at home*. She also grabbed the building's layout and scrounged up an ownership roster from the city. Unit number 1012 was owned by Lamar Holdings, Inc.

"Never was the most imaginative sack of shit," Mick observed, then blushed. "Apologies for the language, ma'am."

Kate left the comment be, to not embarrass him further.

"They're on the tenth floor, corner unit with a nice view of Central Park down the street. Or they were a few hours ago anyway."

Rikka had morphed the building plans filed with the city into a 3D wireframe of the building on the large screen. The glowing blue lines clearly delineating the wall structures.

Kate had forgotten quite how scary good Rikka was.

"Franco's systems aren't tied into the building's security. Or, if they are, it's a hundred percent passive, so that I can't see it. The building security itself? Lame."

Kate studied the place. Doorman in front, camera in back with a screen at the front desk. That counted as a secure building in a good neighborhood.

"Their system is too primitive; there's nothing to hack. It's like they bought it at Costco and installed it themselves, the cheapskates." Rikka sounded seriously put out at being defeated because something was too simple.

Entry looked like a straightforward enough problem.

Flower delivery in the front. Sleepy gas on the doorman. Teams in separate elevators to the ninth and eleventh floors then meeting on ten using the main stairs—that would avoid any elevator bells on ten and block either avenue of escape. One team up the internal service stairs, one up the outside fire escape would seal the trap.

"Rikka, Paul, Harold, you're staying here."

Only her brother protested.

"Not your kind of dance, brother. It's either going to be fast and ugly or fast and a dry hole. Either way, it's not what you do. This time I need you to just wait. One hour from now it will be over—one way or the other."

He didn't look happy. But when she opened the gun safe in her executive bathroom, the one the NYPD hadn't found, and began arming herself, he subsided.

She turned to the FBI agents. "This isn't exactly above board, are you sure you want in?"

"Cleared it with the boss," Marcus tapped the pocket that held his phone. "We're in."

"Let's do this."

Kate felt as if she was playing a deadly game of Follow the Leader. Sam, three retired Marines including Devlin, and a pair of FBI agents trooped along behind her. Kate grabbed a large vase of flowers from the display table outside the Cooks Network upper lobby elevator. They trooped into the elevator, dropped to the underground level amidst the perfume of exotic blooms, and split up in four separate directions. They'd meet again on the tenth floor of the condo on West Eighty-second Street in thirty minutes. She'd told Paul an hour to keep him safe.

Kate checked her watch. Four-thirty now.

One hour to sunrise.

Five a.m. strike.

Perfect.

71

Kate distracted the door guard acting as the delivery girl for a massive vase of flowers, wearing her best smile. She kept the blooms between herself and the security camera positions that Rikka had identified.

He buzzed her into the lobby. Old World: cherrywood front desk, dark marble floors, oak-covered walls, a small, alabaster-white fountain that trickled merrily in the center of the lobby. Tucked among potted plants were plush but tasteful benches for the residents to wait on while the doorman called a cab.

Sam, his face hidden by a black ski mask, slipped in behind her and clipped the guard on the jaw so fast the doorman never had a chance to cry out. He dropped like a bag of potatoes.

"Out of knock-out gas?" She pulled on her own mask to avoid the cameras and turned back to the door to let in the others.

Devlin had already gone up the outdoor fire escape. He'd been out of shape enough to need a boost past the locked gate, but then he'd moved upward so stealthily that Kate lost track of him by the third floor.

Sam tied up the guard with his own belt. Right, the punch

and belt instead of knock-out gas and zip ties would mark it as an amateur job.

She and Sam took the inside stairs. The FBI agents took one elevator to the ninth floor and the two Marines took the other to the eleventh. They'd pilfered the guard's shoes, each team taking one. They'd use them to block the elevators open so they wouldn't be moving unexpectedly.

Three minutes until *Go*.

72

"I can't stand this. I'm going out to get breakfast." Rikka headed for the elevator at her normal terrifying speed.

Paul was slouched low on Kate's office couch, watching a late-late night rerun of a stupid-ass cooking show that didn't have Kate in it. What was the point of a television that only showed the network's own programming? He needed a Bruce Willis thriller to keep him awake, not some lame candy-sculpture cook-off.

"Wait. What?"

"Breakfast," Rikka called back over her shoulder. "Don't worry, I'll be back before they go in. We've got thirty-two minutes."

"What are you getting?" Paul forced himself upright to follow after her. He was blurry with lack of sleep, but there was no way he'd be asleep while Kate was raiding enemy territory, not even if she was doing it without him. He was cursing himself for not insisting on going along, but he'd never used or ever faced a gun. Then Kate had been so daunting with how casually she pulled on a dual shoulder harness preloaded with nasty looking hardware.

Harold had given in to exhaustion and was tipped back in Kate's office chair and snoring quietly.

"Ratner's," the elevator in front of Rikka dinged. "A couple of pastrami sandwiches."

"But that's thirty blocks downtown, that'll take—"

She stepped into the elevator, then, as the door was sliding shut, she pulled the Ferrari's key out of her pocket and jangled it at him. The door closed on her bright grin.

He slammed the down button and cursed.

It took thirty seconds for another elevator to show up and let him follow her to the garage. And thirty more for the descent.

73

"One minute," Kate whispered, keeping her eye on her watch.

It had been a real workout running up ten stories of the interior stairwell. The masks were hot and there was no internal surveillance past the first floor, so she'd rolled it up onto her forehead.

Sam had done the same and crouched close beside her outside the tenth-floor apartment's rear door which opened onto these stairs.

The other two teams would be sweeping toward the apartment's front door from opposite ends of the lush-carpeted hallway.

Through a small window in the stairwell wall, she could see a shadow on the fire escape twenty feet farther along the side of the building. That must be Devlin. The streetlights didn't reach this high, and the pre-dawn glow was too soft to reveal more than his vaguest outline.

She turned on the radio and fitted the headset. Sam had produced them from a case in his car's trunk. Silence, no clicks from the rest of the team; exactly as planned.

74

———————

PAUL ARRIVED IN THE ROCKEFELLER CENTER GARAGE AS OUT OF breath as if he'd been sprinting, not riding in an elevator.

At least at five in the morning there hadn't been anyone to stop him on any of the passing floors.

Except himself. He'd hit the damn first floor button out of habit before punching for the garage and had to wait for the doors to cycle despite his frantic pounding of the Door Close button.

He shoved himself out the elevator door and turned the corner.

The Ferrari sat there, unmoved and empty.

"What kind of game are you playing at, Rikka?" he asked the silent garage.

Not silent.

He heard the squeal of car tires on the ramp a level above then the hard rev of a large, highly tuned engine exiting the garage.

That's when he saw his Ferrari's key.

It dangled from the driver's door lock.

75

AT FIFTEEN SECONDS TO *GO*, SEVERAL THINGS HAPPENED simultaneously.

Sam shifted into position to kick in the back door of Franco's tenth floor apartment.

Kate could see Devlin out on the fire escape flick loose Vince Tarello's switchblade, the only weapon he'd accept, and her cell phone rang causing Sam to flinch in surprise.

She grabbed her phone.

Paul.

The moment she accepted the call he was screaming at her.

"—a trap! It's a trap! They just took Rikka!"

Kate didn't bother to answer, instead, breaking radio silence, she roared out:

"Abort! Abort! Abort!"

From the fire escape, Devlin turned to look at her through the stairwell window. His switchblade was slid up into the crack between the upper and lower casement window. As he turned to her, the tip of his blade flicked open the inside lock.

Sam tackled her, shoving her aside and up against the hard

stairwell wall. Over his shoulder she could see an explosion as it ripped out the window in front of Devlin.

A rolling blast of flame didn't give Devlin time to scream. It simply blew his glass-riddled, burning body off the fire escape and sent him plummeting to the street ten stories below.

Sam's powerful arms wrapped around her, crushing out any air that had been left after her back had been driven against the concrete wall.

A second later the steel rear door of the apartment exploded into the stairwell.

The blast ripped across where they'd both been standing moments before.

Heat!

Immense heat!

Her cry against the shock was muffled in Sam's shoulder.

The next impact was sound.

The force of the explosion slapped the scalding air at them hard enough for her to cry out again at the pain. But this time she couldn't hear herself.

The door, blown off its hinges, slammed into the far stairwell wall, then tumbled and bounced down the concrete risers—in absolute silence.

Forever passed slowly by, though it couldn't have been more than a few seconds. Then the shock passed and the roar of the flames once again battered at her eardrums.

Sam dragged her to her feet. A glance into the apartment told her all she needed to know, and they staggered down the stairs together. By the time they clambered over the apartment door lying across the steps two stories below, they were at a dead run.

The explosion hadn't been a fake like the one Sam had rigged at his shop.

The apartment was a burnout. Maybe a fuel-air device. Nothing remained unburned inside. It was entirely black char.

Automatic sprinklers were washing away the devastation.

76

RIKKA FELT SO STUPID. IF SHE HAD A BRAIN IN HER HEAD, SHE'D never have done something so damn dumb.

She'd stepped into the garage of the Rockefeller Center studio, walked up to the Ferrari, and spotted someone up on a ladder rigging a camera not twenty feet away. Five a.m. didn't find service crews installing security systems, not even in New York.

But had she run? Cried for help? Been carrying an Uzi in her purse? Been carrying a purse to have the Uzi in instead of a wallet shoved into her jeans pocket?

Stoopid!

By the time the thought to run registered, hands had grabbed her from behind. Her shout of surprise was muffled by a large hand, which she bit. Didn't do her any good, her captor was wearing heavy work gloves. Dirty ones that tasted of concrete dust.

They'd bundled her into the back seat of a midnight-blue sedan and were now racing along the city streets headed uptown.

She could only blame her slowness on the fact that she'd

spent the last thirty-six hours with Paul Stark. She'd long since used up her daily dose of survival instincts.

Either that or she was irredeemably naïve.

She elected for the former but suspected the latter. When she'd been laundering accounts for the Tongs, they'd always treated her as if she was stupid. Now she suspected that it was her naiveté that stood out and made them so protective of her.

It might also explain why they had chased her so tenaciously after Kate had turned her State's evidence. The gangs weren't merely ticked about her betrayal; they'd been personally offended that after all their extra protection and caring for her, she'd turned evidence against them.

Offended?

They'd thrown a major shit storm, that somehow Kate had turned aside.

Well, if this was the new level of storm, she'd pony up for it.

Of course, she didn't have a lot of options at the moment. If she had been one inch bigger or the car one inch smaller, she'd never have fit between the two massive bruisers who sat to either side of her.

Franco Lamar on her right and Manuel Nagalo on her left. That meant the back of the driver's head belonged to Jason Mann. There was going to be no punching one man and diving out the door. Or grabbing the other's gun and forcing them to let her go.

Rikka knew that she was in further over her head than the day that Secret Service agent Kate Stark had knocked on her dorm room in MIT's Random Hall, innocently asking a question about an Ancient Greek History class.

Yeah right.

Kate had looked like any another college student; the kind Rikka had seen every day in the back of a class or on the quad. And Rikka had totally fallen for that too.

Well, at least she'd gotten the latter part right, Kate had indeed been shadowing her, apparently for months.

She just hadn't been a student.

They rocketed over the Queensboro Bridge, thereby avoiding the toll stop at the midtown tunnel where she might have screamed. Screaming would do her no more good now than it would have five years ago.

77

Kate had been friendly, likeable even. Something Rikka missed at MIT. Maybe if she hadn't been carrying a four-point-oh across so many credits, she'd have had the downtime to make friends. Or maybe there was something wrong with her. She always knew she was different though she couldn't quite see how.

After she and Kate had talked through a tricky point in *The Iliad*—Rikka wasn't sure why she'd decided to take a course in ancient Greek culture—Kate had suggested getting pizza at the place down the street. It had sounded great.

Naively—there was that word again—she'd gone along with no clue of what was happening.

She remembered the experience of that meal with Kate Stark in minute detail. They'd been sitting across from each other in the far back of the restaurant, elbow deep in a large Chicago-style Meat Lovers plus mushrooms and extra cheese.

She'd been using the name Shirō Usagi at the time. If *White Rabbit* was good enough for Neo to follow into *The Matrix*, that was a good enough working name for her:

"I've got a job you might be interested in," Kate made it sound as natural as could be.

As her mouth was full, Shirō shrugged her bare interest. She liked Kate, but the Tongs were giving her plenty of ready cash as a freelancer. With no rent and no tuition, life was sweet and easy.

Kate took a companionable bite before continuing, "A Secret Service counterfeiting team is currently tearing apart your apartment."

She'd said it so casually that Shirō had finished chewing and taken a sip of beer before answering.

"Not funny, Kate."

Kate responded with a shrug that mirrored Shirō's own of a moment before, but didn't look away.

"Really not funny, Kate."

"Wasn't meant to be."

Shirō considered what little she knew of the Secret Service and what they'd find in her apartment and decided she wasn't worried.

"We can put you away for a decade, maybe two." Kate could have been chatting about Hector's motivation for facing Achilles without a second warrior of Troy to assist him. "And that's just with what we already have, even without cracking your hard drive or the USB jump drive in your front left pocket. But I'd rather not do that."

"You wouldn't?" had been all she'd managed past a throat gone suddenly dry.

Kate took another bite of the pizza and indicated for her to do the same. She managed it, but didn't taste anything.

"Nope. We don't want the Tong particularly," and Kate had proceeded to name each of her contacts, several of which she had thought safe behind her double-blind data wall. But Kate had them.

That was the moment Shirō realized how out of her depth she was. She'd always prided herself on being a **Smooth Criminal** *like Michael Jackson said.*

Not so much.

"*It's the North Koreans who are running the Tong that we want.*"
"*North Koreans?*"
Shirō had had no idea what Kate was talking about.

78

———————

Now, five years later—as Rikka figured out that they were roaring toward La Guardia airport—she understood that Kate Stark *always* knew what she was talking about, because she only ever spoke *after* she was sure.

The North Koreans had torn apart the Tongs in the following weeks and would have gotten to her if Kate hadn't protected her. In the process Kate had seriously damaged the North Korean counterfeiting distribution system.

And now?

Here Rikka sat, once again in over her head and about to be handed off to the North Koreans. This time there was no Kate and no Witness Protection Program between them. Instead, there were three bad guys roaring through Manhattan in a luxury sedan and one small, very scared Asian American woman.

Fear is the path to the Dark Side.

Thanks a buttload, Yoda.

Okay. She might be helpless now, but she'd keep an eye out for the first opportunity.

Kate would be coming.

These guys had no idea the world of Class A hurt they'd signed up for, but they were going to find out.

And when Kate arrived, Rikka would be ready to help.

She hoped.

79

———————

P ER PLAN , THEY MET IN A PARKING GARAGE TWO BLOCKS FROM Franco's apartment.

Sam saw that it was a good thing that the people on the streets were few and far between at five a.m.; Kate's team was a sorry looking lot.

Everyone accounted for, other than Devlin.

He had led Kate through the alley-side exit rather than the front doors. There was hardly enough left of Devlin to bother declaring him dead. There would be time later to claim the body, he hoped.

Kate had muttered a foul curse, turned, and shifted from a full run to a fast walk, shedding her mask as they exited the alley.

Sam had never so respected the woman as he had in that moment. She had learned that so-hard lesson of shoving the mourning and grief aside until the mission was done. He'd seen whole teams of Marines immobilized when their first member took a hit, often leading to more losses that could have been avoided if they'd only kept moving. Yet another reason so few made it into Recon. When you could watch your best friend die and could recover his radio to call in the next air strike coordinates, you had the necessary mindset.

Once in the garage, no one spoke. He and Kate had taken the worst of it, their jackets were badly singed. The ends of Kate's hair were light with ash.

Blood trickled from one of her ears. He snapped his fingers close beside the ear and she turned to look at him strangely. At least her hearing worked. He turned her head back sideways and saw that the blood originated from a scalp cut up in her hair. Not a bad one. Her hiss when he probed it was more of annoyance than pain.

His Marine Recon buddies had slight scorching on their backs and both FBI agents had singed eyebrows, though the rest of their clothing was fine. That told him that the Marines had tackled the FBI out of harm's way at the *Abort!* signal. FBI trained as partners; Marines trained as teams. The difference showed and had saved the agents' lives.

Kate pulled out her phone and glanced at the screen, which Sam could see over her shoulder was still connected.

She pressed the button for speaker phone.

"Hey, Paul."

Her voice sounded strange in Sam's own ears. He snapped his fingers beside each of his own ears in turn and heard only a muted sound. A quick touch revealed no blood. Shock. The hearing loss shouldn't last more than a few minutes longer. Hopefully.

"Kate, thank God. Are you okay?"

She scanned the group before answering.

"We're fine." Her face was grim enough that Sam knew she wasn't forgetting Devlin but forcing herself to ignore his loss for the moment.

"I screwed up," Paul's voice sounded fast and desperate—nothing like Paul Stark.

There was a roaring in the background that Sam at first

thought was in his ears. But it was coming through the phone: the fast shifting of a highly powerful engine. Paul was in his sports car.

"I let Rikka head down to the garage without me," Paul continued breathlessly. The engine climbing from first to fourth or fifth, then back to second as if he was street-racing a block at a time. "She said she was going to get breakfast. I wasn't more than thirty seconds behind her, I swear I wasn't, but they grabbed her. She's gone."

Sam didn't hear a word after that, Paul's voice now merely an annoying buzz in the background.

Franco, Jason, and Manuel had kidnapped Erika Albert. It wasn't possible. That sweet girl caught up by...

He couldn't risk the thought or his head might explode.

They'd just signed their own death warrants.

80

"I HAVE NEWS," CAPTAIN RANG JIN-HO HAD WAITED UNTIL PARK had paid off the Panamanian whore and shuffled her off the boat. She'd be bound to make more money en route from the two crewmen manning the skiff.

He and Park had decided not to wait at the dock in Cuba for the kidnapping and delivery of the Japanese translator. They should continue their homeward trek. The more that their movements seemed normal, the better.

They were now anchored in Bahia Limón, the bay at the north, Atlantic-side entrance to the Panama Canal. Not that Rang would be stupid enough to transit the Canal with the weaponry and UN-sanctioned luxury goods stored in the special containers; diplomatic seal or not, they would be opened.

Rang had also suggested the move because of American-Cuban relations. Collecting their hostage would be far easier here in Panama and then they could take the Cape Horn route home around the southern tip of South America. The longer route was dangerous and had upset Park with the several weeks' delay. But in the Straits of Magellan there would be no one to investigate their cargo or discover their prisoners.

Rang shivered at the thought of the last time his ship had tried to pass through the Canal. His leg had been crushed in a hurricane, and he'd been flown home to recover. The substitute captain, flown out from the DPRK, had ignored P'yo's advice and Rang's own strict secret orders not to transit the Canal but rather go around the Horn. The substitute captain was of a lower rank than Rang. He hadn't been told about the missiles and jet that had been purchased in Cuba because those were behind official seals.

The Canal's Customs inspectors, knowing the *Chong Chon Gang* belonged to Office 39, had searched the vessel. Of course they had uncovered the illegal weapons being transported from Cuba.

Then the fool had tried to kill himself. Pity he hadn't succeeded.

Rang spat. It had cost Office 39 seven hundred thousand dollars in fines to recover his ship and his crew. They hadn't dared use any counterfeit bills.

Panama kept the fool captain and the two officers he'd brought with him—as if Rang's men weren't to be trusted. Office 39 had disavowed them. Let them rot in the Panamanian jail. The day they returned to the DPRK would be their last on this Earth.

"What news?" Park dropped into a chair in Rang's office with a satisfied sigh implying he'd slept little last night.

Rang had discreetly questioned the whore as he'd escorted her to the skiff. Park had managed only two forays, neither lasting more than minutes, and six hours of sleep. She'd only been aboard for eight. Rang had tipped her an extra hundred dollars US for the information, which had cost him a hundred won—a bit over an American dime. He did love the DPRK supernotes.

"We were right," Rang had offered to call Park's contact with the details of the delivery of the translator when they moved from Havana to Colon, Panama. He'd taken possession of that important contact for himself. The man, Franco, had sounded like a thug—kept asking for his money *before* he had kidnapped the woman.

"The Stark woman was inaccessible," he continued. "But the Japanese one has been captured. She is now en route and will be delivered here in the next twelve hours."

"Good. And how long do you think, Rang, before the Stark woman follows? You are still sure she will?"

He was. Rang considered his memory of those blue eyes and the fierce loyalty of her followers.

He was so sure that he half wondered if the Stark woman might arrive before her interpreter.

No matter what Park thought, Rang didn't think they'd have any better luck holding onto Kate Stark this time than they had three days before. This time she was warned, and he knew that would make her more dangerous.

He had no illusions of bringing back the woman. And forcing her to create a North Korean cooking show was perhaps the dumbest idea that he'd ever heard.

Look in the shadows, Su-jin often said.

So, rather than point out the idiocy of Park's plan, he was looking. Park was not stupid. There must be another reason to hunt Kate Stark.

He must watch the shadows most carefully.

For now, knowing they would be unable to hold her when she arrived, he must plan. What would he need to do to make sure that the fault of the imminent failure landed squarely on Park and didn't touch him? He'd have to prepare a private cable to Su-jin. She knew Park better than anyone else.

She'd made sure of it.

Maybe this was the opportunity they'd spoken of for Rang

to finally have a seat among Office 39's Council of Five. Could it be?

81

———————

"I'm so sorry, Kate. I should never—"

She put a hand on Paul's arm to stop him as they rode back up to the offices. He'd been waiting for them at the garage elevator beneath Rockefeller Center. A very tight squeeze.

"If you think you can control a force of nature like Rikka Albert, you haven't a clue what she's like. The question now is where are they taking her?" She and Sam had shed their scorched jackets in a dumpster in Central Park. A quick brush of her hair had knocked off the worst of the ash.

When they reached her offices, the sun had risen to the east and washed over Harold asleep in her office chair. The man was so cute. As she watched him, he awoke. Quietly, neatly, no big ordeal; one moment asleep, the next awake and studying her through heavy-lidded eyes.

"This doesn't look good," his voice was a rough mumble.

"Thanks, Harold." Kate fluffed her hair with one hand. She had to tease someone so that she didn't scream.

He didn't try to backpedal or say that he hadn't meant her. Instead, he simply smiled at the tease with perfect understanding. Man kept looking better the more she knew of him.

"Okay," Kate turned to the group. "Any theories of why they kidnapped Rikka and not me?" She grabbed a water bottle and dropped onto a couch.

Harold sat bolt upright, now fully awake and paying close attention.

"Duh, sis!" Paul dropped to sit beside her.

"What am I missing?"

Paul rolled his eyes at her and pointed his water bottle toward the other occupants of the room. "Surrounded by a personal army. Hello! As far as we know, Franco has two guys left. You went into their apartment with six. Where's Devlin? Slippery dude disappear again?"

Kate tried to hide it to protect Harold, but her twin read her reaction as easily as always and whispered a soft, "Shit."

Harold's shock was deep and complete. Then, in a shift that surprised her, his look shifted directly to pissed; as if he'd be glad to seek revenge on them for Devlin's sake. It wasn't a typical civilian reaction, but it was one she could respect.

It was easy to recognize as it burned hot through her own bloodstream.

82

Paul had never understood Kate's past in the Secret Service back when it was happening. Sure, it was dangerous. She was always wandering in, bruised from training, sore from an overlong session on the firing range, or exhausted from a hard day that she couldn't discuss.

In the last three days she'd been drugged, kidnapped, and nearly died in an explosion. She was now surrounded by a pair of FBI agents, three of the US military's most elite warriors, and had just watched a fourth die.

Whereas he hadn't been able to keep track of one pint-sized computer geek / sushi chef. He hadn't even known that Erika Albert was a computer geek until she'd slapped open one of the cabinets in her Bronx kitchen and keyed a code into a hidden pad. In moments the room had transformed around them: six screens, three keyboards, and a server rack big enough to run a small corporation. And that was only the equipment he'd recognized.

She'd tracked Kate's cell call in seconds, as he'd—

"Idiot!" Paul's curse had everyone in the Cooks Network office spinning to stare at him. He slapped his pockets and found his cell phone. He pulled it out and shouted, "Ha!" in triumph.

"What?" Kate and Sam shifted to look over his shoulder.

"Earlier I traced Rikka using her cell phone. I had a buddy give me a GPS geographic locator using something he called *The Find* routine."

"Well, that's illegal as hell," Leona, the dark and sexy FBI agent glared at him. "And there's no way they didn't dump her phone."

"We didn't find her phone by the Ferrari," her partner put in.

"Then we'll find it on the street."

Paul ignored them and called up the locator. It popped up right away.

"She's at La Guardia."

"Or at least her phone is," Leona wouldn't let it go.

"Uh," the view shifted. "No, I was wrong she's in Brooklyn, close by Sam's place."

Sam reached over his shoulder and did the finger stroke to expand the view. As soon as he did, the screen jumped again.

"Coney Island," Paul wondered what was wrong with his phone.

"She's in an airplane headed south," Kate stated.

She was right. It was the only thing that would explain it. She always was sharper than he was regarding such things.

"Right over there," she pointed out her office window.

They raced to the glass and, with hands shielding eyes against the newly risen sun, tried to look out, though there was no possible way for them to see it. The windows offered a sweeping view of the Manhattan morning.

Paul could imagine he saw a glint of silver in the dawn sky to the south but knew he was fooling himself.

"Why wouldn't they turn off and disable her phone?" Leona sounded distinctly unhappy.

Paul didn't see why that was so odd, but clearly the others did, so he kept his mouth shut. He'd never been a professional sneak, only an amateur one. At least he was one up on Harold.

"They'd never miss that," Harold confirmed.

But...

"So, either they sent Rikka's phone on a trip to lead us astray..." Harold was figuring it out faster than he was, and Paul didn't like that one bit. That the man had obviously gotten into his sister's pants was bad enough, that he was wearing Paul's own clothes was irritating as hell, but that he was a step ahead was insufferable. Paul was always the one who—

"Or" his sister continued, "they want us to follow."

"But that would mean..." Paul finally caught up with what was going on and wished he was nearer a chair so that he could collapse into it.

"Yep," Kate looked at him with sympathy. "It's a trap."

83

One look told Kate that Sam and his Marine Recon buddies were in for the long haul. They'd watched Devlin die. It was no longer a question of a favor to Sam or a donation to the Wounded Warrior Project.

It was now a question of honor and a fallen brother.

A brief phone conference with Marcus Reynolds' FBI boss achieved several things. The warrants for Harold and her were lifted and Vince Tarello was charged in their place. Warrants were also issued for the remaining members of Franco's team. Not that it would do any good. Not a chance that they'd be landing on US soil anytime soon.

Kate stopped Marcus before he mentioned Rikka's name.

Marcus muted his phone, "Why?"

Kate scanned the room, trying to decide who could know what. Finally, she dragged Marcus off to her executive bathroom and flushed the toilet.

"You know what Erika Albert can do, and she had a past connection to your suspect, Rafe. She's in the Witness Protection Program. You are now one of only a handful, literally," she held up four fingers then added a fifth, "who know that. Her name is not in the Department of Justice files nor on the US Marshals Office roster as those were already breached once. Thankfully a marshal caught it the first time and notified me. I was able to extract her from her prior life only minutes before an international hit team landed on her doorstep—a fact she does *not* know."

Marcus didn't ask the obvious questions that there was no way in hell Kate would answer. Instead, he was back on the phone before the toilet finished flushing.

The third item to result from the phone conference was that Marcus and Leona were released from their current assignment and attached to the OIO. The FBI's Office of International Operations extended the bureau's sphere of law enforcement beyond the traditional barrier of the US border. They'd been cleared to pursue the kidnapping of a US citizen, unnamed, to the limits of their abilities.

When they reentered her office moments later, her brother was waiting for her.

"I'm in. All the way."

The gratitude that swept through her was immense. He might be a pain in the ass most of the time, but he did come through when it counted. She threw her arms around his neck and let herself be held for a few moments.

"Me, too."

Kate turned toward the new voice.

Harold had come up to stand close beside Paul. "Count me in. She seems like a great kid, and I'd like to help."

The fact the *great kid* was only three years younger than him was beside the point.

"You're cleared now, Harold. No warrants for your arrest. You can go home to your Chicago restaurant."

He simply shook his head.

She gave him a hug, too.

Kate turned to the room and barely resisted the urge to

gush at them, which would only embarrass the Marines and the FBI. And herself.

"Okay," she swallowed again to make sure her voice was steady. "I'll call our pilots and we'll be aloft inside the hour."

"Where are we going?"

She opened her mouth to answer Paul's question but didn't have one ready.

"How about," Harold looked ill but forged on. "How about that ship?"

Kate turned for her computer wondering how Rikka had found them the first time. Agent Leona Edwards held up a hand to stop her and headed for the computer herself.

"Marcus, call La Guardia and find out where a private charter departing at," she consulted her ever-present notepad, "5:47 a.m. filed as their flight plan's destination."

"Nothing says that's a real one. They could have done the same thing that Paul did to us on his flight to Florida."

"Not if they want us to follow them," Kate felt more and more sure that for some reason, she was the one they were after. That meant Rikka was merely bait to make sure she followed, which was even worse.

She hoped so, because then they'd know that the bait would only work as long as Rikka lived. It would also mean that they didn't know who Rikka truly was or they'd have killed her immediately.

Marcus got on the phone.

"Let's see," Leona perched on Kate's chair and woke up her computer, "where they're presently moored."

"Top secret vessel tracking site?" Paul teased the agent, lightening the room's mood.

"No, smartass, NKNews.org. There are a lot more people than our government who don't trust the DPRK. These folks have a dedicated vessel tracking site solely for North Korean vessels and any FOCs they can identify."

"FOCs?"

"Flags of Convenience. American oil companies aren't the only ones trying to find ways around US Merchant Marine regulations."

"They're anchored in—"

"Panama," Marcus hung up his phone and finished for her. "It checks."

Kate sighed. There were times she hated being right.

A one-hundred-percent trap.

84

ANY OF RIKKA'S FEARS OF RAPE OR TORTURE WERE AT LEAST temporarily allayed by Franco telling Jason to *back the fuck off.* She'd been steeling herself for it, but didn't know if her internal preparation could ever be enough and was glad she didn't have to find out.

Best policy of the moment? Stay quiet and listen, see what she could learn.

Which was disgustingly little. They'd assigned watches, so two of them immediately fell asleep while Manuel watched her.

She'd scanned the jet, but didn't see any way out until they landed. Each of the men were heavily armed. There were no secret folders to snitch ore even books to read. All she could do was sit and be terrified. If that's what they wanted, it was working just fine.

The tiny jet had only one thing that didn't belong, other than her.

A coffin with a biohazard sticker pasted across the surface.

If that's where she was going to end up, why was she still alive?

Or was the coffin for Kate?

Oh crap! That was it. She was bait and Kate was the fish. They'd caught Kate once already; they must want her badly for something. And the only reason she could think of that the North Koreans would want Kate Stark...

Double crap! It was her doing! The DPRK was trying to bust Kate's chops for breaking up the Tong's counterfeiting ring five years ago and rescuing Rikka in the process. Which meant, if they found out it was her who'd turned State's evidence against the Tong...she'd be a dead woman.

That was far too much to consider, so she shoved it aside and refocused on Kate. Rikka hated that it was her actions giving Kate so much trouble.

One careful glance at the three men in the small cabin told her that, even if they were willing to answer any of her questions—no way in hell—she wouldn't like the answers.

Not even a bit.

Maybe if she thought small enough, she could disappear altogether and be no more trouble to anyone.

85

RANG HAD PARK MEET HIM ON THE RADAR MAST PLATFORM TEN meters above the command bridge. Climbing the ladder had pained his missing leg, but it was his ship and he would work her.

Park clearly had a secret that he was desperate to share. Su-jin had warned him in their own coded language: *Park likes to believe himself to be the master of secrets. He also likes the sharing of them.*

Well, he wasn't going to have sex with the man to convince him to share them. So, Rang would convince Park that Rang himself was the safest and most discreet man Park would ever find.

Su-jin had also heard a rumor from the wife of the most senior council member that this entire operation was Park's idea.

Therefore, if it succeeded, which Rang deemed highly unlikely, then he needed to be in a position to take credit for it. If it failed, it needed to land so squarely and visibly on Park's shoulders that the other four council members would never trust him again. That the resulting purge would also eradicate

Park's gentle wife Mi-sook was unavoidable so there was no point in worrying for her sake.

Yes! had been Su-jin's only other note. Simply that, no more.

Rang needed no more. It was the absolute confirmation that this was indeed the opportunity they'd both been maneuvering for, through all of the years of their marriage.

Rang smiled out at the waiting ships in Bahia Limón as Park exited the bridge and began the climb up to the radar platform.

Su-jin had masterminded a fine political line for him to walk, a high-wire, but he had not risen to power without placing bets and taking chances himself.

"What are you smiling at, Rang?" Park asked as he arrived somewhat out of breath beside Rang.

"The beautiful morning, Park-ssi." *He* at least would continue to be polite with the honorific.

And it was indeed a beautiful morning. On the water, the heat of Panama felt no worse than on the fishing skiff he'd sailed off Kaesong as a youth. The world's commerce lay before them, awaiting their turns through the Canal. Tankers, monstrous PANAMAX container ships designed to the limits of the Canal, smaller ships like his own, as well as the tiny sailboats of globetrotting amateurs mingled together in the sheltered bay anchorage big enough to hold an entire fleet and safe enough to ride out a hurricane.

For a time they admired the setting in silence. It was eight a.m. local time, the same as New York. In two more hours, the pretty Japanese interpreter would be in Panama. An hour later she would be safely aboard.

And after that?

Then would come the woman with the sea-foam blue eyes.

86

Marcus Reynolds kept trying to get Leona aside, but he wasn't having much luck with that. The drive to the airport had been hurried and a pair of Marine Force Recon soldiers were sitting silently in the back of the car. Speed being of the essence, any planning would occur during the four-hour flight to the Canal Zone.

Kate had crowded into Sam's small car with her brother and Harold.

At Teterboro Airport, unsure what weapons to take, he and Leona had selected nearly identical rigs from the locked case inside their car's trunk. Numerous extra magazines for their sidearms. He'd grabbed an M4A1 sniper rifle with a suppressor in case they needed to be quiet, which he'd equipped with both an Elcan day scope and a TNC night scope. She'd opted for an H&K MP5SD machine pistol that already had a suppressor built in. He'd be able to offer distant coverage, and she was ready if they landed in a Close Quarters Battle situation. He hated CQB and Leona seemed to thrive on it. Yet another reason they made a good team.

That was one of the reasons he wanted to get her aside for a few moments. Through the whole of the day and night that they'd been on this case, he could feel a tension building between them—a good tension, the kind that caused heat. And he needed to find a way to ask if it was only in his head. But everything kept conspiring to keep them apart.

Nearly being killed on the Upper West Side for example. Not exactly a quiet kind of moment and one that still left his heart pounding at the thought.

That close.

Kate's *Abort!* call at less than three seconds to contact. He'd never been burned, blown up, or shot in his eight years of service. In a single night he'd managed two out of three and was not liking the odds on the third.

With a shared look, they each grabbed a Kevlar vest.

The Marines had arrived at Kate's office carrying a duffle bag apiece, and they still carried those. The bags bulged and did not appear to be light.

Again, Kate had refused to arm Harold or her brother.

"That way we'll at least look dangerous," Paul had practically whined, like a small boy being denied a new toy.

"No, you'll look foolish to anyone with a trained eye. You'll look far more dangerous if they can't see how you are armed."

Marcus appreciated her assessment. The last thing he wanted behind him was a panicked civilian armed with so much as a paintball gun.

The pilots had the jet ready before Marcus closed the trunk to his car inside the Starks' private hangar.

Once inside the compact jet, Kate kept her brother and Sam close, taking three of the four forward seats. She nodded to Marcus to take the fourth after shooing her boyfriend to the back along with the other two Marines and Leona.

Well, at least Leona was well away from Paul. Having a

handsome billionaire underfoot and targeting her, well, Marcus didn't like that one bit.

By the time they rotated aloft off the runway at Teterboro, they were only fifty-five minutes behind Franco's plane. It still tracked direct for Panama.

And he wasn't a single step closer to understanding Leona.

87

"It was 1978," Comrade Park leaned on the rail of the high radar platform and looked out at the arrogant Western ships scattered across the bay. How many of them would soon be bowing to the Democratic People's Republic of Korea? The space launches were going well, despite the current failures. Hadn't the Americans destroyed many giant rockets before they sent men into orbit? Stolen designs took time to understand. Soon Korean People's Army Air Force missiles would be able to strike anywhere on the planet.

"Kim Il-sung was the Supreme Leader. The Americans worked so hard in the Vietnam War to win the 'Hearts and Minds' of the people. They failed on both accounts. Not Kim Il-sung; he grabbed the power in 1949 and made the people love him."

Rang, the puppet, made the perfect audience. Next time Park was in Korea he would fuck the man's wife twice as hard until he ruined her for any man other than himself.

"Kim Jong-il had a wider vision than his father. He wanted to reach out to the people of the world. But North Korea didn't have the talent needed. The Great War, in which we were divided from our southern brethren by force, killed too many of our skilled workers. Both men and women. Kim Jong-il made an audacious plan then, following in his father's footsteps, he found what he was looking for and took it."

"Choi Eun-hee," Rang's whisper was reverential.

"Choi Eun-hee," Park echoed softly. The great actress.

"At least that's what I told the Council I would recreate for them with this Kate Stark."

Rang was a most attentive audience, showing proper surprise and respect when Park told him of Kate Stark's true value. [Capturing her was his path to leading the Council of Five, perhaps challenging the Supreme Leader himself, though he'd never admit to the latter.

"And if I take over control of the Council, Rang..." He let the bait dangle.

A respectful inhale of breath through clenched teeth from Rang, "I would be most honored to serve at your side, Park-ssi."

Park offered him a nod, revealing none of his true plan.

The Supreme Leader's father had taken four wives. With his power as the Council's leader, he would see that Rang had an accident at sea that would cost him more than his leg.

Then he could keep Mi-sook as a plaything *and* take the sublime Su-jin to also be his.

88

—————

"I arranged Panamanian Customs clearance for our arrival," Marcus Reynolds had spent the last fifteen minutes on the plane's in-flight phone. "We'll be landing at a remote end of the field and go straight into a hangar. But if these guys are tied into the control tower, we can't hide from them."

"If they turn on their radio, they'll hear the tower calling out our tail numbers for the landing," Mick said from behind Kate's seat.

Everyone had crowded into the back couches so that they could confer. They could each seat three people, if they weren't built like Marine Force Recon. They had turned two of the chairs, but that left a few people standing behind others.

"I want to go in light," Kate told them, "and scout things out. Then we'll go in heavy if we find something. They'll land at ten a.m. and we're an hour behind them."

"Won't they take Rikka and make a run for it?" Paul was thinking, but he was blocking out the concept that his own sister might be the ultimate target. It was sweet of him.

As Sam was shaking his head, Harold answered the question for him. Again.

"Not if it's Kate they want. They're going to wait until they have her. Besides, where can they go? The Canal only offers two or three transit groups each day. If they start a crossing, we can follow them every step of the way."

"With illegal cargo, they won't go through the Canal," Paul corrected Harold, appearing to enjoy it entirely too much. "They'll have to shoot for Cape Horn. The Canal's custom inspectors won't let them through so easily, especially not with what else they might be smuggling in addition to my sister."

"What do you mean by, 'go in light,' Ms. Stark?" She couldn't get the Marine Recon guys to use her first name. Was it a respect thing? Maybe she hadn't earned it yet? Maybe Sam had told them she was a hateful bitch and not to cut her any slack. If that was so, then why were they helping her? For Rikka's sake. Well, she'd take their aid any way she could get it today.

But sometime, other than today, she'd have to gear up and hash it out with him.

That sounded like one of her dumber ideas.

"Well," Kate shoved that problem aside once again. "I think maybe Harold and I should go play tourist along the waterfront. They must get supplies from shore though they're anchored a half-mile into the bay. I don't like the idea of arriving on their ship in broad daylight, so let's do a bit of intelligence gathering."

"What about Rikka?"

Kate closed her eyes. Assuming it took an hour to smuggle her aboard, she'd have eight hours to survive until sunset, surely that was a safer bet than a daylight raid.

When she opened her eyes, Sam stared straight at her.

"We wait."

His nod said she'd made the right choice.

Her gut wasn't so sure.

89

———————

"In the box."

"Are you fucking insane?" Rikka already knew the answer to that. Why did she bother asking?

Jason smiled up at Franco. His smile had a twisted *I told you so* look to it. Like *I told you we should have fucked the shit out of her first* or something equally vile. He spoke almost as rarely as Sam, but the feeling was completely different.

She could really, really, really do with seeing Sam's face right now. Rikka fought back against the tears that idea brought. He'd want her to be strong, so she'd be strong.

Franco Lamar leaned in until his face was so close to hers she could smell his hair mousse and his breath mint. He kept sucking on those flat strips like they were drugs he was addicted to. Franco majorly cared how he looked. Rikka hoped that somebody messed up his face before this was over.

"I forfeit a third of my take on this job if you're damaged. And since my customer is paying two and a half mil to receive you in one piece, I'm not going to hurt you...at least not in any way they can see or that will show up within the first twenty-four hours. But I can make it so that you are your cute and perky self for twenty-four—and screaming in agony as you try to rip out your own guts with your bare fingers inside of thirty-six. Now climb into the goddamn box."

Rikka looked at the coffin resting in the back of the plane's cabin. The lid with its biohazard stickers had been unbolted and lifted aside. The inside had padding.

She wanted out. She wanted away. Jason pulled out a black nylon rollup case like a chef's knife case. Rikka couldn't look away as he untied and unrolled it. Instead of chef's knife, paring and deboning blades, shears...he had syringes, wires, small bottles of murky liquids and clear ones. The last flap revealed pliers and—

Rikka looked away before she could see more. Bravery was one thing, but that was scary and real as shit.

She let Franco's light touch on her shoulders turn her and move her toward the box and did her best to ignore Jason's grunt of disappointment. Without being instructed, she climbed in and lay down. It was made for someone much bigger. Kate or Paul could fit in here. Not Sam though. His shoulders were too broad, weren't they?

Her memory of such things was blurring in strange ways. She could remember everything about the day Kate had taken her out for pizza and ended the existence of money-laundress Shirō Usagi, except Kate herself. It was as if there'd been a thousand holes cut in her world, and every good memory had been snipped out of it. Fighting to recover the memories wasn't working well.

Maybe it would come out alright on the other end. If they were taking her to the North Korean ship—which was as good a guess as any—there would be more opportunities for creativity there. Maybe. She'd hadn't exactly been creative so far.

"Hey, you listening to me, girly?" Franco was squatting at

the head of the coffin so that he looked to be upside down. He was tapping on her forehead to get her attention.

"You've got three bottles of air in here with you. Each is good for thirty minutes. Don't be falling asleep, girly. If you sleep through a bottle change, you'll be dead in minutes, and I will be truly unhappy. Truly. And I will take it out on your friends if they come for you. Even if they don't; I know where to find them. You understand me? Three bottles."

She managed to nod.

"I knock twice on the coffin, you freeze. Not a peep or a wiggle, not a bottle change even if you have to hold your breath. I knock once? You can do the change. One cry and I press this," he held up a small control for her to see. "It floods the coffin with sleepy gas. Then you only live until your current bottle runs out because you won't be awake to change it. We clear?"

She nodded again.

She heard the squeal and felt the bump as the jet's tires hit the runway.

Franco put a mask on her face and opened the valve of the first bottle then he handed her a tiny flashlight and moved out of her line of vision.

"Seal it," he ordered the others. "Remember to check the relief valve; we don't want to overpressure her coffin."

Rikka's world went dark as the lid slammed shut. There was a loud whine of an electric wrench and the high squeal of bolts seating into the coffin's structure.

Her job now was to stay alive.

She didn't dare move—despite the tears she couldn't stop streaming down her cheeks.

90

———————

Kate split them up into teams to check out the Bahia Limón and the port of Colon, Panama—the northern, Atlantic entrance to the Canal.

Mick and Rio had taken a couple of scopes with them and would make tactical evaluations of the ship and the shoreline.

Sam and Paul would pose as buddies on holiday—Paul was certain to talk enough to make up for Sam's silence. They'd take a sightseeing helicopter flight over the bay to *Look at all the pretty ships.* It was a common enough and therefore invisible activity, even if their interest was focused on one particular ship.

Marcus and Leona would meet with their OIO counterparts to learn what they could and arrange for on-call backup. Neither had worked with the FBI's Office of International Operations before and this was their chance to see what was possible.

Kate and Harold were headed for the waterfront, but Harold had stopped them while still inside the Enrique Adolfo Jiménez Airport's terminal.

"This will never do, you know," Harold led her by the hand toward the shops.

"What won't?"

"You. You're too damn beautiful, Stark. You stand out way too much in a crowd. Come on." Harold tugged her sideways into the tackiest tourist store of them all.

"I didn't come here to shop."

"But you did, sweetie. There. This is perfect for you," Harold's voice was practically campy as he handed her a floopy straw hat with a ridiculous pink ribbon and a wide brim. In moments she also had large sunglasses that might have been chic on a sixty's movie star.

Kate wasn't going to—

"What size t-shirt do you wear, honey? A women's large because you're so tall, I'm sure. Here, go put this on."

When she tried to protest, he shoved a bundle of thin cotton cloth into her hand and turned her toward the tiny curtained-off corner. After she'd turned, he patted her butt to send her on her way. For that, she might have to maim him.

"No bra," he whispered as she stalked off.

She'd *no bra* him smack between the eyes if he kept this up. She saw that he'd given her a medium size t-shirt, but when she turned back, Harold merely mouthed *trust me* and shooed her behind the curtain.

It was a good thing she took off her bra, there wasn't room for it under the shirt. The fabric was so cheap and thin that it was practically sheer. She put on the hat and sunglasses and stepped back into the store.

Harold had pulled on a bright blue t-shirt emblazoned with *Life's a Beach, Baby*, a touristy hat, and techy shades that looked like they'd been copied from one of Rikka's movies. He also looked surprisingly unlike the patrician and impeccably dressed Harold Merritt.

Kate looked at herself in a courtesy mirror. The t-shirt was small enough that it exposed her midriff. And the Panamanian flag was being stretched far out of proportion by her breasts. It was ridiculously revealing. He inched the lower hem of her t-shirt up.

"Damn, Stark, nobody honestly has six-pack abs. One thing for certain, not a man on the planet could look at your face while you're wearing that."

"Not one woman on the planet could respect herself while wearing this."

"You'd be surprised." His smile spoke volumes about a book she'd rather not open.

She glanced in the mirror again and decided she looked like a cast member of *The Real Housewives of New Jersey* on a Florida holiday. She had to admit that Harold was right, she couldn't have looked less like herself if she'd tried. He held out a ridiculous pair of heeled sandals. At least they were only mid-heels, so she'd be able to walk. With a sigh she sacrificed her comfortable sneakers.

Harold had recovered his wallet from the locker back at the studio, so he paid off the shop clerk. They put their own clothes in a shockingly bright *I (heart) Panama* bag and stepped out of the terminal to hail a cab.

91

Captain Rang Jin-ho's missing leg itched as the Americans unscrewed the coffin lid on his ship's main deck. It didn't take an idiot to recognize a biohazard symbol. The spiky symbol looked scary all on its own.

Park was practically bubbling with anticipation.

Rang also didn't like Park's American thugs with their odd names: Franco, Manuel, Jason. They were so tall and big-framed that it was hard to take them seriously. In hard times, it was the soldier who could slip by unseen and could thrive on a handful of rice who won. But the Americans hadn't learned that lesson in Korea, Vietnam, or Afghanistan. They still didn't understand.

The *slick* one was the clear leader. The *muscle* looked like a brother of the Cuban whore he had enjoyed in Havana, dark skin and curly dark hair. The third American looked like a rabid dog who should be put down, too dangerous for Office 39's uses. That one gave him the shivers and Rang looked away as casually as he could.

P'yo remained stationed out of sight with a Zastava M76 sniper rifle that Rang had given him as a gift when they were officially assigned the prestigious command of the *Chong Chon Gang*—immediately after the voyage where they'd taken it for themselves.

P'yo had always been a better shot than Rang. Once he was captain, Rang had set up a special shooting range belowdecks for P'yo. He was now lethal. His friend would know if his firepower was called for.

The act of thinking about him might attract the Americans' attention to his hideout, so Rang blocked it out.

Instead, he positioned himself to have the first view inside the coffin. The lid cracked open. It was her, the Japanese interpreter.

Her eyes were squeezed shut against the midday sun. Her face and clothes were drenched in sweat; her clothing clung to her slender frame leaving little to the imagination. A wave of heat and stench issued forth; she had nearly been cooked alive by her own body heat and had emptied her bladder. It had taken them over an hour to unload, negotiate their way through airport Customs, and reach the boat. The results were a cruelty.

That didn't bother him, but that it was an unnecessary cruelty did. With imagination there would have been a hundred easier ways to move her. He'd been right the first time, nothing better than thugs.

"Take her to my cabin," he barked out the order before Park could open his mouth. He pointed to two of his most trusted lieutenants. "Put her in my bathroom with fresh clothes and stand guard outside the door. No one gets in except me. No one." Maybe Park would be stupid enough to try. Rang hoped so. If he did, one of the lieutenants would shoot Park and save Rang the trouble.

Park would think to take liberties with the woman once she was cleaned up; a risk Rang was unwilling to take. Well, Park had not met the Stark woman and he had. When she came—

Rang had no doubt that she was on her way—he wanted to have the interpreter unharmed. It might be the only thing that would save his ship and his life.

The path becomes narrower and narrower with each step, Su-jin, but I am past turning back.

With no pleasantries of greeting, the Americans turned to Park and demanded their money.

Hired thugs.

92

———————

"NORTH KOREAN?" PAUL WAS CHATTERING AWAY UP IN THE FRONT seat of the Robinson R44 tourist helicopter painted a garish red.

That gave Sam free rein of the rear of the helicopter. There were only four seats in this model, two front and two back, and thankfully there'd been no solo sightseers waiting for a ride who might have joined them. The two of them had paid for their thirty-minute view of the Canal, but Paul had them circling over Bahia Limón with his questions about the ships there.

"I bet you don't often get to see a North Korean ship, do you? How do you know that's what it is?"

The pilot launched into a long explanation about the ship being impounded here once before, in 2013 for six months.

Sam ignored them. He sat directly behind the pilot, so there was no way for the man to turn and see him. He pulled out the rifle scope he'd tucked into his jacket and inspected the *Chong Chon Gang* from above.

She rode at anchor five hundred meters due west of the Cristóbal pier; so rusted it was a wonder she was afloat. She boasted three cranes forward and one aft of the five-story crew quarters and bridge. Five large cargo hatches, each twelve meters square and raised a meter above the main deck. One was open because the containers were stacked too high to seal it. That had included Kate's container.

Loaded to the waterline, there remained less than five meters of freeboard. Still a step up from a tug or pilot boat. Perhaps they could liberate a power yacht for the evening and slide it alongside with no one the wiser.

No helipad, nor a decent spot to slip one in. Perhaps something as small as this Robinson helo could be landed on the cargo hatch immediately in front of the living quarters tower. It was the only open space on the deck, but it would be too close for anyone less than a top military pilot. With that option out, they'd have to use the bridge wing as they had the first time with the Marine Corps Super Stallion helo, or travel by water and go over the main deck rail.

Riding at anchor, the command bridge was not a strategic necessity, though it was high ground.

A cluster of men stood on the main deck close by a small boat ramp that had been lowered to the water.

Paul glanced back at him.

Sam made a motion for a single circuit around the boat, more than one would be suspicious.

"Hey," Paul turned his attention back to the pilot. "Could we circle it once? I want to take a picture so I can tell my friends that I really saw it. No, don't go any lower; it already fills my screen." He had his smartphone out and was snapping away.

Sam flipped to a higher magnification, braced the scope against the window to steady it, then took a half breath and held it.

It took a moment to find the group at this magnification. Most were dressed casually in the standard sailors' attire of khakis and a white shirt that he had observed when they were aboard the first time. One wore a uniform jacket, though it didn't look military.

Three were dressed in black jackets over black t-shirts, slacks, and boots, despite the heat. No need to guess who they were: Franco, Manuel, and Jason.

The group stood around an open box, a coffin. Sam had enough angle on the lid to see the garish yellow and black biohazard sticker on the top. That's how they'd smuggled Rikka through Customs. Probably with phonied-up embassy paperwork for a burial on her home Panamanian soil. It would have been far easier to give her a *goofy* drug and walk her through as a drunk girlfriend. Idiots.

And she was no longer in the coffin, which meant she was alive.

He pulled back on the magnification and quickly surveyed the ship.

Possibly, just possibly, he caught three shadows—two escorting a third—the moment before they disappeared into the first story of the crew living quarters.

He shifted back to a lower magnification and took a breath.

Erika Albert was alive. In captivity on a hundred-and-fifty-meter-long ship—the primary vessel of the most clandestine agency of the most paranoid country on the planet—but she was alive.

He spotted the sniper atop the command bridge, six stories above the deck and completely hidden from below. Invisible, yet with a clear field of fire on the entire group, his position was perfect. They had a real sniper on board. Correct that, at least one real sniper on board.

Smart. As Kate had told him, the captain was smart and brave.

Franco and Jason would suspect such a thing, but it was a wise move nonetheless. As the captain had demonstrated when he'd walked up to Kate to hand her the container shipping manifest on their last visit, he would perhaps be a man who could be dealt with. Not trustworthy, but neither reckless.

As the helo finished its circle and headed out to investigate the wonders of the third set of locks that were a part of the Canal expansion project, Sam focused on the group of men one last time.

One of the men dressed in black turned to look up at the helicopter.

Sam couldn't make out his features, but he didn't need to.

He could feel the vicious anticipation of Jason Mann's gaze.

93

Park stared up at Franco.

"Money?"

"Yes."

At a signal he didn't detect, Franco's two thugs shifted a half-step closer. One of them a tad slow as he'd been so childish as to be distracted by a tourist helicopter.

"First," Park affected a calm he didn't feel as much as he'd like, "close that noxious box. It is stinking up the entire planet."

One of them slapped the lid. It clanged shut with a crash of heavy metal that echoed the entire length of the ship's deck.

He smiled to himself. They thought to scare him, so assured of their own mental superiority. Every one of them. The Americans probably thought to dump him in the box if he didn't pay them.

Rang thought he was so sly with his tiny hopes of climbing onto the Council. If Park could be assured that Rang was in his pocket, he might let him on the Council; get rid of Yon perhaps. But Rang was too slippery, he'd survived Office 39 politics for decades and risen to first below the highest level.

Park kept his voice and manner casual as he faced Franco. "Would you care to double your money? Today?"

Franco's eyes narrowed with avarice before he controlled himself.

Park knew that he had him.

"I'm not going to gamble two-and-a-half—"

"No. No." Park assured him. "The same amount again." He had a report from an underpaid Customs official about the arrival of Kate Stark's plane and the departure of four pairs of people from the plane. One had matched Kate Stark's description, but the fool had lost them shortly afterward. It didn't matter, Park had the Japanese now, and Rang had been right that Stark would follow.

With a shower and fresh clothes... How typical and short-sighted of Rang to be greedy and take the little woman for himself. Park might use the man's wife, but he had no interest in plowing the same furrow right after Rang had planted his own seed.

"What's the catch?" Franco had signaled his men to back down.

"Kate Stark is in Panama. She will be arriving shortly aboard this ship. Help me to secure her and I will pay you the full amount. Tonight."

"You will pay what you owe me now, plus our standard deposit."

"What I owe you now, yes. Then the whole second payment when Kate Stark is unharmed and secure. Others are with her. I would prefer them intact as well, though I shall not make that a condition of payment. But Stark must be untouched."

"Done."

Exactly the payment plan Park had wanted in the first place.

Franco held out one of his massive hands. Park shook it, managing not to wince at the power of the grip. He also didn't wipe it on his pants though he would certainly wash it at the first private opportunity. After they had Stark, he'd have Rang remove these three and that would save himself the entire second payment.

With a flourish, he pulled out his smartphone.

Rang eyed him strangely. He must wonder if this was a perk of joining the Council of Five. It wasn't. The Council didn't truly understand what was necessary to conduct business overseas and issued crappy Korean-made flip phones that couldn't send a text message or place a call to anywhere outside the DPRK. He'd couldn't have Rang reporting him. Maybe he'd dispose of Rang himself after the man had dispatched these greedy Americans for him.

Not something Park would worry about at the moment.

In minutes the money for capturing the Japanese was moving. Two million. It had cost twenty thousand dollars to print that many high-quality American hundred-dollar bills and twice that amount again to launder the money before moving it into Franco's account.

Sixty thousand American, all-expense paid. A bargain.

And as he had no intention of allowing them to live to ask for the second payment, a true bargain.

Now they merely had to wait for Kate Stark to show herself.

94

———

"You sure know how to show a girl a good time, Harold."

Kate could see the hulk of the *Chong Chon Gang* floating a half mile away. But compared to where they were presently, the rust and gray-colored ship looked idyllic floating on the blue-green waters of Bahia Limón.

The shores of Cristóbal, in Colon, Panama were a combination of industrial piers busy with loading, unloading, and repairing ships, and third-world hovels overflowing with services for the world's sailors.

But they weren't only whores and trinket sellers. There were also local handicraft stalls, one of which sold them a pretty, over-the-shoulder satchel of worked beads which let them lose the *I (heart) Panama* shopping bag. She'd also wanted a shawl to cover her ridiculous exposure—every man in the city had ogled her breasts—but Harold had vetoed the suggestion.

He nudged her hip toward a group of food stalls.

"I'm not hungry. Besides, I'd probably get dysentery."

"Won't hit for a couple days. You can get antibiotics. Besides, I'm not interested in the food." Harold changed speed from excited tourist to curious traveler. He was no longer poking about, looking into everything. He'd shifted to a casual, approachable stance.

Kate hated being on show like this, yet she often was. Sometimes she played the imperious judge and sometimes the eager announcer. On yet others, she played the chef interested in learning from the others around her. She decided that this third guise—which is when she was her most natural self—was what the situation called for.

Harold began engaging the merchants and Kate played along. It wasn't long before a man was splitting the thick green rind off a coconut for them. He wielded a massive machete with an apparent lack of care—though he still retained all his fingers to prove the success of his long practice. In moments, he handed it to her with a straw slid into a notch he had hacked out of the hard inner brown-husked nut. Kate could only hope that the straw hadn't been used before.

The milk was sweet, fresh, and surprisingly cool on the hot day. It slaked her thirst and made her feel far more amenable to the miserable conditions of the market stalls.

Harold showed no signs of moving off, instead chatting with the merchant in Spanish. She was able to follow most of it with her high school Spanish, though she'd be lost had she tried to join the conversation.

"Yes, many sailors come ashore. Including the ones who have not met the customs man. We trade with them. Have many types of money. Dollars, pounds, euros."

Harold kept him on the topic of money for reasons Kate didn't understand.

When she'd sucked the coconut dry of its sweet milk, the merchant waved for her to give it back to him without interrupting his conversation with Harold.

He threw out the straw, Kate was relieved to see. Then he split her coconut neatly in half with a downward stroke of his blade, holding the coconut from beneath. In lieu of giving himself a bleeding stump with that maneuver, he now handed the two halves back to her along with a plastic spoon.

She'd expected to find the usual thick hard white meat inside, instead there was a thin layer of translucent goo clinging to the shell. The man signaled for her to scoop it up with the spoon.

When she hesitated, Harold handed over his coconut for the same treatment. When he took it back, he scraped up a large spoonful and ate it. "Young coconut. Very special."

She tasted it tentatively and was surprised by the soft sweetness, as rich as commercial coconut milk but more subtle. It was a new flavor for her.

"*Delicioso,*" her high school Spanish managed to unearth.

The man smiled before returning to his conversation with Harold.

"I like the colors of the Canadian money and the euro. My child collects coins. Do you have any coins?"

Harold dug out a few.

The man reached out a long finger and flipped through the quarters, "Alaska. I don't think my son has this one."

Harold handed it over to him with all due ceremony.

"Do you ever collect any won?"

Kate finally understood what they were doing here. *Well done, Harold.*

"South Korean won are boring."

"The North Korean ones?"

The man shivered in a way to make them laugh. "They are so ugly. Worse than American money. And they are no use. You can only exchange them for more won. They do me no good."

"Then how do they trade with you?" Harold had asked about the North Koreans without ever naming the country or the ship. Kate would never have been so smooth. The man kept surprising her in the most pleasant ways.

"Most don't," the man began breaking another coconut

from its thick rind for a boatman who had hauled his craft up on the beach.

Kate would have to congratulate Harold on a good try at least; it was more than she would have learned.

"But that boat," the man pointed his machete at the *Chong Chon Gang* floating offshore, "they pay with American hundred-dollar bills. Always tell us to keep the change. We were suspicious at first, but the bank always says they are good."

"Have they been ashore this time?"

"Yes, their cook is here often. Would you like to meet him?"

Before they could answer, the merchant was waving at a short Korean man in tattered clothing.

"*Señor* Bok. Come. Come."

When the short man—who she'd last seen weeping on the floor of the *Chong Chon Gang's* command bridge—arrived all smiles and stared at her chest, Kate was finally thankful for Harold's disguise. *Damn well done.*

95

Captain Rang Jin-ho had been biding his time.

Through the long hot afternoon, one or the other of the Americans had patrolled the length of the ship. In the meantime, the other two slept, ate prodigiously while complaining bitterly about the food, and would have whored prodigiously had women been available.

For her own safety, Rang quietly moved the interpreter into a smuggling locker that could be locked from the inside as well as the outside. He had spoken with her in his office before locking her in, his bad leg propped on a desk drawer.

Once he was over his own unease at her heritage, she seemed a pleasant enough young woman.

"The woman with the blue eyes will come for you, won't she?"

Her eyes shot wide at his knowledge, then he could see her struggling to hide that surprise as if she'd given away a great secret.

It reminded him of his eldest daughter and the first time she'd taken a boy to her bed. In the morning, she'd showed the same surprise and inept attempt to hide it when he'd confronted her. The one she'd chosen had been deeply unworthy of her; her choices since their conversation were much more considered.

Had Rang himself ever been so innocent? Before the first time he had been with Su-jin? Perhaps. Not after. Even their first time together she had opened a world to him. She had only been awaiting the right man and for thirty years now, he was proud that it was him.

"Are you lovers?"

She shook her head hard enough to swirl her hair. Pity. A fantasy image he would have to toss aside. He should not have asked, then he could have kept the image for his own.

"She is already here, in Panama," he told the woman unsure why he wanted to reassure her.

"Alone?" the interpreter's voice was a bare whisper.

"Not alone." Rang watched her carefully.

She gained confidence from that statement. A great deal of confidence for a defenseless woman locked up on a smuggling ship of Office 39.

"Are they that skilled, those who come with her? The big man who carried the machine gun onto my bridge the last time?"

Again the hesitation, then the confirming nod. She truly was pretty. It was a pity that she would be so dangerous to keep.

"He is more skilled than the three who brought you?"

Again the nod; no uncertainty this time. In fact, she appeared to take great courage from her own answer to that question. To be so certain that there were no shades of doubt. That she had such a positive view of the world, in one small area, was such a gift. One he had lost somewhere, long past redeeming.

Everything existed in shades and chance. The time when he must place his bet was fast approaching.

And Rang Jin-ho was a betting man.

From the moment he had elevated Su-jin, the greatest whore of Kaesong, to be his first and only wife, he had gambled.

It was as if he'd played *Hwatu* and captured the five bright cards when his first captain had been tragically and—inexplicably to others—lost overboard during a typhoon. Rang and P'yo had stepped in to save the ship. Thankfully no one except his childhood friend knew how close that had been to disaster. In those three long days he'd learned that the bitter old man had taken far more knowledge of the sea over the rail than he had ever taught Rang.

When he and Su-jin had agreed she should slip into the bed of both Park and the ever-so-secretly lesbian wife of the great Gil Jang Yong, the most senior member of Office 39, they had taken the risk together. For if one of them had fallen, so assuredly would the other.

Yes, the time was now, and he was ready to bet it all.

So sorry, Park-ssi.

"Let us speak of possibilities."

At his simple suggestion, the woman settled. Her uncertain jitters evaporated as if they'd never been.

Suddenly, he was no longer reminded of his daughter, but rather of a young Su-jin; at least as smart if not yet as wise.

Yes, he would remain prepared for Park's success. But as a wise man, he was going to bet on a woman who earned such absolute faith from this young woman and who wore red silk upon her breasts.

96

––––––––––

Kate had fed them an early dinner from the supplies on the plane. They'd gathered back aboard and began sifting through what each of the teams had learned.

Marcus and Leona were disgusted. "The Panama OIO is all legal attachés. There isn't a single field agent among them. I started talking about physical security—not even an actual raid. They began mouthing off about which Panamanian authorities and agencies would have to be notified, which couldn't be done until tomorrow because of a banquet tonight at some embassy that—" He sputtered to an angry halt.

Leona patted him on the shoulder, "At least three times today he threatened to quit the Bureau and go join the CIA, so that he could get something done. Sorry, Kate. We tried so hard." Then she slid her hand down Marcus' arm and took his hand in hers.

Kate shared a smile with her. Well, at least the day hadn't been a total waste for them.

Mick rolled out a map of the harbor across their knees and Rio ran a finger along the shore. "We could swim in from here. The water is warm enough, and there's not much current.

Tossing a grapple would gain too much attention, but we can climb the anchor chain."

"The problem with that," Mick picked up as if they were one voice, "is that it's flat calm and the harbor lights are wrong. They'd spot us a thousand yards off and then we'd be toast. SCUBA gear would leave an obvious bubble line, never mind approaching by a surface craft. With Franco, Manuel, and Jason aboard, they'll be expecting that approach. I don't know if Dräger closed-circuit rebreathers would be sufficient to fool them even though there'd be no bubble trail; that's if we could get our hands on the gear on such short notice."

Paul and Sam had ascertained that Franco, his henchmen, and assuredly Rikka were aboard. Sam had also drawn a detailed plan of the boat deck itself including hatch cover elevations, crane sizes, and the sniper's position.

"What's the weather prediction, Ed?"

"Ceiling at a thousand feet," her chief pilot, Ed Carmichael, had been keeping quiet in the background throughout the discussion. "Winds flat calm, which never happens here. No moon behind the clouds, so the sky is going to be extra dark. You only have to worry about surface lights."

She looked at the team. They were good people, every one. And they were looking to her for the answer. Sam waited quietly for her plan too. She supposed that if someone had to cook up a plot, it should be a chef.

"Well, to start. Harold and I have a date tonight."

RANG HAD MUCH PLANNING TO DO AND MANY PEOPLE TO organize if this was going to work. The one thing he couldn't do was appear to be in a hurry, for that would attract Park's attention to his plans. Which was a good thing. With the constant climbing up and down he'd been doing throughout the day, his leg was already in pain and the day was far from over.

Yet Park would not finish his meal and get out of Rang's office.

P'yo finally came and rescued him at sunset.

He gave P'yo his instructions.

Together they checked discreetly on the girl. He introduced P'yo so that she would not be forever trapped behind steel if something were to happen to himself. He relocked the outside of the door as he heard her relock the inside; couldn't have her wandering out of hiding at the wrong moment. If something happened and neither he nor P'yo survived to free her, well, that was karma.

The three Americans had set up several traps. One of the men squatted forward by the anchor chain where he could survey the entire bay ahead. The other two patrolled the deck.

Shortly before sunset, he left an officer on the command bridge—as the Panamanian officials required—but warned him to do nothing no matter what happened. If the anchor chain parted, he was to let her drift; it would be the safest choice. To call to duty the necessary engine crews and deck hands would only put his own crew at risk.

The heart of Rang's plan was simple: keep out of the way.

He only wished that he knew when it was beginning. That would be useful knowledge.

He went below and advised his own crew that this might be a good evening to go to their bunks early. Most took the warning. But the cook came up to him once the others had gone.

"Captain Rang-ssi. I know I should not ask. I truly do. I should never have said yes, but I—" he faltered.

"What is it, Bok?" He tried to use his kindest voice to soothe the perpetually nervous man. Bok was the best cook Rang had ever sailed with and that was worth a bit of patience, though he didn't have time for much tonight.

"On the beach today, while buying papaya and star fruit for your breakfast, Rang-ssi, I met two American tourists. I...I...I liked them. They wanted to come see my galley. The man offered me a wonderful recipe. We were merely going to cook together and talk. I promise Rang-ssi. It is so innocent. They're coming tonight."

Rang somehow managed to keep his temper from blasting the man into the bulkhead so hard that he never walked, talked, or pissed again. This was a secret ship of Office 39. And the man had invited aboard strangers without his asking? Insufferable!

When you feel the greatest emotional surge, then you are best served to stop and understand why. Su-jin's advice *did* stop him.

He had taken that advice to heart, other than when they were driving each other into soul-wrenching orgasms—for she had trained him exactly how to most please her. Whores frequently complimented his technique, often sharing their personal favorite techniques for him to take home to Su-jin.

So, he took a breath. Another.

At his signal, Bok collapsed onto a nearby seat.

"An American tourist you say?" he asked when he could be sure of his voice.

"Two. A man who spoke good Spanish, which I also speak enough to see to the buying of food, and a woman who did not."

Was it possible? Rang sat across from Bok after double-checking that no one, not even P'yo was nearby.

"Describe the woman to me, Bok."

"It is difficult, Captain-ssi. She wore a large hat that shaded her face, large sunglasses that hid her eyes, and…"

"And what?" Was he going to have to beat her description out of the man?

"She wore a t-shirt of the Panama flag," Bok inspected his shoes. "But it was much too small. She had magnificent breasts and no bra. The material was so tight you could easily see the bumps of…I'm sorry, Captain-ssi. I did not look at her face. I have failed you. I am so sorry."

Rang felt the thrill rush through him. She was coming. Bok had stood as close to her as he and Bok now sat.

He patted his cook on the shoulder, "When is she coming?"

"The man said an hour after sunset, at full dark."

Park's American mercenary thugs had sounded so certain that nothing would happen until three a.m. or perhaps an hour before dawn. They were wrong.

Rang glanced at the porthole. The sun was already set. They had less than thirty minutes.

"You have done extremely well, Bok," he reassured the

quaking cook. "Now..." He hesitated before sending Bok to cower in his galley.

Kate Stark had as good as told him through his cook exactly when she was coming aboard.

Why?

Why had she warned him?

If Park's plan worked, then he might have both the Japanese and American of the blue eyes aboard his ship. To circle Cape Horn, for that was the route they must take with such a cargo in addition to the illegal items they already carried, was a long and rough journey.

Much could happen during such a long crossing.

Stop thinking with your dick! Su-jin's frequent warning echoed through his thoughts. *I too enjoy what is between my legs, my husband, but I don't keep my brain there.*

Rang set aside the image of what he might do with two such women—an idle fantasy in any case.

Kate Stark must know it was a trap, yet she came. This woman was no fool. If he could trust Park's information, she alone had cost North Korea billions of dollars when she broke the Boston smuggling rings. The cascade had ripped along much of the American eastern seaboard and reached inland to Chicago.

Proof of her true identity as more than a cooking show performer was evident in the way that the interesting Japanese woman followed her as unquestioningly as the man who had wielded the massive gun on his command bridge.

The command bridge.

When they had first met on his command bridge two days ago, he'd felt her eyes pick him out as captain before he'd said the first word.

Then he had walked up to the gun whose name was death and stood close enough to hand her the manifest.

Her nod had acknowledged him as a worthy adversary.

Ah! There was the key.

It was because of that meeting that she had told him of her arrival time through his cook. She was betting he was intelligent enough to use the information wisely.

Rang was certain of that.

The cliff-edge path beneath Rang's feet had now narrowed past even turning about. How narrow could it get without shattering beneath his feet and plunging him into the ocean depths?

The time had come that he must carve a new course if he planned to survive the night.

Su-jin would agree. Would encourage him in his decision. Of that too he was certain.

Rang considered if there was enough time to send a message to Su-jin to tell her how perfect she was and to apologize if he was about to prove that she had married an idiot.

There wasn't.

He stood and clapped a hand on Bok's shoulder.

It took coaxing to convince the man to stand on his own feet.

"Come, Bok-ssi. I will wait with you. We shall greet your guests together."

He went to the deck of his ship and sat at the lip of the cargo hatch closest to the head of the stairs that led down to the small floating dock they'd deployed for ship-to-shore use. It bumped gently against his ship's hull. The only other sound was soft music drifting over from the shore where it must be truly loud.

It was a quiet and beautiful night, the calm moment before the storm. He was the Senior Captain of Office 39, in command of her most successful ship, and had the love of an amazing woman.

He was as ready as he could be.

98

"Your plan is insane. You know that, don't you?"

Kate considered that Harold might be right, but the wheels were now in motion and there was no turning back. They sat side-by-side in the middle seat of a small water taxi as it pulled away from the beach by the coconut merchant's stall.

"I offered to let you stay ashore and pretend you were sick or passed out drunk on coconut liquor."

"The way you speak Spanish, Kate, you'd be toast without me. Until you find Rikka to interpret for you, the fact that the cook and I both speak Spanish is your best bet."

Harold had pointed out earlier that for this to work, there also had to be two of them. If Kate arrived alone, they'd simply grab her, and it would be over. But with two of them there it would slow everything down, buying them the precious moments that were needed for her plan to work.

Kate had struggled against the idea of involving Harold, up until she'd seen Sam's simple nod confirming the need.

Damn the man!

He had been right every step of the way so far. But Harold was an innocent and, even with his consent, she was the one putting him in harm's way. There wasn't a chance he'd be playing along if he truly understood the dangers.

If that was what she thought, why hadn't she grounded Harold and her brother back in New York? She could have, should have. She hadn't. So now she was carrying a double load of worry aboard.

"If I don't get a chance to say it later," Harold's mouth was so close to her ear that it tickled, "you're welcome."

"What?" Crap but the man could make her smile at the strangest of times. She understood the joke. "Uh right... Thanks, Harold. I'm glad you're here."

The brightly lit Cristóbal piers passed alongside them. Far ahead, barely discernible from the ships behind it, lay the looming darkness of the *Chong Chon Gang*.

99

———————

"WHAT ARE YOU DOING HERE, RANG?"

Rang could become quite irritated that Park never used either his first name or his rank; and he had long since dropped any honorific. Park wasn't arrogant. Perhaps he *was*, but not as deeply as the unmourned political officer Ro. Park had simply been in power for too many years and didn't know how else to be.

Well, the years would tell their own tale tonight.

"I am sitting with my chef and enjoying the night, Park-ssi. The water is so quiet. You should join us, Yeong-suk." There was a first time for everything, including using the Council of Five member's first name as only an equal or a friend would dare.

And they weren't friends.

If Park detected the threat to his own position, he made no comment. Instead, he sat beside Rang.

"It is quiet," Park said after a while.

It was.

But because he was listening for it, Rang could hear the distant murmur of a small engine.

100

Captain Ed Carmichael wound up the dual Honeywell HTF7250G turbine engines to their full fifteen thousand pounds of thrust and lifted off the Starks' jet from Panama's Enrique Adolfo Jiménez Airport. He headed due north out to sea, climbing rapidly through five thousand feet.

His flight plan said that he was traveling to Costa Rica.

But once over the water, he didn't turn west to follow the coastline north and west. Instead, he shut off his transponder that would let traffic controllers know where his plane was and who it belonged to. Then he shut off the exterior lights and descended until he was headed out to sea at a mere fifty feet over the waves. A tricky maneuver in the dark at five hundred and fifty miles an hour.

He ran the turbines to the edge of yellow line and made sure he was trimmed for best speed.

Once at the correct altitude—high enough above the waves to maneuver without catching a wingtip in the water—and on the team's schedule, he turned around and headed back toward Panama.

101

───────

"THAT'S QUITE A BOAT, YOU HAVE THERE." A MAN SWAYED drunkenly at the edge of the dock staring at their patrol boat.

The two *garda* of the Panamanian Customs Service looked at each other. It was going to be one of *those* nights: drunken tourists and boring as hell.

"Is that two hundred all y'all got on this here boat?" The American drunk might have been staring at the engines mounted on the stern. It was hard to tell with the way his head was wobbling.

"There are two of them, *Señor.*"

"Shit!" the man took a slug off the bottle he held clenched in his fist. "I'm so drunk I'm seeing single instead of double."

They laughed.

"Hey, you want some? You guys looked bored as shit. It's Crown Royal. Damn good."

"For Crown Royal, we'll take you for a free tour of the harbor."

Quite how the drunk managed to climb into their boat was something neither of the *garda* could remember afterwards.

What they did remember was when he turned around.

321

He had a pistol aimed at them, then a man and a woman, one light and one dark, appeared from nowhere carrying fearsome-looking weapons. Weapons with silencers already mounted.

"A tour of the harbor sounds like a great idea boys," the drunk said with no slur in his voice. "You don't mind if my friends join us, do you? Or if I drive?" He stuffed his pistol into his belt, with the safety off, which was crazy; nobody was that stupid unless he didn't mind accidentally shooting his balls off. Or he didn't know any better.

The man moved to the controls.

The two on the dock with the large guns clearly knew how to handle their weapons though. They untied the Customs Patrol boat and jumped aboard without either of their aims wavering in the slightest.

The man with the bottle handed it over. "Drink up boys, your night is only going to get worse."

As one of them took the bottle, the man started the engines and maneuvered away from the dock with an ease that spoke of much practice. Then he turned to speak to his companions.

"I can't believe she gave me a gun but wouldn't trust me with any bullets."

"They're called cartridges or rounds," the woman with the machine pistol corrected him.

The first *garda* took a long drink from the bottle and handed it to his mate.

The night was definitely going to get worse.

102

RANG WAS AMUSED THAT PARK WAS THE LAST TO NOTICE THE noise of the engine as the water taxi approached the *Chong Chon Gang*. The man knew nothing of the sea.

The slick American, Franco, arrived from wherever he'd been patrolling before Park noticed anything.

"What's going on? Why are you sitting here like a bunch of goddamn pigeons?"

Rang waved toward the water, "I am enjoying the night and awaiting guests of my cook, the honorable Bok-ssi."

"Guests? Tonight? Shit! What is it with you people? We're going to have a mess on our hands when Stark arrives, and you invite guests?"

Rang kept his smile for himself. It was fascinating the way it was unfolding. Again, he wondered how deep the Stark woman's plan might be.

At times, the best option is to wait and watch the world unfold around us. Only then do we know where to step.

His money was not on Park-ssi or this Franco. Though his lone foot wasn't planted yet, he expected he must make the final choice in mere moments.

"Guests?" Park turned to look at him in shock.

"I think that you will like to meet them," Rang told them both.

Franco merely grunted; his rifle hung across his shoulder as he stared out at the approaching craft.

Rang felt quite content with the moment. His attempts to understand which pieces would move and how they would do so had borne less fruit than an ornamental cherry tree. Yet he felt no particular worry or fear which was curious in itself. For once, he found contentment being a mere pawn in someone else's game. He trusted this Kate Stark to be wise, as easily as he had found his trust of Su-jin during their first time together.

The initial move of the game lay firmly in the woman's hand, and he would wager she'd play it well. Further into the match, he had a few moves of his own—if everything happened as he suspected it would.

The taxi bumped gently against the floating dock. Franco leaned on the rail staring down on it and sucking on one of his pieces of green paper that he kept in a small plastic case in his pocket.

The woman's voice carried easily from below. It was bright and cheerful. No fear at coming aboard a North Korean cargo ship. If there was anything wrong with her role, it was that she was too cheerfully American. To her advantage, she didn't sound the least bit like the woman who had stood on his command bridge in such barely controlled rage.

As they ascended the ramp under Franco's lazy gaze, the water taxi turned and headed back for shore.

The man arrived first. He was American tall and wearing a tourist t-shirt.

"Bok, *mi amigo*," he called out as soon as he arrived on the deck. Rang also understood some Spanish. "We are going to cook tonight, aren't we? I brought food and wine!" He held up a bright shopping bag that declared, *My (heart) lies in Panama.* It brimmed over with produce.

103

KATE LOOKED AT THE MEN LINED UP AND WAITING ON THE DECK of the *Chong Chon Gang*. They had discussed a hundred different ways to handle this moment.

Enter with guns blazing.

Grab the captain and hold a gun to his head.

In the end she had decided on keeping the recipe simple.

"Captain, a pleasure to see you again," she managed in weak Spanish.

His quiet nod of greeting showed that he was exactly as she'd expected, a smart man who played his cards most carefully.

"*Señor* Bok." Under the deck lights, she could see the man blush. When he went to stand, his captain kept him in place with a gentle hand on the man's arm.

Kate smiled. Smart indeed. The captain was the man she'd have to watch above all others.

His half smile in return was interesting if not illuminating. He'd chosen to play a waiting game, at least she hoped that's what was going on.

Time to add the next ingredient. After all, that was why she and Harold stood here.

She pulled off her hat that had kept her face shaded and shook her hair loose before turning to Franco.

"Good evening, Mr. Lamar."

The man's jaw dropped, "Holy shit!"

The third Korean, who she didn't recognize, looked as if he'd been electrocuted.

104

Approaching the outer breakwater that protected Bahia Limón, Colon, Panama, Ed Carmichael knew that in the next few seconds he would freak out every flight controller in the area. An unidentified aircraft appearing abruptly on their scopes at fifty feet above the water and over five hundred miles an hour would be enough to upset any radar technician.

It was freaking *him* out. Many of the ships in the harbor were significantly taller than his current flight altitude and offered serious collision hazards.

At the breakwater, he slammed the turbines' throttles to idle. His jet became a nearly silent high-speed glider.

Ed pulled back on the control yoke, sending the Gulfstream soaring aloft. He punched up into the cloud layer that had blanketed the Panamanian night, trading speed for a near vertical climb to four thousand feet before leveling out. Rolling through the top of his climb at nearly a dead stop, he thanked God that his hobbies included flying gliders. He'd kept only enough speed to maintain flight control. The stall-warning buzzer screamed, but he'd expected that.

He hung deep in the clouds at his new altitude.

The Gulfstream would be splashed bright across the scope of every traffic controller. Except now, instead of flying at fifty feet where the radar would think he was noise from surface clutter, it was at four thousand—dead in the middle of the approaches to Enrique Adolfo Jiménez Airport. His radio snarled on the local traffic control frequency.

He ignored that along with the stall warning.

The red light showed as his copilot opened the passenger door; Ed compensated for the drag of the fold-down stairs now sticking out the side of his fuselage. There was no need to signal the men in back, they were already diving off the stairs, tumbling under the wing, and gone. His copilot closed the door. The door sealed, and its indicator light turned back to green.

With the last bit of remaining control, Ed nosed the plane over, using the dive to gather speed once more. As soon as he dared, he turned back toward the sea. At five hundred feet he once more flew over the Atlantic Ocean and began adding throttle. At fifty feet he leveled out, hopefully below where any upset military patrol planes might come looking for him.

He turned the jet for Costa Rica as his copilot returned to sit beside him. They had been instructed to stick to the flight plan for the night. At ten minutes and eighty miles out, he climbed to a proper cruising altitude and turned on the external navigation lights.

He'd always enjoyed flying for the Starks, but damn, that had been the best yet.

105

———

Kate amused herself by counting seconds. A full seven seconds passed before anyone aboard the ship reacted to her presence.

She had the feeling that the captain was also counting the seconds. He still wore that half smile.

It worried her; what hadn't she anticipated that he was seeing? She'd built a plan in three hours to raid a North Korean smuggling ship. What unanticipated holes did it include?

The cook remained huddled by his captain.

The third Korean, by far the best dressed of the trio, was the first to break his lethargy and jerked to his feet with the grace of a broken string puppet.

That had Franco slapping for his sidearm. When he pointed it at Kate, she raised her arms to the side and turned slowly. No weapons. Not even an ankle piece which she found to be disconcerting. Back on land, Sam had watched her silently as she'd started to strap it on. That had stopped her. With a sigh, she'd restowed the piece. They were playing by her plan, but Sam knew battle tactics and she'd be stupid to ignore his experience.

Aboard the ship, Harold handed his food bag to the cook who clutched it to his chest simply for something to hold on to. Then he also raised his arms and did a slow turn before the one-eyed gaze of Franco's M45 pistol.

"Manuel! Jason!" Franco shouted out. When there was no response, he called again, louder.

The sound of one pair of running feet accompanied the man rushing toward them from the bow. Manuel Nagalo arrived with his rifle at his shoulder and quickly aimed it to cover both of them. He halted, as Sam's Marines said he would, ten meters back and crouched partly behind the raised cargo hatch.

Step One of the plan had worked, they were gathering around her. Only twenty or so steps to go.

106

FBI Agent Marcus Reynolds hung on as Paul Stark slalomed the Customs boat across the bay. Though the man knew nothing about guns, he was expert in a speedboat. Might have his own personal America's Cup boat too, Marcus thought in disgust.

The *Chong Chon Gang* started to take shape out of the darkness.

He and Leona had disarmed the two *garda*, but at Paul's insistence had left their hands free and let them keep the bottle. The crossing to the ship was under ten minutes, but they were already well on their way to drunk.

After checking that the tiny cabin had no hidden arms cache, he escorted the *garda* and their bottle inside and locked the door. Under the face of Leona's weapon and stern gaze, they moved without hesitation.

Damn but the woman was magnificent. In the night, out on the water, only the faintest wash of shore lights graced her dark skin and revealed her eyes which saw everything.

Once the *garda* were locked up, she moved up to him.

"You better come out of this alive, Marcus, or I'm gonna kick your goddamn butt so hard." Then she laid a kiss on him.

He'd been unaware of her holding his hand during the briefing on the plane. There'd been a deep humiliation churning in his gut that he'd had nothing to bring to the rescue plan. The Bureau had always made perfect sense to him. National security against internal threats. But now, for the first time, he had become aware of a wider world and found the Bureau wanting. Badly. So badly he'd felt betrayed.

The man he'd been this morning before his meeting with the legal attachés of the OIO had been so naïve.

Marcus had thought Leona was merely comforting him by holding his hand.

Now, her kiss was proving that he was more clueless than he'd thought. She filled his arms as he'd always imagined she would; her curves fitting against him in all the right ways. Just like the woman, her kiss had the power of a hard right cross delivered by a velvet fist.

Come back alive? Hell, for more of this, he'd come back from the dead.

<h1 style="text-align:center">107</h1>

"WHAT NOW? DID YOUR COOK INVITE THE ENTIRE CITY OVER FOR dinner?"

Kate looked down at the rust-brown deck to hide her smile.

Franco glared over the side toward the roaring engines. But his actions belied his casual manner. He yelled out Jason's name again, then ducked close against the solid side rail of the ship. He flipped the safety off his weapon and held it at the ready.

Step Two, the distraction, had now arrived.

Looking downward also saved her eyes as Paul snapped on the big floodlight mounted on top of his approaching Customs boat. That also provided a degree of invisibility to the two FBI agents with him in case they needed to provide covering fire.

"Damn it!" Franco Lamar cursed as he threw up an arm to block the glare.

She and Harold remained immobile in order to not draw attention. The well-dressed Korean also rushed to the rail to see what was happening, but didn't have the most basic survival instincts that kept Franco low and behind the ship's protecting metal. Desk jockey, perhaps a powerful one, but not a man of action.

The captain glanced over the rail without rising from his seat, then glanced at her before speaking, with Harold offering a quick translation. "I believe that is a Customs Inspection boat of the Panamanian government."

His calm, which had initially been worrisome, now felt less so. If she didn't know better, she'd think they were on the same side.

Manuel shifted his position from behind the hatch cover to ducking behind against his own section of the rail. He peered over the edge but kept his weapon facing Kate and Harold.

The important thing was that his position was now exposed toward Kate and Harold.

Kate listened, but she couldn't hear any sound other than the roar of the fast-approaching boat.

Step Two complete; except where the hell was Jason Mann?

108

Using the GPS locator on his wrist, Sam knew he was perfectly on target. This afternoon in the tour helicopter he'd marked the exact location of the ship's hatch. She hadn't moved since.

He let himself freefall until he was through the cloud cover. After he broke through at eleven hundred feet and could see exactly where the ship lay, he waited another six hundred feet before opening his parachute.

The black rectangular ram-air chute snapped open with a crack, but no one on the deck reacted, though he was close enough to see them clearly.

As planned, the full-throttle roar of the Customs boat's engines masked any noise he might make.

Through his night-vision gear he could see the body heat of the man once again perched in the hide atop the Monkey Island—the highest deck, immediately above the bridge. His team's manpower was so thin, they had decided to trust the captain's man and focus on the deck.

Sam guided the chute down to land on the ten-meter-square hatch cover immediately behind where everyone faced toward the racing Customs boat.

He didn't bother unslinging his rifle. He dumped the chute, slipped up behind Manuel, and dropped him with a sharp chop to the neck before he could move. Sam stripped him of weapons as he collapsed to the deck.

Franco turned and raised his sidearm.

Mick had landed right behind Sam, but it was Rio who had the honor of taking out Franco. At the last instant, he bellied his chute to gain a few more meters of flight—and planted both feet firmly into Franco's back.

Franco slammed into the rail, his pistol sailing out of his hand and into the ocean below. He flopped back onto the deck like a beached fish, the air driven from his lungs by the unexpected impact. In moments, Mick had hopped down from where he'd landed on the hatch and was standing over Franco with his M4 carbine aimed point-blank at the man's face.

Rio floated over the rail, released his chute, and fell the last ten feet into the water. By the time he surfaced, Paul was pulling up alongside him in the Customs boat and the FBI agents hauled him aboard.

Moments later they were gathered on the ship's deck, Franco and Manuel sitting cross-legged on the deck with their hands behind their backs, secured with zip ties.

He signaled Mick and Rio to strip search them before he turned to Kate.

She had the three Koreans lined up along the hatch, with the FBI agents behind her providing the firepower to convince them that moving would be a bad idea.

Step Three, the takedown, complete.

Except where the hell was Jason?

109

———

Sergeant Jason Mann Marine Force Recon (retired)—it still pissed him the hell off that his retirement had been neither voluntary nor honorable—lay on the Monkey Island and looked at the entire main deck of the *Chong Chon Gang* spread out below him. The captain's loyal right-hand man lay ten feet back and was starting to irritate Jason with his groaning.

"Shut up, P'yo, you useless bag of shit." Even if he didn't understand the words, the man didn't miss the tone despite how his head must be ringing. His groans became quieter.

He'd had a Zastava M76 sniper rifle, pretty sweet for a Communist punk. Jason wouldn't try for anything past a half kilometer with it, but from here to the main deck was under thirty meters and he could hit that with his back turned if he had a pretty aide to hold the mirror for him.

He amused himself by sighting through the scope. The Stark woman. Cast-iron bitch with breasts. She didn't know when to go down. But doing it like this would be too easy—and much less fun than what he had in mind.

He could trim her boyfriend; there'd be a real boo-hoo for absolutely nobody. Like the newsies who hadn't cared about the Marianne Rimaldi broad enough to learn her name. Zania the screen hooker hadn't been his to leave behind. Damn that klutz Vince for screwing that up; she'd have made for good sport, if she'd survived the overdose. Just as well Vince was dead.

Franco. Jason smiled to himself. Now that was a seriously tempting target. Mister Prep School and college degree was far too sure of himself.

Sam Fierro.

Jason flipped off the safety and zeroed on the top of Sam's head but stopped before fingering the trigger. There was no fun in shooting him dead if Jason couldn't look him in the eyes first.

Manuel. Sitting there cross-legged on the deck, trussed like a pig for the slaughter. Bastard had no balls; he'd collapsed after a single blow.

Now here was a way to wake up this whole boring party.

Jason was going to enjoy this.

Manuel? Not so much.

110

Kate watched as Sam and his Marines faded into the shadows. The FBI were now guarding Franco, Manuel, and the Koreans. A stern look ascertained that Paul and Harold would stay safely out of her way.

Kate turned to face the Koreans and decided to address the captain. Perhaps by working together they could solve this without any more bloodshed.

"Captain, there are two more people we are missing here." Harold sat close enough to translate.

"The woman is safe," the captain clearly knew what was important. "The man—"

Manuel, who'd been sitting quietly on the deck, looked at his own lap—and screamed!

The rolling crack of a gunshot echoed across the ship.

The captain looked at the highest level of the crew residence tower aghast. Something had gone wrong with his plan.

That was Kate's last thought before Sam crashed into her and drove her along the deck until her back slammed flat against the hard steel of the residence tower.

In moments, the FBI had herded Harold and Paul beside her.

The Koreans, left on their own, rushed off in the other direction.

Kate saw the captain hesitate then duck low and double back to arrive breathlessly beside her and flatten himself against the steel plate.

"Not my man," he managed in broken Spanish, worse than her own. She nodded her understanding. Whatever he'd been planning, he felt it was important for her to know that he wasn't attacking her people. That was good to know and, because he'd doubled back under a sniper's range of fire, she believed him.

Franco was yelling for someone, anyone to cut him loose.

Beside him Manuel was curled up on his side and screaming. By the amount of blood, he was already a dead man —the shot had cut an artery. By the pattern... An angle of fire from high above, he'd had his balls shot off.

Mick and Rio were at opposite corners of the cover hatch. They were hunkered low and had both of their weapons aimed high into the structure. But the deck lights were against them. The shooter would be in shadow; they were in bright light.

They shot out the lights, plunging this section of deck into darkness.

Sam rushed into the door leading up into the residence complex.

Kate had been staring straight up the face of the structure and saw a muzzle flash atop the tower.

Mick ducked for cover; Rio fired back at the muzzle flash.

Kate knew that a hit would be pure luck. She turned to the captain, "Where is Rikka? The one you took."

He scanned left then right. Then he grabbed Kate's arm and led her along the front of the living quarters. They entered a doorway and began climbing metal stairs that switchbacked their way upward.

On the fourth level, the one below the bridge, he slipped through a doorway guarded by a heavy hatch that looked as if it hadn't been closed since the day the ship was built.

Along the corridor.

The captain slowed.

111

Rikka stayed crouched in the hidey hole in the captain's office. Air was getting in, but not much. It was hot, stuffy, and there was only so long she could remain alert by panic as hour after boring hour dragged by.

She'd tried to keep herself awake by reciting food poetry she'd memorized. But a Basho poem was only so long:

Coolness of the melons
flecked with mud
in the morning dew.

Maybe she'd learn Robert Frost next time or a couple of Shakespeare plays.

Rikka hadn't meant to curl up in the corner, it had just happened. And closing her eyes hadn't changed the quality of the dark.

She snapped awake to the rattle she'd come to recognize, the captain's key unlocking the hidden panel.

Groping around in the darkness, her fingers located the interior deadbolt. It was only as she drew it back that she registered she hadn't heard the captain's voice.

Maybe she'd slept through it.

The door was jerked aside, the bright light of the office blinding her. A powerful hand grabbed her around the throat and dragged her out into the open.

She struggled, but it was pointless.

The hand around her throat felt massive, powerful, omnipotent. Her battling? No more than a fly to so strong a man. All her struggles achieved were choking herself worse.

As her eyes adapted, she saw who had her.

Oh God, she was in so much trouble.

112

———————

"Jason!" The captain had pushed open the third door on the left, Kate followed a step behind.

At his exclamation, Kate dragged him back against her.

A shot rang out and a round thudded into the wall directly opposite the door, punching the steel hard enough to leave a deep dent with the bullet embedded in the well of it.

"Let me guess," Jason's voice called from within the room. "Captain Rang and Katie Stark. You have three seconds to show yourselves or I snap Albert's neck. One! Two!—"

Kate cursed Sam roundly that she didn't have a backup weapon of any sort and stepped into the doorway.

The captain's office. Desk right, three chairs middle, a sofa to the left. Several file cabinets, none positioned to offer a safe harbor. A few tattered posters of exotic locales.

On the floor lay a semi-conscious Korean bleeding from a broken nose and a knife cut along his chin, but he breathed. Kate recognized him as the captain's officer, P'yo.

In front of an open section of wall stood Jason Mann. Directly in front of him he held Rikka pinned against his chest.

Jason kept ducked low behind her with a hand clamped around her throat.

The captain earned her respect by stepping in beside her.

Kate felt the air shift behind her and saw Jason's slow smile build.

A cold shiver ran down the base of her spine that she couldn't quite suppress.

A shiver as cold as steel.

113

Manuel had bled out by the time they figured out that the shooter had moved.

Leona checked for a pulse, none. The bullet that neutered him had ricocheted off the deck steel and cut his femoral artery. He'd been shot twice by the same bullet, once from in front and once from behind. By one of his own team. Real nice.

"Gotta be more careful choosing your buddies next time," she told the corpse.

Franco Lamar was shouting as if the world was coming to an end. She traded a look with Marcus.

At his nod, she clipped *Slammer* Lamar hard enough on the chin with the butt of her MP5 machine pistol for the man to collapse in a heap. She lay him down and zip tied his ankles to a handy stanchion. Not going anywhere. There was at least kidnapping against him, times three for Kate, Harold, and Rikka, and a couple murders. She'd wager that any digging would turn up much worse.

The two Marines were gone.

"They followed Sam," Marcus pointed over his shoulder at the five-story crew quarters structure that spanned the width of

347

the ship and comprised fifty or more rooms. Any number of those could have cowering, trigger-happy North Koreans in them.

Oh joy.

Marcus looked no happier about the scenario.

Harold and Paul crouched side-by-side in the safety of a shadowed doorway.

"Stay there."

"Couldn't pay us to move," Paul reassured her.

A man came toward them, slipping from one shadow to the next. The well-dressed Korean. It took experimenting to discover that Paul's fluent Japanese and the man's grade school command of the language were the only overlap in their whole group. He didn't look happy.

"You help me. I help you."

"Help?" What did he need their help with?

"Assassinate Jason. He very bad. Much trouble. I pay much American money."

"How much?" Leona wasn't interested but she needed to buy time to figure out his game. Covering the main deck and protecting the civilians was plenty at the moment.

"As much as want," the man promised. "One million. Two. No matter. Good quality."

Great. Now they were in the middle of a North Korean counterfeiting scam?

Oh wait. More of the pieces were connecting up. Kate Stark busting the counterfeit distribution ring. And Marcus had told her that Ms. Albert had been at the heart of that bust.

Great.

What else was going on that they didn't know?

114

"HELLO, SAM." JASON'S VOICE SOUNDED AT FULL SNEER.

Sam moved Kate and the captain aside. P'yo lay crumpled against a side wall.

He wished he could shoo everyone out of the room, but he recognized Jason's grip around Erika's throat. Thumb pressure from behind combined with a quick jerk to the side and her neck would snap. He couldn't do anything that might aggravate the man.

"Long time no see, bro. Lose it. All of it."

He could feel Kate look at him but couldn't let himself look away from the terror in Erika's eyes. It felt as if he was the single thing holding her together.

Her terror eased visibly as she focused on him. Jason's hold around her throat was too tight for her to nod, but he knew she'd be ready. Damn but that was his kind of woman.

As he'd stepped in behind Kate, he'd slipped his suppressed M45 backup piece into the rear waistband of her trousers. He hoped to hell she wouldn't do anything too rash with it.

Stepping to the desk, he set aside his M40A5 sniper rifle. Then reached for his M45A1 pistol.

Jason didn't stop him, so he continued until he was stripped of weapons, shoes, and only his boxer shorts remained. He shifted a step to the side after dumping all his clothes on the desk in order to mostly block Kate from Jason's sightlines. Rang Jin-ho stood two paces behind her—full credit for not running while he had the chance.

When he stood there barefoot, Jason rolled his eyes.

"I meant everything, Sam. Let me show you."

Without shifting his pistol from covering them, Jason slid a hand from Erika's throat and around her front.

In a single motion, he slid his hand up inside her shirt, grabbed her bra, and yanked down hard.

With a snapping of straps and a cry of surprise, Erika's bra came free. The momentum caused her to double over forward.

Jason wore body armor.

The distinct, loud double report of an M45 reverberated in the captain's cabin.

Two .45 cal rounds caught Jason Mann in the face.

The subsonic hollow-point Federal rounds that Sam kept in his backup piece snapped Jason's head back then expanded to splatter his brains into the open smuggler's space behind him.

The result was nearly bloodless in the captain's office as Jason toppled backwards through the opening, and left Erika unmoving, unaware that she was safe as her lacy spring green bra fluttered to the deck by Jason's feet.

Sam looked over his shoulder at Kate. Having stepped enough to the side to not deafen him, she now held the weapon in two hands, pointed toward the ceiling, her finger alongside the trigger.

"What? You didn't think I was going to let you two go at it *mano-a-mano,* did you?"

That wouldn't be Jason's style; he'd proven his cowardice on Manuel.

But, exactly as he'd counted on, this was definitely Kate's.

115

It wasn't until Kate had booked them into a suite at the Hotel Meliá overlooking Gatun Lake that Rikka felt her brain slowly re-engage. Kate had declared that they needed to stop and that the Stark jet would take them home to New York in the morning.

Rikka had been moving through a murky and shadowed world that nothing in her life had prepared her for. The terror of her own possible death had been nothing as horrid as seeing Sam standing nearly naked and unarmed, knowing Jason would shoot him in the next few seconds, and being helpless to stop it.

He'd put his life on the line for her.

Scrubbing herself over and over in the shower, she'd tried to cleanse every place that Jason had touched her. Her throat and where he'd dug at her breasts were raw with it, but she still felt unclean.

Kate hovered, apologizing repeatedly for getting her involved. Paul's sad-puppy-dog look at everything that had happened made her not despise him—almost. Though she could see him slowly rebuilding his devil-may-care self. She'd bet he'd be out hustling sexy heiresses within the week. Perhaps within the day. That image was enough to make her smile.

Then she remembered.

"Kate," her voice was rough. It was the first word she'd spoken other than, "I'm fine," since the ship. "I don't understand, in the captain's office after you shot Jason, what was that message you had me interpret to Captain Rang Jin-ho?"

116

"WE ARE DEAD," PARK COULD SEE NO WAY TO SALVAGE THE situation. His plan had failed. He'd spent millions, inauthentic, but still millions to make this work. He stood at the bow of the *Chong Chon Gang* and wondered if this was the last sunrise he would ever see.

They'd had the Stark woman twice aboard this ship and been unable to retain her either time. He now understood what Rang had meant about her, he'd been lucky to escape alive. But the Council would not be so understanding; he had made many promises to them.

"We are dead, Rang. There is nothing I can do to stop it." They were still anchored in Bahia Limón; the entrance of the Panama Canal lay a few miles straight ahead. Rang's crew had quietly disposed of Jason and Manuel's bodies. At the present, they were busy cleaning Rang's office.

The FBI had taken away the moaning Franco Lamar. Park would kill the man if he could. He'd been useless, lying on the deck pleading like a woman.

Ah, he sighed. No more Mi-sook. No more Su-jin. What a pity, but they were certainly forfeit. He couldn't even save himself anymore. If he were to try and defect to the Panamanians, they would turn him over to the Americans. The remaining Council of Five members would never allow him to live long enough to talk.

"Park-ssi," Rang addressed him quietly from where he stood a respectful step behind. "I may have a way to resolve this matter, but I must go ashore. I will take P'yo to a doctor as an excuse. He will reset P'yo's broken nose and stitch his cut chin."

"There is a chance?" He turned to face Rang, not daring to hope. "Do that and I will make sure that you are placed on the Council immediately."

Rang's face was hard to read; his smile perhaps too broad, but his words sounded steady. "You are most kind, Park-ssi. I would be most honored to serve the Office in any way I can."

Obsequious man. But if he could salvage this situation, he might indeed belong on the Council, for his loyalty was unquestioned and his modest underhanded work on behalf of the Office had proven to be a most effective asset time and again over the years.

"Go," Park told him. "Do what you can. How may I help? Should I accompany you ashore?"

"You are most kind, Park-ssi. Yes, you can help, but here. From the safety of the ship."

117

———

There was a knock on the suite door one hour after their arrival at the hotel.

It had taken more time than Kate had anticipated to depart the ship, return the Customs boat and its two inebriated officers, and tidying up other minor matters.

They'd eaten breakfast, but no one had slept.

Kate had forewarned everyone that she expected visitor.

At the knock, Mick and Rio slid out of sight into one of the bedrooms in case it turned out to be a trap. They had Paul and Harold with them for protection.

Marcus and Leona lounged in the living room area, their weapons at the ready but hidden from view by the generous cushions. They had returned from delivering Franco Lamar to the OIO's legal attachés for extradition to the US, Marcus grumbling something about *finally finding a use for those people.*

Kate kept Sam and Rikka close. He stood out of sight behind the hotel suite's front door, weapon drawn. Rikka remained invisible on the far side of Sam's broad frame.

When she opened the door, the Korean captain stood in the hallway of the hotel. He had dressed simply but well, in white

355

shirt, slacks, and loafers. Sunglasses were perched up on his short, gray-speckled hair. He looked like nothing more than a Korean on holiday.

He said something brief in Korean that didn't sound threatening. His hands were empty, there was no weapon at his side, and he appeared to be alone.

"He says hello," Rikka interpreted to Kate from where she stood behind Sam.

Kate took a deep breath to make sure she was calm before leaning out to check the hallway. No one to either side of the door, the man was indeed alone. She held the door wide for him to enter.

"Please tell him," she addressed Rikka, "thank you for accepting my invitation."

As soon as she closed the door, Sam frisked him, unearthing only a wallet and a hotel key card. The captain submitted to it patiently without looking away from her or showing any slackening of his self-satisfied smile; the same she'd seen him use aboard his ship only a few hours ago.

Sam held up the room key in question.

"As you advised, Ms. Stark, I used the excuse of transporting my first officer to a doctor. He is presently asleep in a room on the first floor. It is not as extravagant as this penthouse suite, but it is comfortable. You have exceptional taste in hotels, madam, which does not surprise me in the slightest."

Rikka interpreted simultaneously as he spoke. It was hard to focus on two voices and two sets of facial expressions, one slightly delayed from the other. It was like watching a magic act and never knowing quite where to look to see the trick. For the moment, Kate would simply be thankful for Rikka and watch Captain Rang Jin-ho carefully.

Sam opened the suite door, checked the hall, then tried Rang's card three separate times in the door lock.

Kate could see that the card failed, and the lock remained red after each try. So, it seemed unlikely that a team of North Koreans would be coming quietly through the door anytime they felt like it.

Sam returned the wallet and the key card, which the captain tucked away.

She led them out onto the suite's balcony and indicated that he should sit with her at the small table overlooking the view. Rikka sat to Kate's other side. Sam loomed protectively behind her.

The captain didn't show the least concern, not even when the others approached, heavily armed, and ranged themselves at the other table or behind him.

Far below the balcony were the hotel's three swimming pools—one with a pretty fountain. In the distance, shining beyond the dark green thickets of several varieties of palm and banana trees, Gatun Lake's surface shone beneath the mid-morning sun.

The morning's passage of ships had exited the locks and dotted the Canal's surface in a long southbound line.

118

———————

RANG KNEW HE HAD PLAYED THE GAME WELL. FOR ONE, HE WAS still alive. For another, his gamble on the woman's victory had paid off.

But the game was far from over and that worried him.

He used the moment she took to pour him a glass of iced tea to assess her team. They were strategically placed as if he was far more dangerous than he knew himself to be.

Most of them he could discount as long as he was no physical threat. Four were heavily armed, three men and one woman; they remained in the background. There was a man with clothes a size or so too small for his chest, the same one who had greeted his cook.

Ah, his anger showed that he was the other one in the container with the blue-eyed Kate Stark. Had he been a lucky man? Rang would have to answer that question with a yes.

However, while the man must have been aboard the helicopter, he had been hidden while Kate Stark and three others who had rescued them came back aboard his ship. So, despite his furious glare, he could be discounted as well.

That left the three of them who had come aboard his

358

command bridge from the helicopter with their leader. The interpreter, the muscle, and the man with eyes as strange as... his sister's. He had to be. Though he clearly had no military training, Rang could see a mind working behind those eyes.

Yes. That's what this was, a meeting of the minds. It would be he and the two Starks. Those were the ones he would watch.

He recalled Kate Stark's earlier message while they'd yet been aboard the *Chong Chon Gang*.

"We have a problem," she had said through the pretty interpreter. *"Are you interested in solving it?"*

He was. *"Unless we,"* he'd chosen the word so carefully, *"are brilliant, Park and I will be dead soon. He is the key, somehow."*

"Perhaps, we should speak ashore, away from other's ears."

Park had been constantly nosing around as the Americans prepared to depart on their stolen Customs boat. It had taken maneuvering for the two of them to find a moment alone with the interpreter.

"That will be difficult."

"Say that your officer needs a doctor."

"Not enough," Park would know they had a medic on board.

"Tell him..." she'd looked thoughtful, then smiled, *"you may have a solution to my escape."*

Ahh. This woman was a worthy adversary.

"I want to make sure we are left alone," she'd continued. *"You want to live through whatever will happen because you no longer have us in custody."*

"That will require making Park, ah, ineffectual." A game piece he *still* could not understand how to safely remove from the board, because it must be a permanent solution, and it must not be Rang's doing.

Her smile then, as she'd given him the name of this hotel and the suite number, had been as pleasantly enigmatic as it was now.

"Tell me if I am guessing correctly, Senior Captain Rang Jin-ho," she opened this morning's conversation showing far more respect for him than his own fellow-member of Office 39. She also arranged his name in the proper Korean order instead of the confusing way of the West who identified the person before their family as if the individual mattered so much more. "This Mr. Park is the man who wanted me and the others kidnapped?"

"Yes. Kidnapping you and the other chefs was solely his idea." To play this game well, he would have to show her most of his cards, hoping only that she didn't see the few he held back for himself. "A fact well known to the other members of our head council."

"So, your council will see this as a failure on both of your parts."

"A disgraceful failure, but perhaps survivable," Rang realized too late that he had closed a door.

"But if I do nothing, the chances are that you both will die. Then my people and I will be left alone?" She shrugged to indicate how little she cared about the costs of that possible outcome on his account. Rang appreciated the effect the motion had on other parts of her body. He was becoming used to the strangeness of her light skin and bright eyes. She was a truly attractive woman.

And a terrifying one.

He did not see the anger in Kate Stark's face, but he certainly heard it in the interpreter's words. Were it left to the Japanese, he could roast in Hell for many reincarnations for his part in the kidnappings.

If Kate Stark did nothing, then he truly was dead. Park would kill him if the Council did not.

He must think quickly.

"Unless..." he dragged it out hoping for inspiration. Ah! "Unless Park somehow convinces the Council to try again." *Ah, there is our salvation, Su-jin.*

"And why would they do that?"

He sipped his tea and let her people discuss this possibility for a moment or two before he continued.

"There is a secret that Park has told me. A dangerous secret, about you."

Her teammates, especially the armed ones, tensed.

Kate looked unworried. Formidable indeed.

"Park has said that you, Ms. Stark, were the one who destroyed our entire East Coast network by convincing the Tong's key programmer to change sides."

Kate Stark did not even blink—but the interpreter's reaction was dramatic. She stumbled and had to restart the interpretation. Twice.

Why, Su-jin? Why would the woman react to that simple fact...

"This missing programmer..." he hadn't meant to say it aloud, but the interpreter's reaction escalated as if... *"Jin-jja?"* His astonishment too great to contain.

"Yes, for real." The interpreter did her best to glare at him, but she was too gentle a soul to make it work.

He'd held the missing programmer on his ship. In his own cabin. She was perhaps the most wanted individual anywhere in the world from the Council of Five's view.

When she caught up the translation for the others, his comment caused a galvanic reaction among the others. Kate Stark's muscle man, who had stood unspeaking behind the interpreter, had pulled a massive weapon that centered on Rang's face from far too close.

He heard safeties snapped off on weapons behind him and to either side. Kate Stark's hand shifted below the edge of the table but made no other motion. He did not doubt that she had a weapon of her own close to hand.

Smile in the face of adversity.

He would. He simply wished it was as easy as Su-jin always made it sound. It wasn't.

"I...find that..." Rang struggled to find the words, finally managing, "...fascinating."

The weapons did not waver.

He tried another tack. "What you will want, my dear Ms. Stark, is to have a friend on the Council of Five. I am that friend, for I have no use for Comrade Park or his plans. I think his secrets are best forgotten."

"But you are not on that Council."

Yes, Su-jin would like her directness very much. At the moment, he did not appreciate it himself.

"Not yet. However, it is I who must sit in Park's chair to guarantee your safety. And for that to happen, Park must..." He shrugged his indifference despite that being the one key he could not understand how to turn. Park could not die at Rang's hands, nor would death be enough. Disgrace was required to neutralize that threat.

Rang decided it was time to keep his peace and hope that this woman would help him find the solution. One that would allow him to step from the grave to the Council in a single move.

The big man's weapon had not wavered by the thickness of a single supernote.

119

PAUL STARK PACED ALONG THE BALCONY RAILING BUT WAS HARDLY aware of the bird's-eye view of the swimming pools below. That's where his attention would normally be, upon those bikini-clad bodies at one of the finest resorts in this tropical country. Staying here meant money. Being at the poolside meant great gobs of beautiful money and trophy wives.

But here, now, in this suite—this was Paul's kind of game. He could always feel it when it came along. Always. When that happened, he always went for the ride, enjoying whatever and whoever crossed his path.

There'd be this buzz.

This quiet hum that he felt clear to his toes. When that happened, he dropped into the groove and the game was on. That's when anything was possible.

They'd sat here for over an hour after the flare-up over Rikka's identity—she had a past that was too cool for words— listening to Captain Rang talking about Office 39.

Or rather *not* talking about it.

Kate had kept directing the man toward operations,

363

apparently not catching the way the man pulled back each time she did.

But when Paul had grown bored with the smuggling and counterfeiting crap, he'd thrown out a question about the other Council members.

That's when the captain had opened up.

The commanding Council of Five of the illicit Office 39. Damn, if it weren't for these guys, the whole country would have folded. North Korea was backed into a hard corner. That it was of their own making didn't make the corner any less tight.

Without Office 39 bringing in its five billion or so a year, North Korea's thirty billion a year gross national product wouldn't keep the country afloat. And if they couldn't make money...they'd make war. Then, boom, the most over-equipped and underpaid army in history would explode.

So, they needed to keep the Council intact. And this Rang seemed like a reasonable guy, if Paul discounted his working for the evil empire and kidnapping his sister, Rikka, and Harold along the way.

"Your ship?" Paul didn't know quite where that had come from, but he'd long since learned to trust his instincts in situations like this.

"My ship?" Rang blinked at Rikka's interpretation and then up at Paul.

"It has a certain...reputation with the officers of Panama's Customs department."

"It does," he acknowledged.

"A reputation," Paul remembered the story from the helicopter pilot yesterday, "of smuggling UN-sanctioned military supplies through the Canal. Your boat was fined a million dollars and was impounded for six months the last time it tried to pass through the Canal."

"The fine was reduced to two-thirds of a million."

"Provided the captain and his officers were arrested and

would face the Panamanian courts. Didn't he try to kill himself?"

"I wish he had succeeded. The fool," Rang sounded deeply offended. "We told him not to go through the Canal. He lost several missiles, two Mig-21 airframes, and many engines that were...ah...to be repaired by North Koreas technicians."

"That had been bought in Cuba to refurbish your older jets," Paul countered. It was a guess, but the man's uneasy shrug said it was an accurate one.

"And how many containers are aboard your ship right now with illicit content?"

The captain started to answer, but Paul cut him off to keep up the pressure.

"Nine of them, now eight. The ones off the trucks including the one that was switched."

Rang did not cover his surprise in time. Paul knew he had him on the run and kept pushing.

"How many of the eight have contents so secret that you, the captain, weren't told what they contained?"

That rocked him back on his heels. More than just on the run. Several of those containers worried him a great deal.

Paul stood close beside him, nearly blocking Kate, way inside the guy's personal space. "You say you didn't know Kate and Harold were in that one container. What about those others?"

The captain kept his mouth shut and looked unhappy.

"An inspection would not be a good thing, would it?"

"The local Customs officials' attitude toward my boat did not improve last night when the Customs boat you stole was reported visiting my ship." Rang sounded both worried and deeply irritated at the moment. His earlier careful complacency had evaporated. Angry-worried men made mistakes.

Kate watched the both of them carefully, but staying out of his way. *One more minute, sis. I'm close.*

Paul turned as if to attack, and Captain Rang Jin-ho of Office 39's *Chong Chon Gang* braced for it.

So, Paul did the opposite, and made his voice utterly calm as if he were asking an idle question. He casually rested a hand on the man's shoulder.

"Whoever captains your ship through the Canal will be in a whole world of hurt, won't they?"

"We wouldn't do that. With our cargo, we must go around the Cape Horn."

He didn't see it. Paul only did just now.

"But if you *did?*"

"Then I would most certainly be arrested. And my senior officers. Why would I want to do that?"

Paul smiled at Kate.

She understood, of course. The last question had been more than enough for her to read what he was thinking. His twin was an uptight and A.J. Squared Away-Roger Ramjet— and sometimes a touch slow when being sneaky was called for. But she was also the best sister a guy could ask for.

He'd give her credit for being the one to get them off that ship alive and to set up this meeting so neat and slick.

But he was the one who brought the hammer to the endgame that no one else brought.

He considered taking the chair next to Rikka, but Sam's looming-right-behind-her thing looked damn formidable.

Instead, he circled around to the other open chair that was between Rang and Harold. Harold looked stunned-puppy lost. Right where Paul wanted him.

Paul sat and turned his back on Harold to give the captain the final key to the puzzle.

120

After they had finished working out the details and a few discreet messages had been sent, Rang sat back and considered the beautiful day.

For the balcony of the Meliá hotel afforded a truly splendid view.

"A pity that you chose this hotel," Rang sipped his iced tea and admired the vista of the American woman and the Japanese, side-by-side. Not on the command bridge under the cover of Panamanian customs' rifles; instead sitting at their ease in luxury beneath the soft morning sunlight of the tropics.

"Why a pity?"

Rang liked the way the two women's voices mixed and overlapped as one spoke and the other interpreted.

"Had you chosen..." he sipped the tea, fine quality. There were many things to appreciate in the West. "...to stay at the Washington Hotel in the heart of Colon city, we might have had an interesting sight at this moment."

Kate Stark offered him her silence, so that he might relish the moment. A woman who understood the importance of silence. It was a skill Su-jin had taught him, though he'd found it hard to learn. His wife would approve of this woman.

Yes, Su-jin, I have been wise to trust in this woman's skill.

She was so like his Su-jin. It was a pity he could not have Kate Stark *and* Su-jin at his side. If he had them both, Supreme Leader Kim Jong-un would not sit so comfortably in his chair.

Comrade most-high Park-ssi would be ordering the weighing of the anchor even now. The short passage to the Customs dock for the pre-Canal crossing inspection would be the last freedom the man would ever know.

Park did not know the sea and wouldn't know the insanity of such an act.

Rang had *suggested* that Park use two of his officers in particular—the two who had run away when the giant Marine Corps helicopter had hovered over his bridge wing.

Rang had also called the chef, Bok, and had him warn everyone else to stay away from the bridge and to not open their mouths.

It was going to be a complete and perfect disaster.

The eight containers would be bad enough with the Tesla roadster, the disassembled American attack helicopter, and RPGs which only accounted for five of the eight. He'd been unable to discover the contents of the other three, which did not bode well for Park at all.

What had Park hidden away on his ship without telling Rang so that he could be prepared?

It did not matter; Park would pay the price.

"What precisely did you tell Park when you telephoned him?" the interpreter asked on her own.

Kate and her slippery brother would of course already know or guess well enough to not matter.

"If your Comrade Park," the brother had said, *"were to be convinced to go through the Canal himself, what might happen to him?"*

"I told him that I had paid the bribe to the Panama officials so that our ship might pass, which, I will of course deny saying when asked later. I also told him that P'yo and I must stay ashore, for I would deliver Kate Stark at the Balboa docks on the Pacific Ocean end of the Canal."

She thought considered that a while then asked innocently, "But you aren't going to do that?" But it wasn't innocent. Her smile said how greatly she enjoyed the joke. A smart woman who had been careful while aboard his ship. Yes, much like a young...he was going to say a young Su-jin, but that was wrong. She was like a young Kate Stark.

"No, my dear girl, I am not," he assured her of her safety anyway.

Safety such as the unlamented Park would never find.

And when the ever-so honored Comrade Park-ssi attempted to accuse Senior Captain Rang Jin-ho of complicity, he would deny it easily.

"Oh no," he would tell Panama's Customs officials. "You saw the seals on those containers. Only the most honorable Park-ssi could know what was in them. See, the manifests he gave to me. They say *Farm Supplies!* I do not know why he would lie to a ship's captain unless he was doing something illegal for fear I would try to stop him. That must be why he sent me ashore to take care of my injured first officer."

"No," he would tell the remaining four members of the Council of Five. "I ordered the idiot Park in front of witnesses, my esteemed first officer P'yo and the ship's cook, Bok, not to take the ship into the Canal while I rushed P'yo to a hospital for the grievous injuries he sustained at the hands of the stupid thugs Park the Incompetent had hired."

The Council would make sure that Park didn't survive prison for he had too much knowledge that the Americans would be desperate to possess. If his two incompetent junior officers were taken by the Panamanian law as well, Rang would not be one to complain.

He would leave it to Su-jin if they should save Mi-sook, Park's soon-to-be widow. She was no Su-jin, but she had potential to be useful.

Quite useful.

Mi-sook was young and an especially pretty thing who had caught the eye of more than one other Council member. Now that he had considered the matter, he knew that Su-jin would already have a plan in place for her.

Ah, my wife, you are so wise. Together they would train her, and she would flourish greatly.

Rang Jin-ho had many productive ideas for the Council, none of which would require the kidnapping of Kate Stark. Righting old wrongs was counter-productive, especially when the future held so many interesting possibilities.

For now, Rang would join the Council and P'yo would have his ship. But soon? Perhaps the avaricious Kim Jong-un did not sit so comfortably upon his Supreme Leader's dais. Ah, that he would leave in Su-jin's oh-so-capable hands for another day.

Yes, Rang slipped his hands into his pockets and enjoyed the view. Women who wore deep red silk and spring green lace undergarments that felt so fine in his fingers were meant to be left free to be admired.

As a seaman, he enjoyed the irony of red in his right pocket and the tiny scraps of green lacework, which he'd found on his office floor, in the left. Such were the colors of the marker lights of a running ship.

Yes, fine to contemplate, but these two women were far too dangerous to own.

A lesson Park the Traitor was learning at this very moment.

121

Sam stood in his butchering kitchen. Nadya, who ran the front of his shop, had replaced the ruined doors and windows while he was gone. The city had replaced the melted dumpster. Everything was back to normal.

Vince Tarello had sung like a canary about a variety of jobs.

In addition, Erika had anonymously hacked around and found Franco's files. Two congressmen, a US Senate leader, several building contractors, a New Jersey toxic waste handler...

Agents Marcus and Leona had agreed to never reveal her secrets. Besides, they were far too busy heading up a whole task force crushing the multitude of former employers of Franco Lamar one by one like the line of pestilential ants that they were. Even with the FBI's protection, it was unlikely Franco would live much past the many trials to come.

Kate had made one other thing beyond Rikka's safety completely clear in her deal with the FBI. They could go easy on Vince if they wanted to, but there would be no deals with Franco. He was going down and going down hard.

Devlin would have liked that.

Sam closed his eyes and planted his fists on the work

bench. It was past ten p.m. No Devlin passing by to trip his alarm, to let Sam know he was coming. He would be buried next week at Arlington with full honors; they'd all be in attendance for that.

Master Sergeant Thomas Devlin had recruited a young Sam into the Corps and later into Force Recon. He'd served his country for thirty-five years in the field and suffered on her city streets for a dozen more. At least he had died in action, an echo of his former self showing through.

Damn but he missed the man.

The trip of the alarm when it came was a galvanic shock that left him unable to move.

The back door of his shop opened, a hesitation, the soft sound of a light footstep, and then it closed.

Only one person had that step, and he'd know it anywhere.

"You miss him, don't you?" Erika's voice wrapped around him like a soft breeze of fresh air.

He nodded. Not turning. Not wanting her to see the rawness of his pain.

"Kate told me what Mick and Rio did, donating her gift to them to charity."

They'd refused any payment for their time and risk. They'd done it for him and they'd done it for Devlin. Marine Recon took care of their own, except for twisted bastards like Franco and Jason. Those guys only took care of themselves, but didn't understand why it never lasted.

"They gave me an idea," Erika continued talking to his back. "While I was digging through Franco's files, I traced his US and offshore accounts. I think I cleared everything before the FBI confiscated any. Apparently, Franco Lamar has donated twenty-three million dollars to the Semper Fi Fund—in Devlin's name. It's too late to help Devlin, but maybe it will help others like him."

He turned slowly to face her.

Erika Albert leaned her back against the closed door, dressed in her standard tight jeans and form-hugging black turtleneck. Her hands were behind her, thumbs stuck in back pockets. This was the most motionless he'd ever seen her. She wasn't holding herself unmoving by sheer willpower. Instead, it was as if, for the first time since he'd met her, she'd finally come to rest.

She was so damn delicate and beautiful. She'd also proved herself to be strong when needed. Erika had stood up after her kidnapping and manhandling by Jason better than any civilian could ever be expected to.

He couldn't look away from those steady green eyes as she walked toward him.

She didn't stop until she was in his arms.

He bent down to bury his face in her hair and hold on for all he was worth.

122

———

Harold Merritt knew he should be getting back to Chicago. He had to, though his sous chef claimed to have the restaurant totally under control.

But he felt suspended in time. He knew the plane would be coming for Kate and him tomorrow to ferry them back to their separate cities. Knowing didn't mean he could make himself care.

The balcony of the Hotel Meliá suite overlooking Gatun Lake felt deliciously warm though the sun had already dropped beyond the lake, beyond the Pacific Ocean. He lay at ease on a generous lounger and enjoyed the rich scents on the air: ocean salt brushing across the jungle, gathering hints of ripe fruit and lush trees with its passage.

Kate made no sound upon returning to the balcony. He opened one eye and again appreciated the woman's long curves. The thin silk of the white hotel robe left little, yet precisely enough, to the imagination. Each step exposed an amazing length of tanned leg, each movement a hint of the nicest set of breasts he'd ever had the pleasure to enjoy.

She set the room service tray she carried upon the low table between their loungers and lay across from him.

"There's so much to admire about you," Harold could feel his voice was low and husky with desire.

"Such as?" her own voice a warm tease that had him raking his gaze over her length and feeling aroused anew.

But there were other scents now on the air. Fresh mango, the garlicky tang of beef empanadas, the lemony promise of a *ceviche* of local shrimp and corvina fish.

Over the last days, Kate had befriended the hotel's master chef. Sometimes they ate meals in his kitchen, sometimes he joined them in the suite to share a midnight bottle of wine at the end of his shift, but he always sent the finest local cuisine to their suite.

"Your most admirable traits..." Harold attempted to refocus his thoughts. "For one, your ability to order a truly amazing meal."

"You said 'traits.' That's plural."

"Your smile while your brother was facing down the Korean captain."

"What about it?" Kate lay back looking completely content.

"How long *before* your brother had the solution did you come up with it?"

She didn't answer but did look over at him.

"Before you invited the captain to come visit," it was obvious once he thought it through. "Which was long enough to give your brother a personal win when his ego desperately needed one."

She turned back to admiring the sunset.

"Anything else while you're admiring things?" her languid, self-satisfied voice ramped up his nervous system to a rolling heat.

"That comes easily to mind?" he did his best to keep his

voice steady but knew he wasn't having much luck. "Not a thing at the moment." He couldn't breathe in the woman's presence.

"Hmm, let's see if I can jog your thinking." She rose to her feet like a goddess. With an easy shrug, the silk robe shimmered off her shoulders and puddled about her feet.

The sunset light embraced her in golds and reds.

Kate Stark moved to lay beside him on his lounger.

Dinner would have to wait.

He had other things to feast upon.

AFTERWORD

If you enjoyed Final Taste
please consider leaving a review.
They really help.

More Kate Stark coming soon.
Keep reading for an exciting excerpt from:
Kate Stark #2, Ice Burn

A list of characters and locations may be found at:
https://mlbuchman.com/people-places-planes#KS
And return afterward for a free bonus story
and a recipe from the book.

KATE STARK #2 (EXCERPT)

IF YOU ENJOYED THAT, YOU'LL LOVE…

ICE BURN (EXCERPT)

Maxwell Klugman enjoyed cooking competitions, or he had until he'd almost died in one. He'd never found out if he won, because his competitor's dessert had killed both her and one of the judges. Poisoned. Enough to put a chef off his food.

A week later Kate Stark, the head judge and owner of the entire Cooks Network television station, had called to tell him the criminals were caught and to invite him back. He'd rather give up his grandmother's sausage recipe than ever set foot inside one of their studios again. Hell, he now considered Rockefeller Center in midtown Manhattan to be a no-man zone; especially if that man was Max Klugman.

Been kind of Ms. Stark to ask and he'd told her so, but... shit man.

Death by chocolate ganache?

Nicht. Nein. And no goddamn way.

Then Kate Stark had called again, six weeks later. Not about a show she was judging—she'd be out of the country on another project—but there'd been a last-minute drop-out due to a broken leg and might he be interested?

One day.

Sugar sculpture.

He loved sculpting in sugar. Though he had no idea how she knew about that, he didn't care.

Competitions were a different kind of adrenaline rush from restaurant work—thank God. Keeping everything running smoothly night after night in a busy restaurant like his family's, well, it was both a challenge and a royal pain in the ass. Damn Pops to Hell for stroking out at fifty but not having the decency to die—instead hanging on like a dangling salami and shaming Max into taking over the business.

He'd been well down the road to making it as a sugar chef and now he was worrying about a hundred details he didn't give a rat's ass about. Crappy line cooks too drugged-out to show up. Compromising his own ideas about the menu to retain their loyal customers and not piss the fuckers off. *And* not becoming the Klugman who destroyed four generations of shining success and family tradition.

A sugar competition had cleanliness, purity, and it jolted the nervous system like cocaine had back when he was a younger and stupider chef.

A well-designed competition started as an adrenal high and then climbed from there—a single clear punch that left you wrung out and, hopefully, triumphant at the end.

Instant gratification.

Maxwell liked instant gratification...a lot! Nothing to do with old cocaine habits, of course.

At the highest level of sugar-work challenges, against the top competitors, the jolt climbed over a precipice he could never achieve otherwise—better than sex with his new girlfriend. It carried him into a state of simpatico with the sculpture's hard-crack architecture—a world of precise techniques, not wondering if the bloody lump on his cutting block was grass-fed beef or if the fucking merchant had slipped him corn-fed instead.

He made his living with German cuisine. The towering sculptures made of glass-clear sheets of pulled sugars, swirling cones of hardened ribbon sugar, and blown-sugar figurines—they were his joy. He ran the only German restaurant in New York with an old meat locker turned into a dedicated sugar kitchen, perhaps the only one in the world.

That Kate Stark had known that about him, and thought of him when it wasn't even her show with the scheduling issue, had told him how damned impressive the woman really was. Not his type at all. He preferred his girlfriends to be...no real way to be all politically correct about it, not quite so terrifyingly competent. Kate walked into a room and made everyone want to snap to attention or bow or some such shit.

The other reason he'd agreed to do it? No taste testing during a sculpture competition. When he'd caved to Stark's ever-so-perfectly couched pleading, he figured that no one could poison him, even if he did go back to the Cooks Network studio. He'd stay focused on the competition.

He'd be fine.

Now, three hours into the competition with less than ten minutes left, he wallowed deep in the sugar-high zone. He didn't need to look down at his design sketches, hadn't since the start of the competition because it radiated like shining crystal in his head. He ignored his competitors, the hot lights, the studio cameras and audience, and, most of all, the judges. Couldn't let those bastards into his head while he worked—though he couldn't keep his wheezing father out.

A slacker Klugman. Never thought I'd see the day, you overgrown fairy. That had almost earned the man his death for real.

Screw the old bastard; this morning was his. He'd feed the fucking restaurant patrons later. Right now his sous chef bore the burden.

A quick glance to either side proved that his current

masterpiece existed in a far different class than his two competitors. At six feet tall, two hundred pounds of melted and re-formed sugar, Elsa's castle from Disney's *Frozen* was a shoo-in for the win.

He had built towers, turrets, and battlements; he built and hung the central chandelier of spun-sugar tendrils.

The competitor to his left had chosen a similar scale, but a much simpler depiction. *WALL-E's* junk world was merely suggested—though her *pastillage* of WALL-E and EVE were damn near perfect. He wouldn't mind learning a thing or two about working soft sugars from her. Nice butt too, which he could also think of definite uses for. He'd remember that for when the current girlfriend no longer worked out.

To his right stood an elaborate and gorgeously colored sea anemone that included the weak-finned but undeniably cute Nemo and his worried looking dad, Marlin. Charming, but too small. Read as: *No victory for you, dude.*

He so had this one.

When Maxwell pulled the ball-peen hammer out of his toolkit with less than three minutes remaining on the clock, a surprised murmur rippled through the studio audience.

His ice castle looked complete.

And it was.

It only needed one final touch.

Time to kick serious sugar ass.

He kept his face carefully neutral as he waved a cameraman in for a close-up. When he had the lens in position to spy through the largest castle window, Max made the move he'd practiced a hundred times in private.

The other two competitors stopped to watch what in the hell he was doing despite the last moments of the competition clock ticking down. *Hang on to your silicone mats, you're gonna need 'em to shit on after you see this move. You two can pack it up and go home now!*

Reaching into the grand entrance hall through the towering double doors of his sugar castle, he lightly tapped the hammer in a circle around the edges of the main floor of inch-thick pressed sugar.

It was so retro to use pressed sugar, hardly any chef did anymore. It took an application of pressure and patience, waiting much longer than with other sugars for it to set. In a competition where every second was precious, it was considered a waste of time...by most. Pressed sugar was also cloudy and not a terribly aesthetic look at.

However...

He made sure the camera was in the right position, then he rapped the exact center of the sheet with his hammer.

Hard!

The judges gasped as the sugar shattered with an audible crack—normally a disastrous sound in a sugar sculpture.

A number of people in the studio audience cried out.

His petite girlfriend, who had watched him do this again and again, had her hands over her mouth; her pretty blonde hair covering half her face didn't hide the anticipation and excitement. Oh, it was gonna be good with her tonight. She always did something extra special after a competition and her imagination was amazing.

Maxwell withdrew the hammer. He picked up the tiny figurine of Elsa made of blown-sugar in pale blue, white, and blonde, and tacked her at the center of the crack with a bit of dampened paste. Then he stepped back and let the camera drink its fill.

The pressed sugar base had shattered. The center of the break burst outward from the struck center to terminate at each of the tiny dents he'd made around the edges.

With that final stroke, he had created a snowflake pattern in the sugar floor nearly identical to the one Elsa had created in the floor of her castle with a stomp of her heel—where the figurine's extended heel now rested, covering the shatter point left by the hammer. The pressed sugar's cloudiness looked exactly like ice and snow.

As people saw what he'd done on the studio monitors, they roared to their feet. The judges were standing and applauding. *Eat that, Pops!* The entire television studio went nuts. He could only hope the old bastard was watching.

Unknown to anyone in the studio, a ten-thousand-dollar Svantek SVAN 979 sound-and-vibration analyzer mounted beneath the sculpture's display table measured this unusually loud volume.

The applause and cheering peaked, sending vibrations through the structure of the metal table itself.

The levels exceeded the preset threshold and the Svantek emitted an electronic error signal.

Two tiny explosive charges interpreted the Svantek's error signal as a firing charge, and sheared off both legs of Maxwell Klugman's worktable on the side closest to him.

In slow motion, the legs buckled.

The table tilted.

Then collapsed.

Two hundred pounds of razor sharp towers, spires, and buttresses slowly tilted...then tumbled.

Elsa's ice palace of sugar crashed into Maxwell Klugman's body with a hammer blow of force that drove him to the floor and spiked him there.

His last thought ever was that he'd been burned down by a Disney movie.

Shit man.

———

Coming April 1, 2025
Ice Burn

ABOUT THE AUTHOR

USA Today and Amazon #1 Bestseller M. L. "Matt" Buchman started writing on a flight south from Japan to ride his bicycle across the Australian Outback. Just part of a solo around-the-world trip that ultimately launched his writing career.

From the very beginning, his powerful female heroines insisted on putting character first, *then* a great adventure. He's since written over 75 action-adventure thrillers and military romantic suspense novels. And more than 200 short stories, and a fast-growing pile of read-by-author audiobooks.

PW declares of his Miranda Chase action-adventure thrillers: "Tom Clancy fans open to a strong female lead will clamor for more." About his military romantic thrillers: "Like Robert Ludlum and Nora Roberts had a book baby."

His fans say: "I want more now...of everything!" That his characters are even more insistent than his fans is a hoot.

As a 30-year project manager with a geophysics degree who has designed and built houses, flown and jumped out of planes, and solo-sailed a 50' ketch, he is awed by what is possible. He and his wife presently live on the North Shore of Massachusetts. More at: www.mlbuchman.com.

Other works by M. L. Buchman: *(* - also in audio)*

Action-Adventure Thrillers

Kate Stark
Final Taste
Ice Burn
Knife's Edge

Miranda Chase
*Drone**
*Thunderbolt**
*Condor**
*Ghostrider**
*Raider**
*Chinook**
*Havoc**
*White Top**
*Start the Chase**
*Lightning**
*Skibird**
*Nightwatch**
*Osprey**
*Gryphon**
*Wedgetail**

Science Fiction / Fantasy

Deities Anonymous
Cookbook from Hell: Reheated
Saviors 101

Contemporary Romance

Eagle Cove
Return to Eagle Cove
Recipe for Eagle Cove
Longing for Eagle Cove
Keepsake for Eagle Cove

Love Abroad
Heart of the Cotswolds: England
Path of Love: Cinque Terre, Italy

Where Dreams
Where Dreams are Born
Where Dreams Reside
*Where Dreams Are of Christmas**
Where Dreams Unfold
Where Dreams Are Written
Where Dreams Continue

Non-Fiction

Strategies for Success
Managing Your Inner Artist/Writer
*Estate Planning for Authors**
Character Voice
*Narrate and Record Your Own Audiobook**
Beyond Prince Charming: One Guy's Guide to Writing Men in Romance

Short Story Series by M. L. Buchman:

Action-Adventure Thrillers

Kate Stark
Miranda Chase Stories

Romantic Suspense

Antarctic Ice Fliers
US Coast Guard

Contemporary Romance

Eagle Cove

Other

Deities Anonymous (fantasy)
Single Titles

The Emily Beale Universe
(military romantic suspense)

The Night Stalkers
MAIN FLIGHT
The Night Is Mine
I Own the Dawn
Wait Until Dark
Take Over at Midnight
Light Up the Night
Bring On the Dusk
By Break of Day
Target of the Heart
Target Lock on Love
Target of Mine
Target of One's Own
NIGHT STALKERS HOLIDAYS
*Daniel's Christmas**
*Frank's Independence Day**
*Peter's Christmas**
Christmas at Steel Beach
*Zachary's Christmas**
*Roy's Independence Day**
*Damien's Christmas**
Christmas at Peleliu Cove

Henderson's Ranch
*Nathan's Big Sky**
*Big Sky, Loyal Heart**
*Big Sky Dog Whisperer**
*Tales of Henderson's Ranch**

Shadow Force: Psi
*At the Slightest Sound**
*At the Quietest Word**
*At the Merest Glance**
*At the Clearest Sensation**

White House Protection Force
*Off the Leash**
*On Your Mark**
*In the Weeds**

Firehawks
Pure Heat
Full Blaze
*Hot Point**
*Flash of Fire**
Wild Fire
SMOKEJUMPERS
*Wildfire at Dawn**
*Wildfire at Larch Creek**
*Wildfire on the Skagit**

Delta Force
*Target Engaged**
*Heart Strike**
*Wild Justice**
*Midnight Trust**

Night Stalkers Reload
*Guard the East Flank**

Emily Beale Universe Short Story Series
The Night Stalkers
The Night Stalkers Stories
The Night Stalkers CSAR
The Night Stalkers Wedding Stories
The Future Night Stalkers

Delta Force
Th Delta Force Shooters
The Delta Force Warriors

Firehawks
The Firehawks Lookouts
The Firehawks Hotshots
The Firebirds

White House Protection Force
Stories

Future Night Stalkers
Stories (Science Fiction)

SIGN UP FOR M. L. BUCHMAN'S NEWSLETTER TODAY

and receive:
Release News
Free Short Stories
a Free Book

Get your free book today. Do it now.
free-book.mlbuchman.com